A LADY'S HEART DECEIVED

A Duke of Strathmore novel

SASHA COTTMAN

Also by Sasha Cottman

SERIES

The Duke of Strathmore

The Noble Lords

Rogues of the Road

London Lords

For other releases and international editions please visit

www.sashacottman.com

The Duke of Strathmore

Letter from a Rake – eBook, Audio, Print

An Unsuitable Match – eBook, Audio, Print

The Duke's Daughter – eBook, Audio, Print

A Scottish Duke for Christmas – eBook, Print

My Gentleman Spy – eBook, Audio, Print

Lord of Mischief – eBook, Audio, Print

The Ice Queen – eBook, Audio, Print

Two of a Kind – eBook, Audio, Print

A Lady's Heart Deceived - eBook, Print

All is Fair in Love - eBook, Print

Mistletoe and Kisses (novella) – eBook, Print

A Wild English Rose – exclusive eBook, Print

The Noble Lords

Love Lessons for the Viscount – eBook, Print

A Lord with Wicked Intentions – eBook, Print

A Scandalous Rogue for Lady Eliza – eBook, Print

Unexpected Duke– eBook, Print

The Noble Lords Boxed Set

Rogues of the Road

Rogue for Hire – eBook, Print

Stolen by the Rogue – eBook, Print

When a Rogue Falls – eBook, Print

The Rogue and the Jewel – eBook, Print

King of Rogues – eBook, Print

London Lords

Devoted to the Spanish Duke – eBook, Print

Promised to the Swedish Prince – eBook, Print

An Italian Count for Christmas – eBook, Print

Wedded to the Welsh Baron – eBook, Print

Bound to the Belgian Count – eBook, Print

Join my VIP readers for your FREE book

Regency London's wild child is about to meet her match...

If Lady Cecily Norris' parents are ashamed of her, they only have themselves to blame.

As a young girl, she was sent to live at a country estate along with other unwanted children of the *ton*. Her upbringing could only be described as unconventional and haphazard.

Cecily has now become a young woman both beautiful and wild at heart. Returning to London, she is determined to set her own rules for how she lives her life. As far as she is concerned, the *ton* and all its expectations for how a young unmarried woman should behave, can all go hang.

But she cannot fully escape her future, and her dismayed parents demand that she make a suitable and sensible marriage.

When Lord Thomas Rosemount trips over Cecily in a dark garden, he falls hard. His heart quickly follows.

In Thomas, Cecily encounters a man very different from those that she has lived with all her life. He is reliable, sensible, and dare she say a little boring?

But Thomas offers her something that she has never known before. A home and a future with someone who loves her.

Thomas knows it will take more than pretty words and a kind heart to win Cecily's hand, and he will have to look deep inside himself to discover whether he is truly the man who can tame a Wild English Rose.

Join my VIP readers and receive your FREE copy of A Wild English Rose.

Grab Your FREE BOOK

Chapter One

❧

Office of Military Records
Horse Guards
City of Westminster
15th September 1817

Dear sir,

I refer to my letters of March and July this year, regarding the late Captain Robert Eustace Taylor who served with the First Regiment of Foot Guards, and who was mortally wounded during the battle of Waterloo.

As noted in my previous correspondence, I am seeking to have a statue of the captain erected in his home city of Coventry. In order to do so, I must furnish the city with a copy of a letter stating the details of his military record and any notes of his heroic efforts during the battle.

Since my other letters have gone unanswered, I must press upon you that this has now become a matter of urgency.

I request that you furnish me with this information forthwith.

Yours faithfully.
Miss Margaret Radley
Fulham Palace
London

By the time Captain Piers Denford got to Miss Radley's letter late on a chilly Thursday afternoon, he was not in a particularly pleasant mood. His reply, unfortunately, reflected his less than generous frame of mind.

Miss Margaret Radley
  Fulham Palace
  London
  2nd November 1817

Dear Miss Radley,
  I am in receipt of your correspondence of the 15th of September and have also retrieved your previous letters from the bottom of one of the large piles which are currently cluttering the top of my desk. I apologize for not having replied earlier, but there are several hundred letters currently bidding for my attention.
  I have looked into your request and can advise the following: There is no record of a Captain Robert Eustace Taylor having ever fought in His Majesty's British Army. This is especially true of the regiment formerly known as the First Foot Guards, as I am a serving officer of that particular regiment.
  Please cease and desist from any further correspondence regarding this matter as I will burn all future letters.

Captain P. Denford

His Majesty's, Grenadier Guards

He didn't bother with *yours faithfully* or *regards*. Week after week, Piers had to deal with requests from the families of real soldiers, men who had fought in the bloody battle which had cost thousands of lives on both sides. His patience with women writing to him regarding imaginary war heroes was limited at best. Whoever this Robert Taylor chap was, he was more than likely a figment of Miss Radley's mind, or some scoundrel who had lied to her. Either way, the man did not exist anywhere in the army records that Piers had wasted several hours searching.

It was only after he had sealed and sent the letter, and was well on his way home to Denford House, that a horrible thought struck Piers. The young woman's name was Margaret Radley. The Radley family name rang loudly in Piers's mind.

"Oh, no," he muttered.

In his bad-tempered haste he had just sent a terse letter to the daughter of Lord Hugh Radley. The address, Fulham Palace, was the home of the Bishop of London. How the third most powerful man in the Church of England would react to having such a blunt missive delivered to his daughter Piers didn't wish to consider.

He slipped his hat off his head and slapped it hard against his thigh. The way his luck was running these days, Piers was certain that there wasn't a snowball's chance in hell that the letter wouldn't return to bite him on the ass.

"You let your anger and frustrations get the better of you."

Piers stuffed his hat back on and continued marching across St. James's Park. The green expanse was at least something of a blessing; it allowed him to stretch his legs. Sitting all day at a desk wasn't what he'd had in mind when he signed up for the army.

You used to be an even-natured chap, Piers Denford. Since when did you become such a foul-tempered and uncaring cad?

He didn't have to ponder the answer to that prickly question. The exact moment was forever burned into his psyche.

An officer didn't ever forget when the word *incompetent* was written next to his name in official dispatches from the battlefront.

Chapter Two

Maggie downed the last of her lukewarm tea and set the cup on the saucer with a loud clatter. She had been in a foul mood since opening her eyes. The letter from Captain Denford had arrived the previous day and pushed her blood to boiling point. The nerve of that man.

I'll give him cease and desist. Cheeky devil.

With an indignant huff, she rose from her seat at the breakfast table, pushed back her chair—then stopped.

Across from her, Claire sat with a quizzical expression on her face. "Aren't you waiting for Mama and Papa to come down for breakfast? It is not polite to leave before they arrive."

Maggie's gaze darted to the other end of the table. Her parents were usually in the breakfast parlor at this time of the morning, except for the days when they ...

She shuddered at the thought. Her parents had been married for many years. It was unseemly that they still indulged in marital activities. Or that they did it in the light of day. But if Hugh and Mary were late, it was more than likely because they were still abed.

"I have somewhere to be this morning. I cannot wait for them. Papa must be finishing up his Sunday sermon and having Mama check it for him," she replied.

Claire picked up a piece of toast and, with a practiced air of disinterest, placed it on her plate. She reached for the butter. The silent agreement that no one was going to mention what they both suspected their parents were up to hung lightly between them.

Unlike many of their peers, Mary and Hugh Radley's marriage had been a love match. It was not unheard of in the Radley household for Lord and Lady Radley to disappear into their bedroom for entire afternoons, only to finally surface in time for a late supper.

Maggie secretly envied her parents—their decades' long romance, was still fresh and very much alive.

I wonder if Robert and I would have known such a strong connection if we had been married and then blessed to grow old together.

She shook the painful thought away. Robert was dead. Buried, along with many thousands of other soldiers, in an overgrown field in Belgium. All her hopes for a happy life had slowly turned, like him, to dust.

"Are you headed into town? I could accompany you if you like?" offered Claire.

Her sister was always one for an impromptu visit to the shops of central London. Claire Radley was a dedicated follower of fashion, and also good fun. On any other day, she would be more than welcome to join Maggie in the Radley family carriage. But not today.

Maggie slowly shook her head. The last thing she needed this morning was for her sibling to bear witness while she gave an officer of the British Army a severe tongue lashing. Her intention was to give the insolent Captain Denford a piece of her mind.

A very stern one.

By the time she was finished with him, the officer would not only regret his decision to send her that letter, but he would vow to never do it again to anyone. No other grieving widow should be subjected to such ridicule.

She glanced down at the simple, unadorned betrothal ring on her finger. It might not be a wedding ring, but in her heart, she and Robert had been as good as married. No one had the right to cheapen his memory. Or his efforts on the battlefield. There was no doubt in her mind that whatever had befallen Robert, his would have been a worthy death. That of a hero.

"Thank you, sister dearest, but I don't plan to be in the city that long. I have one appointment at the Horse Guards, after which I shall return straight home," said Maggie.

Claire gave an all too familiar sigh, then went back to eating her breakfast. The rest of the Radley family had wisely adopted the practice of not saying anything when it came to the subject of Robert. Occasionally, they would offer their condolences, but these days, they usually left things well alone.

In the two years and almost five months since that fateful day at Waterloo had robbed Maggie of her future happiness, the rest of the world had continued on. She, however, was content to bide her time, treasuring Robert's precious memory.

Her kind family had been supportive. Never more so than when they didn't press her to move forward with her life. If she declined to attend a social function, they took her refusal with good grace. Even her reluctance to give up the pale lilac gowns of semi-mourning was not challenged.

She would come out of her time of grief when she was ready.

~

Maggie was headed for the front door when Hugh and Mary Radley finally made it down the main stairs. Her father, clad in his bishop robes, hailed her. "Don't we even get a good morning before you leave?"

She greeted her parents with a tight smile. "Good morning, Papa. Good morning, Mama."

"Where are you off to in such undue haste?" asked Mary.

"Town. Some errands. And to speak to someone regarding Robert's statue," she replied.

When Hugh and Mary exchanged an all too familiar look, Maggie ignored it. Her father was the only member of the family who seemed to find it odd that she wanted to commission a statue for her late fiancé.

"I see. Is your sister going with you?" asked Hugh.

"No. I am perfectly alright going on my own. Two footmen and the driver will be with me. Besides, I'm only going to the Horse Guards."

Only a reckless fool would attack a young woman riding around town in the Radley family carriage. A coach which had both the Strathmore coat of arms emblazoned on the side as well as the personal insignia of the Bishop of London.

After giving Mary and Hugh a quick hug, she hurried out the front door and crossed the courtyard of Fulham Palace to the waiting carriage. She did not wish to discuss either her life or her plans for the future. She had important business to attend to, a man to see.

And if Captain P. Denford was foolish enough to get too close, Maggie could guarantee he would be left with bruises where her finger would stab him repeatedly in the chest.

"Cease and desist. How dare he?"

Chapter Three

T he six-mile journey into London took the best part of an hour. Travelling in from Fulham via Chelsea to Westminster was always slow-going in the morning. Carriages and heavily laden carts crowded the way. Maggie stared out the window, lost in her thoughts. On the seat next to her was a leather satchel stuffed full of papers.

In the eight months since she had decided to go ahead with Robert's memorial, Maggie had written a significant number of letters. Leaving nothing to chance, she had painstakingly made copies of all of them. Nothing and no one were going to deter her from her mission.

Thousands of British and allied soldiers had died at Waterloo, but only one had held her heart. Only he deserved to have a statue standing in his home city for the world to know of his sacrifice in the service of King and country.

The Radley carriage drew up out the front of the Horse Guards in Horse Guard Parade. One of the Radley household footmen quickly leaped down from the carriage and opened the door. Maggie collected her belongings and stepped out. Today was a day for getting things done.

No sooner had she checked her skirts and tucked her satchel under her arm then a loud shout of, "You cannot leave your conveyance there" arose from behind her.

She turned. A smartly dressed soldier marched with great purpose across the parade ground toward the carriage. His arms and legs moved in time with one another. Up, down, up, down. He pointed furiously at the carriage as he approached. "Move it! Move it!" he bellowed.

The startled footman looked to Maggie for guidance.

"Ask the driver to take the carriage around to the other side of St. James's Park. Once I have finished my business at the Horse Guards, I can walk there and meet you. I shall be quite safe," she instructed him. It was only a matter of a hundred yards or so. The chances of her coming to harm in such a short distance were quite remote.

"Very good, Miss Radley," replied the footman.

The soldier stopped in front of Maggie and stood stiffly to attention. "This place is for army business, miss. If you wish to take a stroll, the park is the place for you. I suggest you follow your footman and return to your carriage."

Maggie straightened her spine. She had come prepared for a confrontation and was more than ready to begin with the man standing in front of her. "I am not here on pleasure. I have business with the British Army. And as for your edict about me not being permitted to stop my carriage, I must confess to a degree of ignorance. I didn't realize that the army had rules against young women being allowed to alight safely from their chosen method of transportation. My behavior is clearly scandalous. Would it help if I promise that next time, I shall endeavor to leap from my conveyance while it is still in motion?" She raised her eyebrows, cool and composed. If he wanted to argue the point, she was more than willing.

"Now if you don't mind, I shall continue with my morning."

Unless that is going to break yet another of your rules.

She nodded in the direction of the main entrance to the large cream brick building. "Is that where I should go if I wish to speak to someone from the Secretary at War's office?"

The soldier frowned. He opened his mouth as if to say something but stopped and clamped it shut.

Don't try to give me a lecture or instruct me this morning. I am not in the mood.

"I have important business inside," she added.

"Yes, it is the door to the war office, but civilians are not permitted to use it under any circumstances," replied the soldier.

Clutching the satchel to her body, Maggie rounded on him. "Riddle me this—how am I to speak to someone on the staff of the office of records if I cannot get inside? Or should I climb in through a window? And if that is the case, then I would be obliged if you could point me in the direction of which window has the easiest exterior access. As you can no doubt imagine, long skirts are rather difficult to hitch."

"I am only following orders, miss," he replied, his tone more than a little defensive.

Maggie was fighting to keep her temper under control. "I shall inform all and sundry who challenge me that you tried your best to stop the attack on His Majesty's Horse Guards. They will surely understand the terrible threat that a young woman posed to the hundreds of well-trained soldiers who were cowering inside."

Certain that she had wasted enough time already this morning, Maggie headed toward the front door. Fearful that the soldier was going to draw his weapon, she hastened her steps. Her heart was pounding hard by the time she reached the main entrance.

It was guarded by two sentries standing stiffly to attention on either side of the door. Maggie gritted her teeth and went to step past them. Two sharp, shiny swords crossed in front of her face. The soldier who had followed her, gently pulled her out of harm's way.

"No civilians without orders," said the guards.

The sorely put-upon soldier gave a resigned huff. "I have already told her that, but she wouldn't listen."

Maggie took a moment to compose herself, grateful that neither sharp weapon had actually touched her face. She was determined to continue with her mission, but it was becoming all too clear that neither a haughty demeanor nor pleading was going to do her much good. A change of approach was in order.

Time to invoke the family name.

Her gaze went from left to right, then focused on the path ahead. Maggie loudly cleared her throat. "I am Margaret Charlotte Radley. You will let me pass."

A long silence followed.

She took a deep breath. "My uncle is Lord Ewan Radley, the Duke of Strathmore. My father is Lord Hugh Radley, the Bishop of London. If you do not let me enter this building, I shall let the three of you decide which of those two gentlemen shall be the first to come down here this morning and pay a visit to your commanding officer."

The guards gave one another a sideways look, then slowly lowered their swords. The other soldier held up his hands in surrender.

Thank heavens. Now perhaps I might get somewhere.

The last thing Maggie wanted was for her father or uncle to get involved in this dispute. But only a fool would think it wise to disregard someone who was related to two of the most powerful men in England.

"Speaking of officers, who is on duty this morning?" she asked. Her heart continued to pound hard in her chest; she sensed she was pressing her luck.

"The officer on duty is Captain Denford. Though I must warn you, he is not a man to be trifled with at the best of times," replied one of the guards.

Don't I know it.

"Capital. I would be most obliged if one of you excellent guardsmen would please show me inside and then escort me to Captain Denford. He is exactly the man to whom I wish to speak."

The soldier and guardsmen conferred amongst themselves deciding who would take her in. Maggie wasn't surprised but could confess to being more than a little relieved when the mention of her uncle and father gained her immediate entrance to the military offices. She had gotten her way; she could only hope it didn't get back to her family.

She followed the first soldier inside, leaving the sentries to continue safeguarding the front door. From whom, she wasn't entirely sure. Europe was currently at peace, but there was every chance that Britain was probably at war with someone.

Partway down a long corridor, the soldier stopped at a closed door. He motioned for Maggie to stand a few feet back. "Let me go and speak to Captain Denford, miss. He may not have time to see you."

Maggie narrowed her eyes at him. "Captain Denford will see me. Or he will see my father."

She was determined to get the answers she needed. To finally be able to put construction of Robert's memorial into effect. No bureaucratic army officer was going to stop her. She was filled with glorious purpose.

Maggie took a polite step back and waited. She could be gracious if the moment called for it. Especially if it got her what she wanted.

The soldier rapped sharply on the door and a muffled "enter" came from inside. He disappeared into the office, closing the door behind him.

She grinned to herself. It was quite a feat to have made it inside the hallowed halls of the Horse Guards. In a way, it was a pity that Claire wasn't here to witness it. Her sister would no doubt be thrilled to hear of Maggie's exploits. She made a mental note to relate every detail of them to Claire as soon as she got home.

The door quickly swung open, and the soldier reappeared. He bowed to Maggie and motioned for her to step inside. "Miss Radley, Captain Denford will see you."

Gripping her satchel tight, Maggie took a deep, fortifying breath. "Thank you. I appreciate your assistance."

She headed for the door, ready to meet the man who would hopefully finally be able to solve the mystery of her missing fiancé.

Chapter Four

P iers had expected some repercussions from his terse
letter to Miss Margaret Radley. What he hadn't counted
on was the recipient turning up on his doorstep and
demanding a meeting. But considering the tone of his correspondence, and the lofty titles of her relatives, he wasn't in
any position to refuse her an audience.

He nodded to the private who had knocked on his door
and announced Miss Radley's arrival. "Please show Miss
Radley in."

Rising from his seat, he came around to the front of his
desk, and made ready to receive his unexpected visitor.

His mental image of a haughty, sharp-edged daughter of
the *haute ton* shattered the second she stepped through the
door, her black cloak billowing behind her.

While her attire might have been less than riveting, her
gown an unappealing washed-out lilac, she more than made
up for it with her stunning raven hair and piercing blue eyes.
Piers rocked back on his heels as he took in the vision of
loveliness which seemed to sail into the room. An apparition
of elegant beauty which instantly took his breath away.

He quickly dusted his hands over his military jacket before standing stiffly to attention. He saluted. "Miss Radley. Captain Piers Denford, at your service."

She halted mid-stride as their gazes met. Her lips moved silently for a second or two. It was almost as if she, too, were caught up in the moment. Taken aback by this encounter as much as he was.

Deuce. You are a beautiful woman.

Piers blinked himself out of his near stupor. He turned to his desk and began to clear papers away, making a space.

This place is a mess. I wish I didn't have to work in this blasted department. All this paperwork it just keeps piling up.

It was times like this when he wished the army would hurry up and bring charges against him. Until he could clear his name, Piers would be chained to his paper laden desk.

He dumped a stack of the correspondence on a nearby chair before it suddenly dawned on him that he should have actually offered for Miss Radley to sit in it.

"Sorry. I won't be but a minute," he said, flustered. Scooping up the pile of letters once more, he searched frantically for somewhere to put them.

Miss Radley dropped her satchel onto the floor next to his desk and held out her arms. "Perhaps I could take them for you."

Before he knew what his muddled mind was doing, Piers had handed them over. She carried the papers over to a small table which was tucked in an out-of-the-way corner of the room and placed them on it.

Piers was still trying to get his thoughts straight by the time she returned, his gaze lingering on her form as she bent and retrieved her satchel.

"I ... I am so sorry for my unforgivably rude letter," stammered Piers.

Miss Radley righted herself and gave him a shy smile. "I

am the one who owes you an apology. When you said you had piles of letters stacked on your desk, I naturally assumed you were exaggerating the situation. But it is clear that you were speaking the truth. You are indeed a busy man."

Placing her hand on the top of one of the tall piles, she sighed. "I expect there are hundreds of families all wishing to know what happened to their loved one. To their brave hero."

"Three and a half thousand dead. Almost the same number missing. And that was just on the British and Allied forces side. From what I hear, the French lost at least twenty odd thousand. A bloody toll, by anyone's count. Then you take in the battle which we fought at Quatre Bras two days earlier, and you can add another eight thousand to the tally of the dead."

Her face paled.

Oh, sweet lord, what did you just say to her?

He was so used to quoting the figures to other officers and around the army barracks that Piers hadn't thought twice about making mention of the terrible cost of the battles.

"I. Oh. I."

Words failed him.

"It's alright, Captain Denford. I am well aware of the terrible toll of the final campaign. I have several family members who fought in both encounters, and they have kindly given me a comprehensive account of what went on," she replied.

Piers frowned; what fool told a young woman the gory details of battle? Especially one where her beloved fiancé was supposed to have perished.

He was still struggling to get his mental bearings when Miss Radley pulled up a chair and took a seat. She opened the satchel and withdrew a stack of papers. "As I said, I can see you are a busy man, so let me get straight to the purpose of my visit."

Piers crossed around to the other side of the desk and sat. He accepted the notes from her. On the topmost piece of paper, a few details were written.

Captain Robert Eustace Taylor. Born City of Coventry. Date 1790?

"Why is there a question mark next to the date, Miss Radley?" he asked.

She softly sighed. "I think that was the year Robert was born, but I cannot be completely certain. It's a little embarrassing to admit that I didn't know some of the most important personal details of the man I was going to marry."

Yes, that is odd. I would have thought a young lady of your social standing would find out as much as she could about a chap before accepting his offer of marriage.

She shifted in her seat, and her gaze dropped to the desk. "Ours was a brief courtship. Robert was worried that he would be sent to war without us ever marrying, so he proposed in late April. On the day after we were betrothed, he offered to take me to Coventry to meet his family. His regiment was based in Coventry. He went home to pack, then I received an urgent letter telling me he had been ordered to ship out for Europe that night. HMS *Ville de Paris* sailed from Portsmouth, and I never saw him again."

A cold dread slid down Piers's back. He had sailed from Portsmouth on board the same ship, but that had not been until mid-May. Before then, the allies had still been discussing the strategy to deal with a resurgent Napoleon. A vastly undermanned British Army hadn't been in a position to send troops in April.

Something wasn't quite right about Captain Robert Taylor and his supposed military service.

"And Captain Taylor told you he was serving with the First Regiment of Foot Guards?"

Miss Radley lifted her head. "Yes."

It was only one word, but it carried a great deal of weight. An unspoken question. Perhaps even an accusation. Was he daring to call her a liar?

Steady your hand. Focus on what you can prove.

"I did read your letters, Miss Radley. And I also spent an entire afternoon in the military records trying to find Captain Taylor. I'm sorry, but I couldn't locate him."

A nervous twitch started in her right eye. She blinked rapidly, but it still remained. Piers couldn't imagine what might be going through her mind. Two years of grieving over someone and yet, the army said they couldn't find any record of him.

This was either a case of poor record keeping on the part of the army—highly unlikely, but not impossible —or it was something else. Something more sinister. From the evidence before him, Piers would wager it was the latter.

He wanted to help her. To fill in the gaps and give this young woman some much-needed answers. But if his growing suspicions were indeed correct, he had to tread carefully. "Excuse me for a moment, Miss Radley, I just need to check on something."

Piers quickly left the room and headed for the open doorway of another nearby office. The corporal seated at the small desk shot to his feet and saluted. Piers returned it, with all due respect.

"Corporal Bates, you are from around Coventry, are you not?"

"Yes Captain. Born and bred."

"Excellent. Then would you know which regiments are based at the barracks in the city, and also if the First Foot Guards were ever there?"

The corporal's brows furrowed. "There are no regiments at the barracks these days. Hasn't been for a number of years. It's used as a stopping place for the various regiments moving up and down the country. They rest in the barracks during their movements. As for the old First Foot, no. Why do you, ask sir?"

Piers's unease over Captain Robert Eustace Taylor was growing by the minute. "I have an inquiry regarding an officer who was supposed to be in our regiment in Coventry. I can't find him anywhere in the records. But his widowed fiancée is adamant that that is what he told her."

"I see. It doesn't sound right, sir."

"No, it doesn't. Thank you, Corporal."

Back in his own office, Piers closed the door behind him. He took a slow, deep breath. There wasn't going to be an easy way to deal with this, but he had to try. "Miss Radley, I think we may have a problem. As I explained in my letter, I have checked the records. If your fiancé had been an officer, we would have his details. The muster rolls clearly show birthplaces, dates of death, regiments, and other notes when necessary. No Captain Robert Eustace Taylor appears in any of them."

After the end of the battle of Waterloo, a great deal of effort had been put into collecting the names of the men who had fallen. While Piers hadn't been directly involved, he understood it had taken many weeks. Allied army staff and their French counterparts had worked their way through the bloated bodies on the battlefield, taking copious notes and making long lists of names.

A man could, of course, be missed in amongst all that carnage, but if a man hadn't existed in the first place, finding him would be impossible.

"Please don't take this the wrong way, Miss Radley, but what else do you know of this man?"

He had a horrible feeling it wasn't going to be much.

And that she would indeed take his words to heart.

Chapter Five

Perhaps he hadn't meant to be insulting, but Maggie couldn't take his accusation as anything but. She didn't like what Captain Denford was implying—that she had made it all up. Her fiancé hadn't been a figment of her imagination. Robert had been lovely.

He had also been very real.

Her temper rose quickly. "What are you saying? That he exists only in my head? I am not some simpleton. You can ask my family; they met him. He dined with us at Fulham Palace."

Captain Denford slowly shook his head. "I am not suggesting anything of the sort, Miss Radley. But the fact remains I cannot find him in the records. He is not anywhere in the muster rolls. And no regiments are based at the barracks in Coventry."

She went to protest, but he held up his hand. "Add to that my personal knowledge of events of that time, and I think we have a real problem on our hands. HMS *Ville de Paris* didn't leave England for the final campaign until May. How do I know this? Because I was onboard when she sailed."

Maggie rocked back in her chair, stunned. She put a hand

to her chest, but it did nothing to slow her rapidly beating heart.

That can't be true. Robert wouldn't lie. There has to be another explanation.

"Other ships must have sailed at that time. Could it be that Robert might have not made his designated transport but instead taken another vessel?"

Captain Denford's brow knitted. Maggie took comfort in his response.

You obviously hadn't considered that possibility.

"Yes, some ships did leave for Europe in April. But most went in May. All of them had soldiers on board. It is highly unlikely that an officer would fail to sail with his unit," he replied, his deep brown eyes solemn.

"Unlikely, but not impossible?"

Captain Denford slowly nodded in defeat. "Not impossible. But ..."

"That's what I thought," snapped Maggie. She picked up her papers and, after stuffing them back into her satchel, rose from the chair. It was clear that Captain Denford doubted both her and Robert, so there seemed little point in lingering any longer. "I apologize for disturbing your morning. I won't take up any more of your valuable time. Good day to you, Captain Denford."

A firm, but gentle hand took hold of Maggie's arm. "I am sorry if my words or conduct have offended you, Miss Radley. I shall continue looking for any information I can uncover regarding your late fiancé. The army might move slowly, but it always finds its man."

"Thank you; that is very kind. But I don't know where else you could look," replied Maggie. She pointed a trembling hand at the piles of correspondence which all but obscured the captain's desk. "Besides, you have many more people in need of your attention. I have already used up more army resources than my case warrants."

Gathering up what was left of her rapidly dwindling pride, she clutched the satchel tightly to her chest. "I should go."

Captain Denford released his hold. He'd barely gotten the door open before she dashed out into the hallway. She raced for the front door. Catching sight of the guards standing at the entrance, Maggie slowed her steps.

"Miss Radley. I shall write to you if I find anything else," he called after her.

Maggie's strength was too fragile for her to acknowledge the captain's words. Her focus was solely on getting out of the Horse Guards without bursting into tears. Without collapsing in front of the guards she had so recently berated.

Once clear of the parade ground, she fled. As she rounded the corner into St. James's Park, her eyes frantically searched for the Radley family carriage. For refuge.

This morning had begun with at least a sense of hope. Of finding Robert. Now, she was faced with the heart-shattering notion that the man she had grieved for, the man whose likeness she had been making ready to have rendered in bronze, was someone she didn't know.

The army had no record of him. Captain Denford was adamant Robert hadn't been on board HMS *Ville de Paris* when it sailed for Europe. Nothing made sense.

Robert wasn't a figment of my imagination, and he didn't just disappear into thin air.

Her fiancé had gone off to fight and never returned. Robert had died at Waterloo. He was a hero. But with no army history, she wouldn't be able to commission the statue.

What would she say to people if the man she had cared deeply for, perhaps even loved turned out to be nothing more than a lie?

How will I face my family?

Chapter Six

Hugh was standing in the Tudor period forecourt of Fulham Palace when the Radley family carriage drew up. He opened the door, took one look at her, and murmured, "Oh, dear. That bad?"

The tears were rolling down her cheeks before she had even set foot on the stone paving. He quickly took her hand and towed her toward the privacy of the family's high-walled garden. They were well out of earshot of anyone before he finally stopped to face her. "What happened?"

Maggie had managed to keep her composure for the long ride home, but its façade was quickly crumbling. She had hoped to avoid having to speak to her father for a few more hours but today didn't seem to hold any luck for her. "I spoke to the captain who sent me that terse letter. Captain Piers Denford. It transpires that he was actually a decent chap, and he apologized for having been so brusque with me. He reassured me that he had looked into the issue of Robert's war service. But ..."

"But what?" replied Hugh.

Maggie took a deep breath. "He is adamant that the army

has no record of Robert. It's as if he never existed."

"That's outrageous. Of course, he existed. It's not your fault that the army can't do its job and maintain its records," huffed Hugh. "Don't tell me this Captain Denford has closed your case because if he has, I won't have it. After all that you have suffered, you deserve some answers."

Maggie wiped at her tears. She was at a loss as to where next she should look for clues as to Robert's life. "The captain said he will carry on with his investigations and let me know of his progress. But I am not sure if he is going to succeed in finding anything else. Or if indeed there is any point. Do you remember when I told you that Robert's note said he was leaving on the HMS *Ville de Paris*?"

Hugh nodded. "Yes, I recall him mentioning that in his letter. The ship was sailing late the next evening, which is why he couldn't come to see you before he left."

She had been in a terrible state at the time, fearful of never seeing her fiancé again. Her fears had been well grounded. "Well, Captain Denford explained that when the ship sailed to Ostend, he was on board. And it didn't leave for Europe in April; it went in May. Though the captain did agree that it was possible Robert could have left England on another boat."

The more she thought about it, the more sense that particular explanation made. With hundreds of soldiers all leaving England at the same time, it would have been easy enough for men to have gotten mixed up and put on the wrong ship. And if that was the case, then service records may also have been misplaced.

All of it was such a mess, and there was only one thing of which she was certain: without Robert's army history, she couldn't commission the statue. She felt honor bound to acknowledge his sacrifice. To render him the respect he was due.

Hugh pulled her into a fatherly embrace, holding her tight. He brushed a kiss on her forehead as she rested her cheek against his chest. "I know this might sound harsh, but you must continue the fight to uncover what happened to Robert. The bible teaches us that through the truth we are set free. And while it may cause you pain, you will find a way through the heartache and eventually come to peace."

Her father had always pressed upon his children both the practical as well as the faith-based side of the church's teachings. As the Bishop of London, Hugh was a powerful man in the Church of England. He was also very down to earth. His Sunday sermons at St. Paul's Cathedral were well attended. Calm words of advice were his strength. Maggie would need to draw on them if she was going to see this through to the end.

"If nothing else, I have to find a way to prove that he was real. To honor his memory," she said.

Maggie raised her head and met her father's gaze. A comforting smile sat on his lips. "The British Army is not the only place where records of men are kept. I would suggest that we turn to the church. If Robert was indeed born in the city of Coventry, then his baptism should be noted somewhere in the local church registers. And so would the details of his family."

Maggie sighed. It may very well end up being yet another wild-goose chase, but it could give her some answers.

And, mercifully, an end to all this uncertainty.

No one expected her to spend the rest of her days mourning Robert. Over the past year, that thought had slowly become stronger in her mind. Commissioning a statue of him had been a major part of Maggie's efforts find a way forward. She would forever grieve Robert, but even he wouldn't have wanted her to waste the rest of her years pining for something she couldn't have. *Wouldn't he?*

"You are right, Papa. If I can't find Robert's service history, then I should try to find his birth record. If I am fortunate, I might even be able to locate an address for his family. It would be good to be able to send them my condolences. That's something which is well overdue."

Robert and Maggie's courtship had been so sudden, they hadn't had the opportunity to travel north to meet the Taylor family and inform them of their betrothal—although she assumed Robert would have written to his family and made mention of her before he shipped out to war.

But the prospect of spending yet more endless hours writing and receiving letters from the various church authorities in Coventry didn't hold much appeal. Maggie was tired of the long, drawn-out saga.

"What would you say if I decided to travel up to Coventry? I could follow things up much quicker than if I just wrote to various people," she said.

Her father's gaze shifted to a sudden noise which came from behind her. Maggie turned to see the family dog, King, bounding into the garden. Tail wagging, he made a beeline for her.

She dropped to her knees and gave him a friendly pat, scratching behind his fluffy ears. "Hello, boy. I didn't see you before I left this morning."

King's tail bounced on the ground, an obvious sign he was enjoying the attention. He was a large, whirlwind of a dog, and Maggie loved him.

"There was a big beef bone from last night's supper with the church choir; the cook gave it to him. I don't think he moved until every last lick of meat was gone," said Hugh.

Maggie gave King one last pat before getting to her feet. The blissful dog scampered away in the direction of the garden beds and a nearby lilac bush, which was his favorite.

"So, what do you think, Papa?" she asked, returning to the

subject at hand.

"I think you might be in too much haste. If Captain Denford said he would keep looking, then I suggest you let him finish his work. Give it a week or so, and then follow things up with him. You have been waiting to hear back from the army for many months now, so a few more days won't make any difference."

She hated it when her father made such good sense. Maggie was all for throwing a couple of gowns into a bag and jumping onboard the next mail coach headed out of London.

Hugh was, of course, right. She shouldn't be in such a hurry. Captain Denford may yet uncover the information she was seeking, and then the need for a long journey to Coventry would be rendered futile. Patience would have to be her virtue for a little while longer.

"I will wait to hear from the captain. But if he is unsuc-cessful, I ask that you to consider letting me go."

Her father nodded. "You have a deal. If nothing comes of Captain Denford's work, I shall give serious thought as to who will accompany you to Coventry. Who knows? The army might be keen to close the matter and be willing to lend you the captain's personal services."

Now that was an idea, but more than likely Captain Denford would be far too busy to leave London. All that paperwork he had cluttered around his office would no doubt require his attention.

"Thank you, Papa. I am so grateful for your support."

Maggie headed toward the front of the main red-brick residence, a slight spring in her step.

That night, she slept the best she had in a long time. Instead of the usual fitful dreams of Robert, she dreamt of a tall figure clouded in gray mist. And while the apparition might have been unclear, it still gave her comfort. She rolled over in the bed, deep in sleep and whispered, "Piers."

Chapter Seven

*O*ne *week later*

Piers wiped the dust from his hands and got to his feet. He glanced down at his black trousers and quietly swore. There were dirty marks all down the front of them.

He had hoped to follow up on Miss Margaret Radley's case sooner, but his commanding officer had embarked on an office reorganization campaign. People had been moved, in Piers's opinion, unnecessarily, to new quarters and rooms purely to suit Major Hall's mood. The week of shifting piles of papers, carrying chairs, and cleaning had left Piers with no time to investigate the mysterious Captain Robert Taylor.

Today was the first day in almost a week when he had been given the opportunity to get down into the old records room and search through it. Three hours later and he was still no closer to finding the elusive captain.

Carrying a muster roll upstairs and into his new, smaller office, Piers dropped the heavy tome onto his desk, then sighed. Only a few hours more and he could go home to Denford House. His family's London residence was his place of peace and sanctuary.

He was about to go and avail himself of a cup of hot tea when a fellow officer rapped on the door frame.

"Preston how are you?" asked Piers.

"Good, Denford. I see Major Hall has you doing more bloody paperwork. Will that man ever give in?"

Piers didn't respond. He knew well enough not to say anything against their commanding officer. He might well loathe the man, but he wasn't foolish enough to give voice to his personal opinions of him. Unkind remarks tended to get back to those who had been denigrated by them.

Piers nodded at the muster roll. "Just trying to get to the bottom of a mystery. A captain whose fiancée says he was at Waterloo, but whom I cannot locate. Thought I should take one last run through the rolls before I write to her. Poor woman. I think she was spun a story by a cad."

Captain Preston raised an eyebrow. "Have you checked the regimental colony muster roll?"

The what? "What is that?"

A sly grin crept to Preston's lips. "It's the book which keeps a record of those chaps who don't want to come home from war or army service and who would rather go somewhere else and begin a new life. The regiment allows you to pretend you died on the battlefield, then they send you off to the colonies to start all over again under a different name."

Piers stared at him, dumbfounded. He had never heard of such a thing.

"It's a great way to rid yourself of a troublesome wife or to avoid facing a criminal trial for some misdemeanor. You get to escape your past and in return, the army gets a man prepared to go to the other side of the world."

"I should check the colony muster roll. Where is it kept?" said Piers.

Captain Preston snapped to attention. Out of the corner of his eye, Piers caught a glimpse of Major Hall. He quickly followed suit.

The reed-thin senior officer, resplendent in his full ceremonial military uniform of a red coat with gold facings, strode into the room. Other officers usually wore the more sedate working rig, a simpler uniform for everyday use, but not Major Hall.

Under his arm was tucked a brass-topped swagger stick. Piers shuddered at the sight. Major Hall regularly smashed it across the shoulders of officers and soldiers whenever he felt the need to establish his authority. Captain Piers Denford knew the weapon only too well.

The major cleared his throat. "The regimental colonial muster roll is kept under lock and key in the Commander-in-Chief's private office. And you, Captain Denford, will never be granted access to it. The army doesn't need people to go prying into its affairs. There were several hundred names added to the roll after Waterloo, but I don't recall any officers being among them. Men who were offered a fresh start in New South Wales. New name, no history. All they had to do was undertake the long sea voyage to New Holland and they never had to worry about merry old England ever again."

"I hear that Governor Macquarie is going to recommend to the British Colonial Office that the name of the continent be changed to Australia," offered Piers.

The instant he spoke, he regretted it. Major Hall fixed him with an all too familiar look of utter disdain. "Yes, well, if you put as much effort into your work as you do with listening to rumors, you might be a half-decent ... actually no. You won't ever be worthy of your rank."

You never waste a single opportunity to try and tear me down, do you?

The major's gaze drifted from Piers to the muster roll, and he sighed. "What are you wasting army time on now?"

"A missing captain. His fiancée wrote to the war office some time ago, and early last week, she paid me a visit. I have been trying to discover what might have happened to him."

Major Hall gave another long, weary sigh. "You let a civilian into the Horse Guards? I really ought to put you on report. Then I should have you clapped in irons."

For more than two years, Piers had been subjected to this bastardry. From a man bent on petty vengeance. This morning, he had reached his limit. He wasn't going to stand quietly and take the abuse. "Miss Margaret Radley is the daughter of the Bishop of London. Her uncle is the Duke of Strathmore. Considering her family connections, I decided it was prudent to give her case my attention."

He looked the major straight in the eye, refusing to blink.

It was the tall, thin stick of a commanding officer who eventually flinched. "A duke and a bishop. Sounds like the first line of a bawdy jest. But alright, yes, you should follow up her query. If the muster and pay rolls here haven't given you anything, what's your next plan? Please tell me you have one."

This was a golden opportunity; one which Piers was not going to let go to waste. "Well, since it seems the colony muster roll is out of my reach, I was thinking, with your permission, sir, that I might undertake a trip north. Captain Robert Taylor was supposed to have come from Coventry. I have a possible birthdate and a full name. Perhaps the records at the barracks in Smithford Street might have something. If not, I will check the church records."

He held his breath, praying that the major wasn't that familiar with Coventry or the regiments which operated out of the city. Major Hall was London born and bred, and his previous regiments had served mostly overseas.

Come on, please. This is a perfect chance to get me out of the way for a few days.

The major gave a decisive grunt and slapped his swagger stick hard against Piers's arm. He shook his head as his victim gasped in pain. "Alright Denford. We wouldn't want to incur the wrath of a duke or the Church of England. Pack your things and head to Coventry. Find out what you can about this missing officer. Then return here. Those piles of papers will still be waiting for you when you get back. Carry on."

Piers and Captain Preston saluted. They remained at attention long after the *clump, clump* of the major's heavy boots had disappeared.

Bastard. One day, he would tear that bloody swagger stick from the major's hand and thrash him with it.

Captain Preston put a friendly hand on his shoulder. "Just think. If you go to Coventry and solve the mystery of the missing man, you might win yourself some new friends. If Miss Radley is related to two of the most powerful men in the country, you offering to help her will hopefully go some ways to furthering your own cause."

Piers nodded. He shouldn't need those sorts of friends. He was the eldest son of a viscount. A future peer in his own right. But Major Hall had never bothered to either acknowledge or respect the Denford family name.

"You heard the major; he has ordered me to go to Coventry. And since the man already thinks I am incompetent, I won't bother to go and double check any more of the regimental records." If he had overlooked Captain Taylor on one of the lists, and then happened to discover him, Piers's trip north would be immediately cancelled. He wasn't having that.

Mind made up, Piers promptly marched over to his desk and closed the muster book. He tucked it under his arm and headed for the door. "I shall just return this to the records. Wouldn't want to be accused of misplacing army property."

Half an hour later, he locked the door of his office. In his hand was a letter addressed to Miss Margaret Radley informing her of his intention to travel to Coventry to follow up on Captain Taylor.

There was a spring in Piers's step as he marched out the front entrance of the Horse Guards. He was determined to make the trip north last as long as he possibly could.

Please let there be a hundred churches in the district, all of which need to be visited.

He would be a happy man indeed if Robert Taylor turned out to be a deep mystery that took weeks to solve. For the first time in a very long time, the Honorable Captain Piers Denford had things to look forward to including a long trip out of London, a chance to clear his head, not to mention a beautiful maiden to serve.

Of those three things, one concentrated his mind more than the other. Miss Margaret Radley, the bishop's raven-haired daughter.

Chapter Eight

M aggie set the neatly folded letter from Captain Denford on the breakfast table in front of her and took a deep breath. Her mind was made up, but that didn't make this any easier. Convincing the Bishop of London to allow his unwed daughter to travel all the way to Coventry with a man not of her family was going to take some doing.

Her father may well have suggested it when they were discussing Captain Denford in the walled garden, but she wasn't entirely convinced that he had been serious at the time. Hugh Radley had a habit of promising things, knowing full well they might not come to pass.

After having received the captain's note, Maggie had immediately penned a reply, wishing him well for his scheduled departure on Thursday morning. It was now Wednesday, and she was going to have to move quickly in order to be able to go ahead with her secret plans.

"Papa. Do you remember when I mentioned that I was thinking of taking a trip to Coventry? That if Captain Denford didn't have any success here in London, that I would go north and seek out Robert's family?"

Hugh lowered his newspaper and considered his eldest daughter over the rim of his spectacles. "As I recall, my words were more along the lines of checking the church records. And also deciding who would accompany you on such a pilgrimage if I agreed to let you go."

Why do you have to have such a sharp memory? She tapped her finger on the letter. "While Captain Denford has been most accommodating with his assistance, he still hasn't had any luck here in London. The good news is that his commanding officer, Major Hall, feels that my case warrants the captain's full attention. He is allowing him to make the journey north to Coventry."

Her words sounded a little too rehearsed, which they were, but Maggie held her father's gaze. She hated lying to her family, but there was every chance that Captain Denford would say no to her, accompanying him. And if her parents knew the truth, they would also refuse to let her go.

I have to do this.

"Denford? Would that be Piers Denford?" asked Mary.

Her mother's remark caught Maggie off-guard, but she quickly recovered. "Yes. How do you know the captain?"

Please don't tell me he is some rake of renown disrepute. He seemed so lovely.

Her mother had a nose for such things. She knew all the best gossip in and about high society. Mary Radley was possessed with an almost encyclopedic knowledge of every scandal, both public and secret, which had occurred within the *ton* over the past three decades.

"Piers Denford. Or, rather, the Honorable Piers Denford, is Viscount Denford's eldest son. Lovely family from Northamptonshire. His mother is a delight," said Mary.

Claire clapped her hands together with unrestrained glee. "That's wonderful news. Maggie and the dashing captain heading off into the sunset together with Maggie one day becoming Viscountess Denford. Dearest Mama, what shall I wear for the wedding? That new burgundy bonnet would go well with my cream gown. Perhaps a matching shawl?"

Maggie was ready to throttle her sister.

Fabulous. Just what I need. Mama will now be trying to play at matchmaker. Papa won't agree to me travelling with Captain Denford if he thinks my honor might be at risk, and my sister is in grave danger of feeling the hard toe of my walking boot.

Mary shook her head. "Unfortunately, there won't be a marriage between Maggie and the future Viscount Denford. He is already betrothed to Lady ..." Her brow furrowed, as if she were deep with thought. She waved her hand in the air. "I cannot recall the girl's name. Some family friend, I think. It was early last year that I heard whispers of a future union, but come to think of it, I don't remember ever hearing of a wedding." She pursed her lips. "Most peculiar."

Claire, who had been feeding King bits of bacon under the table, suddenly righted herself. Maggie's heart sank at the expression on her sister's face. Claire Radley loved nothing better than a juicy scandal. Her green eyes danced with mischief. "Gosh, that sounds intriguing."

Hugh shot a hard glare in her direction and cleared his throat. "I shouldn't have to remind those members of the Radley family seated at this table of the cost that comes with scandalous behavior."

"Yes, but not all of it ends badly," grumbled Claire.

James Radley, the eldest of the Radley offspring, had eloped from his best friend's wedding with the bride. It was later discovered that Claire had had a sly hand in the matter. And while things had ended well and the young couple were now happily wed, Hugh and Mary were still coming to terms with it.

Maggie had heard that the rumor mill still bubbled back

to life whenever James and Leah Radley's names were mentioned in polite conversation.

Claire leaned over and met Maggie's gaze. "Perhaps Captain Denford secretly called it off. Jilted the girl. Thought he might do better. Tell me, is he rather handsome? He is, isn't he?"

Yes, he is certainly a dashing looking officer.

She pushed the unbidden thought aside. His looks had nothing to do with her.

Mary wagged a finger at her youngest daughter. "A lady is always the one to end matters. And no one has said that the betrothal was over. One more word from you, young lady, and you will be spending the rest of the day mending dishtowels."

Maggie could see her plans slowly unraveling. It was time to make one last desperate push. "Whether Captain Denford is betrothed is neither here nor there. I want to go to Coventry to find Robert. Well, I mean, details about him, and possibly, his family. The last thing I have on my mind is to fall in love with a stranger."

"I could come with you," offered Claire.

"Out of the question," replied both Mary and Hugh.

Claire went back to feeding the dog.

"I am twenty-six years old. Many people in society view me as a widow, so I don't see the problem with me travelling out of town with the captain. We would be staying in separate rooms at any accommodations along the way. And if, as you say, Captain Denford is already engaged to another woman, he is unlikely to put himself in a position where he would be forced to marry me," said Maggie.

Claire tittered, but neither of their parents laughed. Both sat with guarded expressions on their faces. The reputation of a young, unmarried woman was a precious thing in the eyes of society. Something to be fiercely guarded.

A frustrated Maggie sighed. "We will be taking the public

coach. I doubt he will get the opportunity to ruin me while we are pressed shoulder to shoulder with ten other passengers."

"If he can manage that, you should definitely marry him," said Claire. She broke into a fit of giggles, tipping so far over to one side that she fell off her chair. King barked loudly as she landed on the floor next to him. The dog obviously thought it was some sort of game and jumped all over Claire. The commotion bordered on lunacy.

Hugh shook his head. Mary opened her mouth to speak as a snorting Claire struggled to her feet and headed for the door, taking King with her. "Yes, Mama. I am going to my room. I promise I won't come down until supper."

As soon as the door closed, Maggie turned to her parents. It was time to offer up some well-considered concessions. "If you agree to let me, go, I promise to reenter society when I return. That includes parties, balls, and private dinners."

Mary's eyebrows lifted. "And what about your dull, drab attire? I am prepared to offer my support to this trip if you set aside your pale lilacs upon your return. I want to see my beautiful daughter in colors. And for her light to shine again."

One parent was on the verge of caving; she just had to get her father across the line. Maggie held her breath, waiting for his response.

"The Denford family are solid, dependable people. Captain Denford has clearly been given his orders to go to Coventry and seek whatever information he can regarding Robert. While I am not entirely pleased at the notion of my unwed daughter travelling the countryside, if it means that you are prepared to move on with your life, I will agree to you going," said Hugh.

Maggie nodded. "I know you don't want me spending the rest of my life grieving. And I think this expedition might be exactly what I need. If I can finally get some answers, I shall be able to leave my grief in the past. I will always cherish Robert's memory, but it is time to look to the future."

Hugh and Mary exchanged a brief glance. "Maggie, our sweet girl, we are pleased to hear you say that. I am certain that Robert would not wish for you to spend the rest of your life mourning him. You have done everything to respect his memory; now, the best you can do to honor it is to gently close that chapter," said Hugh.

Mary rose from her chair and came to sit by her daughter's side. "Just remember you have every right to find new happiness. No one would think ill of you if you did."

Maggie clasped her hands together, fighting back the tears. Her parents were right. The decision to move on with her life hadn't been easy, but for the first time in a long time, there was a sense of hope in her heart. She just needed to close this final door, get to the bottom of the mystery surrounding Robert's death, and then she could move on.

"Thank you. I appreciate your faith in letting me go. You can trust that I won't be doing anything rash like James and running off to Cornwall to get married."

Mary placed a tender kiss on her daughter's cheek. "Of course, you wouldn't do something like that. Maggie Radley, you are a sensible young woman. I am sure Captain Denford is already counting his blessings that he asked you to come."

Maggie mustered the best saintly smile she could for her mother. "I expect he is."

She rose from her chair. "I had better go and see what clothes and items I shall need for the journey. Coventry will be cold, and I expect warm woolens will be a necessity. Oh, and I think it would be a good idea if I went and stayed at Strathmore House tonight. That way I will be in town and ready to take the early coach in the morning."

"You know you always have a place at your aunt and uncle's home," replied Hugh. The Duke and Duchess of

Strathmore had an easy attitude when it came to members of the extended Radley family. Anyone who arrived at the door of Strathmore House asking for a bed was welcomed with open arms.

Leaving her parents to finish their breakfast, Maggie headed upstairs. Her mood was subdued. She had only won the first part of the battle.

On her way, she stopped and asked a footman to retrieve one of her father's sensible travel bags. It would be perfect to take with her. As she reached the top of the landing and turned for her bedroom, Claire popped her head out of her own room.

"How did it go?"

"They agreed to let me go to Coventry with Captain Denford. My side of the bargain is that I have to give up the mourning clothes and rejoin society upon my return."

Claire beckoned Maggie over. "That's wonderful news. But why the long face? I thought you would be delighted."

Maggie checked the hallway for servants, then leaned in. "Because I haven't yet told Captain Denford that I am going with him."

What the dashing officer was going to say when she arrived on his doorstep bright and early on Thursday morning and announced that she was going to be his travelling companion was anyone's guess.

Claire grinned. "The apple doesn't seem to fall far from the tree in this family. James ran off with Leah. Papa basically kidnapped Mama and took her to Scotland. And now you are going to be running off into the wilds of Northamptonshire with a betrothed man. I will have to put some serious thought into my own wedding scandal."

"Claire, I think this family could do with a respite from the whispers. And the exorbitant cost of a bishop's license. The best thing you and I can do for our parents is to have nice quiet weddings with the banns properly read. And absolutely not a hint of scandal," Maggie said, but her mind was abuzz.

What would Captain Denford's long-time fiancée say when she discovered he was travelling in the company of another woman?

And just why is she his long-time fiancée?

People didn't tend to delay the journey to the altar once they had made known their intention to marry. Who was holding back on setting a date and why?

She shook her head as she headed to her room. In undertaking this journey, she had a serious task to complete. Her focus was on getting to the bottom of the mystery of Robert. There wouldn't be time for silly games or falling in love.

Captain Denford's fiancée had absolutely nothing to worry about.

Chapter Nine

“Maggie Radley, my favorite niece.”

She endured the warm, bear-like hug of her uncle Ewan, the Duke of Strathmore. Every time she visited Strathmore House, he greeted her this way. She suspected he said the same to all her female cousins, but it was fun to indulge him.

“It is good to see you. Thank you for letting me stay at such short notice. It’s been too long since I visited here,” she replied.

Ewan released her from his hold. “According to your father, it’s been too long for many things for you. I hope you are planning on rejoining society soon.”

She caught the familiar undercurrent to his words. *You are too young to spend your life grieving for a man whom you knew for a short period of time.*

With the coach for Coventry leaving early in the morning, it made sense to stay the night in town. Maggie had arrived at the elegant mansion on Park Lane, just in time for supper.

Her aunt, Lady Caroline Radley, appeared in the doorway of the dining room, a smile lighting her face as she caught sight of Maggie. "Maggie, what a delight. The head butler just informed me that you were here. Are you staying long?"

"Just tonight. I am leaving London tomorrow morning," she replied.

Following Lady Caroline into the room was Maggie's cousin Alex and his wife Millie. The Marquis of Brooke held his spouse by the arm, guiding her as she waddled over to a nearby chair and slowly lowered herself onto it.

"Oh, thank you, my love," Millie said.

A pang of jealousy pierced Maggie's heart. The couple had married earlier in the year and were clearly besotted with one another. Her cousin, the ultimate reformed rake, fussed over his pregnant wife.

They make such a lovely pair. So happy.

Lady Caroline gave Maggie a hug, this one gentler than the one which her husband had foisted on his niece. "Where are you off to tomorrow?"

"I am travelling north with a Captain Denford from the Horse Guards. He has been helping me research Robert's military record. We are going to Coventry to see if we can find out some more information regarding the Taylor family and Robert's birth records."

More lies to my family. I hope this is all worth it.

Maggie could have wept at the sad expression on her aunt's face. It was the same one that each and every member of the Radley clan gave her whenever she mentioned her late fiancé. She was beginning to resent the pity.

And what will they do if it transpires that Robert was a fraud? I couldn't bear it.

Just before she left home, she had spoken to her parents and suggested that if things didn't go well in Coventry, she might travel on to Scotland. If she could seek refuge in their ancestral home of Strathmore Castle and find some solace before the rest of the family arrived for Christmas, it would help set her mind at ease. She would then be well rested and ready to face the wild Hogmanay festivities of the Radley clan.

"I do so hope you find what you are looking for in your travels. You deserve some good news," replied Caroline.

They joined Alex and Millie at the dining table. To Maggie's relief, the conversation soon turned from her to other family members.

"Did you hear that David and Avery are looking into buying more breeding stock for both David's estate at Sharnbrook and Lord Langham's property in Norfolk?" Alex asked.

Ewan set his wine glass on the table. "Yes, I will be most interested to see how it all goes. For someone who was a soldier most of his life, Avery has picked up a great deal of knowledge about animal husbandry in a very short time. Lord Langham says he has a real affinity for the countryside."

David Radley had married Lady Clarice Langham not long after Alex and Millie had been wed. Then their sister, Lucy Radley, had found her husband in Avery Fox, Lord Langham's new heir, a few months later.

Millie turned to Maggie. "Speaking of the countryside, how are James and Leah getting on in Cornwall? Have you heard from them since they made the big move away from London?"

"We received a letter a few weeks ago from Leah. James, of course, is hopeless when it comes to correspondence. Too busy designing his next piece of artwork. Leah says James is painting up a storm at their new home. They seem to be settling in well, and of course, Leah's grandfather is happy to have them living with him at Mopus Manor," Maggie replied.

Cornwall was many miles from town. Maggie was secretly hoping that her brother and his new wife would undertake the long journey north to Scotland for Christmas this year. But after the year they had endured and the scandal which still surrounded their recent marriage, she could understand if they chose to remain at home.

As her generation of the family grew older, and started having families of their own, the opportunities for them all to gather together at the castle each year would no doubt dwindle. The Radley family was slowly being scattered all over the southern parts of England.

Even this year, not everyone would make it Scotland. Clarice was further along in her pregnancy than Millie, and she and David had announced that they would be spending the festive season at their estate in Sharnbrook.

"Uncle Ewan?"

"Yes, favorite niece?"

"I know David and Clarice won't be coming to Scotland this Christmas. And some other family members won't either, so would you consider the possibility of hosting a Radley clan gathering here at Strathmore House in the new year? I mean, once you and Aunt Caroline return to town. It would be nice to see everyone."

Ewan and Caroline exchanged a look, and Caroline winked at her husband. "We could hold a grand dinner and party in the winter ballroom. And if we wait until after Clarice and David's new baby has arrived, we could make it a christening celebration."

The duke clapped his hands together, a decision clearly made. "What an excellent idea. We should consider doing something every year. With the family growing, it would be good to hold a gathering here in London, especially for those unable to make the trip to Scotland," Ewan added.

Happy to have her suggestion so warmly accepted, Maggie picked up her wine glass and took a sip. For the first time in months, she was actually relaxed. Spending time with her relatives took her mind off the worry of the trip ahead. It also helped to put things into perspective.

If disappointment did lie ahead for her in Coventry, she had the family gathering to look forward to, along with the impending births of several Radley babies.

These people will be here for me.

Sometimes she forgot she had such a remarkable family. She had kept her distance from them, huddled in her own world of pain. And that had been a mistake. The warmth and comfort Maggie felt just sitting amongst these people was wonderful.

"You will be back from your own travels before we all head off to Scotland, won't you?" asked Caroline.

"Where did you say you were going?" asked Millie.

Maggie took a deep breath and steadied her nerves; her cousin's wife had been busy getting settled in her chair earlier and had obviously missed that part of the conversation. "I am heading to Coventry tomorrow morning with Captain Denford of the Grenadier Guards. He is helping me with my search for more information on my late fiancé, Robert."

Alex turned from fussing over his wife. "Did you say Captain Denford? Piers Denford. I think I know him from school. Nice chap. Quiet, but studious. More than I ever was."

Millie chuckled. "You are also nice, but yes, there is never a dull moment with you, Lord Brooke." She rubbed her hand on her belly. "This child is in for an interesting life with you as its papa. And a blessed one."

Alex smiled lovingly at his wife. "And with you as its mother, it will have the best role model possible."

Could these two be any sweeter?

He turned to Maggie. "And your trip sounds like it will also be a success if you have Piers Denford at the helm."

"What can you tell me about him?" replied Maggie. Everyone seemed to know her captain. A warm sensation slipped down her spine at the thought. He wasn't her captain, but still, it was nice to hear about him from other members of her family. It helped to settle her worries about travelling with a man she herself barely knew.

"What can you tell me about him?" asked Maggie.

Alex pursed his lips. "He was very good at cricket. An absolute crack of a batsman, especially strong on the off side, and straight down the pitch. I was usually lurking on the boundary, contemplating what might be on the menu for supper when my team was fielding. I wasn't all that interested in what was happening out in the middle. But not when Denford was taking strike. He had me running all over the place, chasing the ball."

It was nice to hear kind words about Captain Denford. Their connection had begun on a misstep, but Maggie was now privately hoping that the trip to Coventry would see them find a way to becoming more than just cordial acquaintances. Perhaps even friends. There was something intriguing about him—an inexplicable attraction which drew her in.

"Oh, and he is the only man I have ever met who can rival David for putting away a full roast in one sitting. Talk about a bottomless pit. If you are travelling with Denford, just make sure not to get in between him and a plate of food. You might lose a hand," added Alex.

Everyone at the table laughed. Ewan and Caroline both shook their heads. David's ability to down his own weight in food was legendary in the extended family. Whenever he was in residence at Strathmore Castle, the servants were sure to have a large boar roasting on the spit.

The door of the dining room opened, and all heads turned. Francis Saunders strode into the room, huffing and puffing. "Sorry I am late. Some sea captains just don't seem able to grasp the simple concept that in order to eat, shipping agents need to actually make a profit."

Maggie grinned at the tall white-haired Francis; her

favorite cousin was the spitting image of a Viking. He was full of mischief but also someone she had always been able to rely upon. Many a night, the two of them had sat up, whisky glass in hand, warming themselves in front of the massive fireplace in the grand hall of Strathmore Castle, talking until the wee hours of the morning and solving the world's problems.

Francis bowed to the duke and duchess, then to Alex and Millie. His mother, Adelaide, was one of Hugh and Ewan Radley's sisters. They might be family, but Francis still observed the social graces of recognizing their noble status.

When his gaze landed on Maggie, he hurried over. "Maggie! Oh, my goodness. I haven't seen you in ages. How are you, cuz?"

She rose from her chair and accepted yet another family embrace. With Francis being over six feet, six inches, Maggie's head was buried in his chest. *I swear he gets taller every time I see him.*

"I am well, thank you," she said, smiling up at him.

Francis glanced around the room, then scowled. "Are you here on your own? Where is the rest of the Fulham Palace crowd?"

There was a definite hint of expectation in his tone. Before Robert, Maggie had regularly stayed at Strathmore House, accompanying her siblings and cousins to the theater and parties. She could understand Francis's reasons for asking; he likely missed those days too.

As do I.

"Maggie is travelling north in the morning with a Captain Denford. They are going to follow up on some information regarding Robert Taylor," said Ewan.

"Ah, that makes sense. So, you are still set on having a statue of him commissioned?" asked Francis.

She reflected on her reply for a moment, choosing her words carefully. If Francis had asked that question of her only a matter of a month ago, her answer would have been a firm yes. Now, she wasn't so sure. "The trip is to discover some more information about Robert, then a decision will be made."

Francis, bless him, merely gave a nod, and moved on. His gaze roamed over the table and the various platters of food. "What is on the menu for supper? Please tell me there is some roast beef; I am utterly famished. A ship arrived at the docks this morning laden with flax. Most of it had gone bad in the sea voyage. My stomach has been queasy all day and I haven't been able to face food. A spot of fresh air and now I am ready to do battle with a plate."

"Tonight's offerings are pork and salted herring. There was a little beef, but Alex and I polished that off this afternoon, washed down with a solid Shiraz," replied Ewan.

The look of utter disappointment on Francis's face was priceless. Maggie bit her bottom lip to stop from laughing. A snort escaped.

"You poor thing," she said.

Francis shook his head. He didn't appear in the mood for exchanging light banter.

Alex rose from his chair and came to stand alongside Francis, giving his cousin's shock of white hair a playful ruffle. "You don't look a happy chap."

Francis rolled his eyes. "That's because I am not. The ship's captain is still expecting me to pay for his soiled cargo. I can't sell it for any decent price, and he is refusing to move his ship until we pay him. He and I spent an hour this afternoon arguing over what is to be done with all the rotten flax. And if he thinks I am going to give him a farthing for any of it, he has another think coming."

Now Maggie understood his mood. Francis wasn't one for making concessions when it came to other people—especially not in business. He and his father, Charles Saunders, ran a successful import and export company at the London docks. And while Charles was a steady hand on the tiller, Francis was always looking for a way to get an edge on their competition.

Whoever this ship's captain was, they were in for a devil of a fight. Knowing Francis, he would cut his nose off to spite his own face. His stubborn temper was its own worst enemy.

"Have you considered asking him what sort of price he would be willing to accept in order to settle the matter? You must be able to find some common ground?" asked Alex.

Maggie smiled at him. Marriage and impending fatherhood had changed the hot-headed future duke. Millie was a calming influence in his life. Prior to her, Alex would have been more than ready to head out the door with his cousin and go rile up the ship's captain.

Francis gave him a look that spoke volumes. He screwed up his nose. "The only common ground he and I will have will be when my fist connects with his fat face."

Ewan grumbled his disapproval. A gentleman didn't talk of violence in front of the fairer sex.

"My apologies, ladies. I let my anger get the better of me," offered Francis.

Maggie gently patted his arm and Francis glanced down at her. "How about you come and eat? I expect some of your grumpiness is from lack of food," she offered.

She knew her cousin only too well. Francis was just like her brother James—both were testy when their bellies were empty. They were happy when they were full.

"You are probably right, Maggie. But enough of my problems, I didn't come here tonight to be the bearer of miserable news. I came to see my beloved relatives."

"And get a feed," teased Ewan, motioning for a servant to set a place for Francis next to Maggie at the table

Alex joined his wife once more. Francis took his seat and

poured himself a generous glass of wine. He raised it to the gathering. "To your good health, Radley family members."

As the tension in the room eased, Maggie smiled. She was badly in need of an evening with family, to talk and share happy memories. These were the things that gave her strength and brought peace of mind.

"Well, Millie, are you looking forward to your first visit to Strathmore Castle?" she asked.

The Marchioness of Brooke wriggled in her chair and patted her baby belly. She was glowing.

"I can't wait to see Scotland. This will be my first real winter in England, and Alex has promised me snow for Christmas Day. And since it will be such a long journey to undertake in my present condition, we have decided to take a week to travel north. We shall stay at the homes of friends along the way. This trip you are undertaking, Maggie—is it far from here? I mean, I have no idea when it comes to places in England."

Millie had been born in Calcutta, India, and had only arrived in London at the start of the year. Maggie found it intriguing to talk to someone who was new to England. The things that she found to be ordinary and dull, Millie often noted as being quite fascinating.

"Coventry is one hundred miles north of here. Travelling via the Great North Road, you won't pass through it on your way to Scotland. In fact, I haven't been there before myself," she replied.

Her journey wasn't quite the same as sailing the many thousands of miles from India as Millie had done, but it still held its own sense of adventure. She was breaking new ground, travelling to a distant city without her family. And in the company of Captain Denford.

Beneath the table, Maggie wiped her sweaty palms on her napkin. She was both excited and apprehensive about tomorrow. Hopefully, when she knocked on the door of Denford House, bright and early, and announced that she was to accompany him, Captain Denford would greet the news with delighted surprise. And if he didn't, he was going to have a fight on his hands.

Chapter Ten

Maggie was up well before the sun the following morning. The Strathmore House servants had a plate of hot eggs and warmed up leftovers from last night's supper ready and waiting when she entered the breakfast room. No one else was up and about at this unholy hour, but she didn't mind.

She needed time to compose herself. In her mind, her case for travelling with Captain Denford was solid, her arguments sound. But until they were both on board the coach, and it was speeding out of London, there was always the chance for something to go wrong.

I don't need his permission. He isn't my family. Nor my protector.

If he said no, she would go it alone. And while that notion was a sobering thought, Maggie wouldn't be deterred.

The hot breakfast was washed down with two cups of tea —a dash of milk, two lumps of sugar, *thank you kindly*—and she was ready to leave.

Maggie checked her notebook. The mail coach to Coventry was due to depart from outside the Swan with Two Necks just before eight o'clock. If she made it to Denford

House by seven, had a brief conversation with the captain, there was still plenty of time for them to make the journey over to Lad Lane and secure their seats on the coach.

With her bag packed, and dressed warmly for the trip, she slipped out of Strathmore House and into one of the Duke of Strathmore's town carriages. It was a short walk to Park Place from Park Lane, but her luggage was heavy.

With the sun yet to peek over the horizon, the streets were still dark. At this hour of the day, it wasn't safe for a woman to be walking anywhere on her own, even in the streets of St. James's parish. Footpads didn't care who they assaulted, and a well-dressed lady of quality would be the perfect target for opportunistic thieves.

As the carriage drew up out the front of number nine Park Place a short while later, Maggie sat forward on the carriage bench and peered out the window.

Denford House was an unobtrusive red brick building, rising over four floors. Its two, triple-windowed, cream-brick bays barely extended out into the street. There were minimal decorative features above the bays—two small scrolls and what she surmised was the Denford family coat of arms. Even the front door was plain, unadorned. A passerby could easily have walked past the house and barely noted its existence.

If the architect of Denford House had been seeking to project a look of 'nothing to see here,' he had well and truly achieved, it. The house wasn't dull, but it certainly didn't catch the eye.

Stepping onto the pavement, she glanced up. The sun had just sneaked above the horizon and the first faint light of day kissed the windows.

"Should we wait for you, Miss Radley?" asked the footman.

Maggie shook her head. "No, thank you. I am expected. I shall take it from here."

She was determined to burn all her bridges before knocking on the front door. If the captain saw a carriage waiting out in the street, he may well just bundle her back into it and send her on her way.

I am going to Coventry today, whether he likes it or not.

While she waited for the carriage to turn left into St. James's Street and disappear from view, Maggie rehearsed the important parts of her speech.

I know a few things about Robert that might help. It would be impolite of me not to accompany you since I was his fiancée. His family would appreciate meeting me. I must do this.

"And I have to find some answers before I can finally accept that he is gone," she muttered.

That last part she didn't intend to give voice to, but over the past few weeks, the notion had taken a firm hold in her mind.

Picking up her bag, Maggie strode up the short set of steps to the front door and rapped loudly on the knocker.

Piers was still rubbing the sleep from his eyes as he walked into his mother's formal sitting room. He had been enjoying a lovely dream about laying out under the night sky at Denford Park, stargazing, when a knock at his bedroom door had rudely awakened him.

"There is a Miss Margaret Radley here to see you, sir."

What the devil?

He'd squinted at the clock on the mantel, twice checking to make sure it really read a minute or so past the hour of seven. No one paid a house call at this hour of the day, let alone a young, gently bred woman. Things had to be serious.

Don't tell me she has changed her mind and informed the war office my trip is no longer required. Major Hall will have a field day.

Piers was desperate to get out of London. If he was going to stay sane, he badly needed a respite from the seemingly endless days of dealing with letters and the abuse of his odious commanding officer.

It was a hurried struggle to get dressed in his half-awake fog, and a good ten minutes before he was in any sort of state to finally leave his bedroom and go to receive his visitor.

At the door to the sitting room, he buttoned up his jacket and pushed back his shoulders.

"Miss Radley, do you have any idea of the time?" he said. With no breakfast, or even a cup of tea in his belly, Piers wasn't capable of finding his manners. He ought to be ashamed of himself. His mother most certainly would have been if she could hear the way he was receiving a guest in her favorite room of the Denford family townhouse.

Margaret Radley stood facing the window. As she turned, she threw back the hood of her long dark cloak, revealing her mane of jet-black hair and soft smile. Piers's gaze immediately settled on her ruby-red lips. The rest of his body leapt to attention, leaving him to hurriedly check that he had indeed buttoned up his jacket and that it covered the top of his trousers.

"Good morning, Captain Denford. And yes, I am well aware of the time. I have been up for several hours making ready for the journey. I expect I shall sleep well tonight."

Journey?

"I am sorry, Miss Radley; you have me at a loss. My brain doesn't function very well until after I have had breakfast. You must forgive me when I ask to what journey are you referring?"

As she crossed the floor, Piers wasn't entirely sure whether she walked or floated. Miss Margaret Radley had the oddest of effects on him.

"Why Coventry, of course." She pointed to a large gentleman's travel bag which sat on the floor. "I am packed and ready to leave. The coach departs just before eight o'clock, so you might want to hurry along and finish dressing. Unfortunately, I don't think you will have time for breakfast, but I understand the coaching inns along the way do serve hot food. You could get something when we stop to change the horses."

Piers scrubbed his hand over his face, desperately hoping he was still asleep and that this was all some sort of horrid dream.

Miss Radley huffed. "The post coach for Coventry leaves the Swan with Two Necks at quarter to the hour of eight o'clock. Lad Lane is a good two miles from here, so we need to leave within the next few minutes if we are to make it."

Piers bit down on his bottom lip and was disappointed to discover it actually hurt. He wasn't asleep. And this wasn't a dream. Miss Radley was really standing in his mother's sitting room, packed and ready to travel north.

His plans had never included her.

He stared at Maggie in disbelief. Her jaw was set hard, her eyes clear and determined. This was a woman whose mind was already made up.

Blast. She is serious about this. Think, man. What are you going to do?

"I didn't expect you to be coming with me. I sent you the letter informing you that I was going to Coventry purely as a courtesy. When you sent me your best wishes for the journey, I didn't think you meant ... well, to be honest, I ... You have caught me by surprise."

She didn't say anything about wanting to come with me. Did she?

His brain and mouth were completely out of sync with one another—neither able to function competently. When she licked her bottom lip in obvious contemplation, his manhood decided to take the lead. It knew what it wanted.

Her.

Settle down, boy. This woman is not for you.

The sudden bout of lust sealed the deal. There was not a chance in hell of him spending time with her. Not without at least a dozen chaperones.

"I have cleared the matter of me travelling to Coventry with my parents. They understand that we will be travelling in public coaches and staying at respectable inns and hotels. You are also engaged to be married, which I must say had a major bearing on their decision. So, there is nothing for anyone to worry about."

She bent and picked up the travel bag. "Shall I wait for you downstairs? I could hail a hack." A soft chuckle escaped her lips. "Not that I have ever had to do that before. I assume it involves marching into the middle of the street and waving one's arms frantically about until a carriage stops. That's how my brother, James, says he goes about it."

Piers shook his head, forcing himself fully awake. He reached for the bag, but Maggie pulled it away. A tight smile sat firmly on her face.

Bloody hell, stubborn woman.

He made a second unsuccessful grab for the bag, then let out a tired sigh. "I am sorry, but it is out of the question for you and me to undertake this mission together, Miss Radley. I'm surprised that your parents permitted it."

How am I going to get out of this?

The mention of public coaches clicked back into his mind. "If you haven't ever travelled in a hack, then I assume you've also not had the pleasure of a cramped, malodorous mail coach. I must tell you that one should only travel in them if there is no other option. The last time I took the coach to our family estate in Northamptonshire, I was sat next to a gentleman with elbows so sharp you could have given yourself a close shave with them."

The smile disappeared from her face, and she fixed him with a hard stare. "So, your answer is, no?"

"Yes. I mean, yes, my answer is no."

She marched purposefully toward the door, and he stepped aside. "Thank you, Captain Denford. I won't waste any more of your valuable time. Good day to you, sir."

The sitting room door was closed firmly behind her.

"Thank God," he sighed. He had expected her to give him a bigger fight over the matter. Clearly, the prospect of having to sit in a horrid, smelly public coach had done the trick. With her privileged background, Miss Margaret Radley had likely never had to experience the sort of discomforts that the working class endured when travelling. Her family would have an elegantly appointed travel coach with heated bricks to keep their feet warm, fine woolen blankets, and plenty of room.

She wasn't to know that he had absolutely no intention of sitting in the mail coach either. His plans for the day included a hearty breakfast and a final check of his papers, after which Piers would be departing London in the private Denford travel conveyance.

By the time Miss Radley made it back to Fulham Palace, he would be well on his way to the town of Luton, Bedfordshire, and tonight's destination. The two-hundred-year-old Cock Inn, a placed famed for its roast beef.

Piers's mouth salivated at the thought of the delicious onion gravy that always came with supper. His stomach growled its agreement. Tonight, his belly would be full of roast beef, gravy, and freshly baked buttered bread. And, if he was lucky, a generous slice of Yorkshire pudding. All of it washed down with a tankard of ale.

The Bishop of London's luscious daughter would unfortunately not be joining him.

"What a pity."

Chapter Eleven

Maggie dabbed at her mouth with her napkin and sat back in the chair. That had to be the best roast she had enjoyed all year. And the onion gravy was divine.

The only cook she knew whose efforts could possibly match such a delectable feast, worked in the kitchens at Strathmore Castle. And since she only got to visit the Radley family ancestral home at Christmas, the surprisingly excellent supper was an unexpected bonus.

It was also a godsend after the uncomfortable coach trip from London. Thirty-four miles didn't seem all that far, but when a body was crushed between two large and very muscular blacksmiths, every one of those miles seemed to last an eternity. She was more than glad to hear that both gentlemen were not travelling on to Coventry.

With a hot meal in her belly, Maggie sat and pondered her day. After leaving Denford House, following her frustrating audience with Captain Denford, she had indeed stepped into the middle of the road and hailed a hack. A smirk now sat on her lips as she recalled how proud she had been with herself as the carriage slowed and drew to a halt.

Fortunately, Maggie had encountered a carriage driver who knew his way across town, and she had arrived with time to spare before the Coventry-bound coach was due to depart. And while she had been a tad disappointed when Captain Denford didn't make an appearance, she had purchased a ticket and climbed onboard. The coach had left without him.

Finding herself unexpectedly travelling alone, Maggie had initially decided to push on and stay with the mail coach as it thundered through the night toward the midland city, but as soon as it pulled into the yard of the Cock Inn, she sensed she had reached the limit of her endurance. She climbed down, unsure as to what she should do next.

As her feet touched the hard ground, Maggie swayed a little. One of the other passengers, an older lady took hold of her arm and helped steady her. "You look exhausted young lady. Perhaps you should stay at the inn tonight. The innkeeper runs a clean and respectable establishment. And they serve a delicious roast here with lashings of gravy. There will be another coach tomorrow to take you the rest of the way."

Maggie nodded. The idea was most appealing. "Thank you, perhaps I will stay here tonight. I could do with a good night's sleep," she replied.

The early start of the morning was fast catching up with her. All she wanted was a warm, comfortable bed. Tomorrow evening, she would climb onboard the next coach as it travelled through the town, working her way farther north each day.

She glanced at her dinner plate, unsure if she had any room left in her stomach to finish the meal. Her fellow passenger had been right, the food was excellent.

Maggie was warm and comfortable, seated in an out-of-the-way corner of the main dining room of the inn. The place was a hub of laughter and chatter, with locals and travelers mixing and sharing tales. On the table next to her half-finished meal was the book she had planned to read on the way up from London. Her fingers idly flicked through the pages. Perhaps later she would attempt to catch up on the story. Sleep, however, beckoned, and she doubted she would make it past more than a paragraph or two.

"What the deuce are you doing here?"

Maggie stirred from her imaginings of soft sheets and warm blankets. Her head lifted, and her gaze settled on a tall, very unhappy-looking Captain Denford. He glanced from her near empty plate and back to her face. "That had better not be the last of the roast beef," he ground out.

A slow blink, and a sly lick of her lips was her reply.

With a tired huff, he dropped into the seat opposite hers. He looked as exhausted as she felt.

How did he get here? He missed the coach. He couldn't have come all this way on horseback, could he?

Maggie pushed the oval pewter platter toward him. "I believe that was the last of the beef and onion gravy, but you are more than welcome to share my supper. We fellow travelers should be generous to one another."

He scowled but picked up the knife and stabbed it into an untouched piece of meat. Maggie pointed at the small smear of what remained of the gravy.

"That was particularly delicious. If you were hoping to get a slice of Yorkshire pudding, you are out of luck. I wasn't expecting company, so I ate all of it. I am glad I chose to stay here tonight; one of my fellow passengers in the coach recommended the food most highly. Said it was well worth delaying my arrival in Coventry just to sample the menu. And they were right."

She found the silent glower in his deep brown eyes to be most satisfying.

Maggie leaned in and smiled at him. "So, Captain Denford, what brings you to the Cock Inn this evening?"

He narrowed his eyes. Maggie didn't flinch. If Piers Denford thought he could intimidate her with his puff and bluster, he was sadly mistaken. She was a Radley, and Radleys never backed down from a fight.

He was going to wring her neck, but not until he had finished the last of her food. Piers and Maggie sat in silence for the next ten minutes. While he stuffed his face, Miss Margaret Radley sat with her nose in a book. Every time he tried to catch her eye, she made a great display of turning the page and ignoring him.

Stubborn woman. Thank heavens she left me some of her supper.

She set the book down and for a moment, he thought she was going to speak to him, but she merely lifted her hand and waved the bar maid over to their table. When the girl arrived, Maggie gave her a cheery smile. "Rose, would you be a dear, and please get the captain a pint of your finest? Put it on my tab. Oh, and make sure you pour one for the old shepherd seated in the booth next to the front door. He looks to be out of coin. Thank you."

"Very good, Miss Radley," replied Rose.

Piers waited until the barmaid was out of earshot, then set his knife down. "You think yourself mighty clever, don't you? I wonder what your father would say if he could see you right now."

She gave a half-shrug. "Considering you are the one who missed the coach and left me to travel on my own, Papa would likely say that I was making the best of a bad situation. Using my initiative and finding the solution to my problem."

Piers shook his head. "And what problem would that be?"

A pair of sparkling blue eyes stared back at him. "Why, the problem of a self-important man who thinks women are incapable of taking care of themselves. And who thought that the notion of a little discomfort would surely dissuade me from the task ahead. You, Captain Denford, have never undertaken a night march on Strathmore Mountain. It's no stroll in Hyde Park, I can assure you. Sooner or later, you will discover that I am no feeble female."

He struggled for the right words to respond. This was a woman who knew how to conduct a rational argument.

I hate it when females are logical.

Piers actually preferred it when some members of the fairer sex attempted to work their feminine wiles on him. He could handle crocodile tears, seeing them for what they were —emotional manipulation. But Miss Margaret Radley had far too much self-respect to play that kind of game. She was cool and level-headed. And that gave her power.

If he didn't watch himself, she would gain the upper hand.

"I never said you were weak, Miss Radley. My comment stemmed more from a genuine concern with regard to your safety. You may have made it to Luton, but have you considered what you will do when you arrive in Coventry?"

The buxom barmaid appeared at his shoulder and set the tankard of foaming ale in front of him. After the day he'd had, Piers was going to need more than one of them.

"Thank you, Rose," he said.

He reached into his coat pocket, searching for a coin, but the girl simply shook her head and walked away. He glanced at his beer and then to Maggie. "You do know it's not the polite thing for a woman of your social station to be buying a man a drink?"

She nodded. "Consider it just another first in a day of many. I am sure it won't be the last time I surprise you on this trip, Captain Denford. And, in answer to your question, I have a pretty good idea as to what I have to do once I reach Coventry. Another of my travelling companions in the mail coach kindly gave me the address of a suitable hotel. I also have enough money to allow me to stay for as long as it takes to get to the bottom of things. In fact, there is a good chance that you might be superfluous to my needs."

I'm not having any of that. "Don't you dare," he growled.

He couldn't in all good conscience leave her to fend for herself. Apart from his own moral code, he knew that the Bishop of London and the Duke of Strathmore would take turns in tanning his hide if he did.

He was stuck with her. They both knew it. But for some inexplicable reason, Piers couldn't muster the energy to be angry about it any longer. The thought of travelling with this woman held a certain appeal—one which he couldn't deny. Miss Margaret Radley was gorgeous. She was feisty, determined, and a breath of fresh air. Piers also hadn't the faintest idea what he was going to do with her.

All he did know for certain was that the next week or so was going to be interesting.

Chapter Twelve

Maggie couldn't quite read the expression on his face. Captain Denford's mood seemed to be constantly shifting. He had arrived a short time ago, full of heated puff and fury. Had sat and promptly polished off the rest of her supper. Now, he was foolishly trying to treat her like she was some sort of recalcitrant child.

She crossed her hands gently in front of her, settling in for what she expected would be a long battle of wills. If the captain had any sense of self-preservation, he would lay down his weapons and admit defeat.

He shook his head. "I might not have climbed Strathmore Mountain, but I have dealt with stubborn, pig-headed people before today. You can't just go off into the unknown and expect me to let you do it on your own."

Under the table, Maggie curled up her toes, desperate not to reveal her amusement at his words. *You have no idea how ridiculous that sounds. Or how much fun this is.*

Being in possession of an older brother and numerous male cousins meant she was well-equipped to handle the temper of a self-important young man such as the captain.

Teasing him was the best fun Maggie had had in ages. She was in no hurry to let him off the hook.

"Well then, Captain Denford, you should be well aware that your being obstinate won't get you too far either. Perhaps you should reconsider your approach."

There. Put that in your pipe and smoke it.

Piers sat silently glaring at Maggie while the barmaid stopped at their table and collected the empty platter. Once the girl was gone, he sat back in his seat.

Maggie secretly admired his ability to hold her gaze.

"I know you think yourself very clever, but I think it's time I set some rules. Like it or not, you, Miss Radley, are going to listen."

Maggie picked up the tankard of ale and, after raising it to salute him, took a long, deep drink. "Go on then, Captain Denford. Tell me all your wonderful plans."

"Firstly, we will be travelling together after tonight, using my private coach which I came up from London in. Secondly, we won't be staying in a hotel when we reach Coventry. My brother, Jonathan, and his wife, Elizabeth, live in the city, not far from the center of town. We shall stay with them." Piers gave Maggie a look which he hoped she would interpret as meaning *you have no choice in the matter*. As far as he was concerned, she had relinquished her rights to claims of genteel privilege the moment she set foot in the public mail coach and left London on her own.

"But ..." she started.

"But nothing. If you are prepared to travel with a group of strangers and sleep in a country inn, all with the intention of travelling a hundred miles from home whilst unaccompanied, you have abdicated all rights to complain."

She picked up his ale once more and took another long drink. It was halfway back to the table when she stopped and raised it to her lips once more.

Piers rose quickly from his chair and took the tankard from her hand, setting it back on the table. "I think you might have had enough to drink, Miss Radley."

She got to her feet, and for a moment, Piers feared she had taken offense at his remark. To her credit, she held out her hand, offering it to him. "Since we are to now be partners in this endeavor, may I suggest we dispense with the formalities? I would much prefer you call me Maggie rather than Miss Radley."

After a moment's hesitation, he accepted her hand, giving it a gentle but reassuring shake. "Alright—partners it is. And my name is Piers. You are more than welcome to never again call me Captain Denford."

He'd hated being stuck in the army. Being referred to as "Captain" was a constant and uncomfortable reminder of his time spent in service. Away from London, and with this most extraordinary woman as his travelling companion, Piers felt a sense of hope. Life could be good, even if it was only going to be for a short time.

Maggie nodded. "Piers it is. I am glad that we are in this together. This calls for another round of drinks. And don't worry about my ability to tolerate alcohol. If I can handle my Uncle Ewan's Scottish whisky, I can deal with English ale."

Chapter Thirteen

The Cock Inn only had a handful of guest rooms, which Maggie was relieved to discover were accessed via a separate, secure entrance away from the public tavern below. An hour and several ales later, she and Piers climbed the stairs leading to their quarters.

"You hold your drink well for a lady of quality," he observed.

She held a hand over her mouth, covering a burp. "I told you, this is nothing compared to the whisky we drink in Scotland. If anyone catches my Uncle Ewan's eye, he has them downing a dram or three. I must confess, I don't have much of a recollection of last Hogmanay, apart from Mama helping me up to bed."

He chuckled. "Sounds like my home when my brother starts in on the cider. He takes no prisoners. And while I haven't endured the forced march over Strathmore Mountain, I have been made to carry a telescope out into the freezing night when my cider-addled sibling decides that everyone must partake in a spot of stargazing. Northamptonshire might not be Scotland, but it can still get bitterly cold, especially on a clear night."

Maggie stopped at the door of her room. The ale and company had been both refreshing and quite lovely. Her night had been made all the better by the surprise arrival of the handsome army captain. And it wasn't just the ale that made him rather dashing.

I can't remember the last time I had such a pleasant evening with another person.

The realization that he had made her smile had Maggie smiling once more.

"Piers, I have a small confession to make. When I first saw you tonight, I know you weren't pleased to see me, but I was more than relieved to see you. I'm not used to being by myself. And while I know I could have made it safely to Coventry on my own, I am happy that we are in this together."

He gave her a respectful but easy bow. "It came as a bit of a shock when I saw you sitting in the corner, a plate of supper on the table in front of you. The fact that you looked quite comfortable probably set my temper off. I was wrong to speak to you in such a way. I realize that you are not a damsel in distress. And I am also pleased that we are going to be travelling in each other's company."

When their gazes met, she could have sworn that her heart skipped a beat.

"Good night, Maggie."

"Good night, Piers."

Once inside her room, Maggie closed and locked the door. She propped a straight-backed chair under the handle. It was a neat trick her mother had taught her from the days when Mary had lived alone at Cambridge University following the death of Mary's father. Maggie Radley might be new to travelling and staying in public places, but she wasn't naïve.

She turned and glanced at the well provisioned bed. It was small, but when she had first arrived, a short nap had proven it to be quite comfortable. Her back was tired and stiff from the long hours in the mail coach, and she was looking forward to a good night's sleep.

After undressing, she slipped into a simple cotton night-gown. From her father's travel bag, Maggie retrieved her diary and a small pencil. She had been making notes in the book since the day the letter had arrived, notifying her of Robert's death. It also contained all the snippets of information she had managed to gather, since she had decided to commission the statue earlier in the year.

Climbing into bed, she pulled up the bed covers and snuggled into the warmth. Flicking through the pages, her eyes catching the odd word here and there, a sudden realization dawned on her. She didn't actually know that much about the man she had once been about to marry.

Piers had been adamant he couldn't find Robert in the army records. And her own inquiries had also drawn a blank.

From the back of the book, she pulled out two pieces of neatly folded paper. The first was the letter from someone in Robert's unit, informing her that he had fallen in battle. Until today, she had never questioned the contents of the note. Grief had enveloped her in its dark embrace the morning the missive had arrived at Fulham Palace, and for more than a year, she had not been able to so much as think of it without falling apart. The following year had only been marginally better. In fact, it was really the last eight months during which Maggie had felt more control of her emotions. Only then had she been able to make any sort of plans.

28 June 1815

Miss Margaret Radley,
My dear Miss Radley,
With keenest regret, I have to inform you that Captain Robert
Eustace Taylor fell heroically in battle at Waterloo on June eighteenth
in the year of our lord eighteen hundred and fifteen.

I am your obedient servant,
Commander-in-Chief
The First Foot Guards

She hadn't ever questioned the contents of the letter before. As far as she was concerned, Robert was dead, and that was all that mattered. But the events of the past few weeks had seeded doubt in her mind. Something wasn't right.

Setting the letter aside, she unfolded the second piece of paper, fighting back tears at the half-finished sketch of Robert. She had made quite a good likeness of him and had asked Robert to sit longer so she could complete the piece. He had promised to do so, but with his sudden call to duty, they had run out of time.

Now she would never get the chance to finish the sketch. Maggie stared long at it.

I will find the truth. I promise.

She packed up the papers and the diary, dropping them onto the floor next to the bed. In the morning, she would show them both to Piers and seek his opinion.

What if this is all a lie? And I have wasted years of my life.

Blowing out the bedside candle, Maggie lay in the dark. There was a hum of noise from the tavern downstairs—locals finishing up the last of their drinks and sharing raucous laughter, no doubt from some bawdy jest.

Her own thoughts drifted as she lingered on the edge of sleep. Comfort came in the knowledge that Piers slept in the room next door. For the first time in what seemed like forever, she didn't feel alone.

Chapter Fourteen

They left late the following morning, their destination, Towcester, some twenty-eight miles away. Piers's intention was to stay overnight at the Saracen's Head, a well-known coaching inn, which he had visited many times on his trips up and down from London.

He was in no particular hurry to make it to Coventry. The sooner he arrived in the city, the quicker he would have to return to town. To his way of thinking the slower they travelled, the better. He was more than happy to be out of the capital and away from Major Hall.

If nothing, it would give him time to think. To ponder his own predicament. And to consider what the future might hold for him, and the Denford family name.

Maggie didn't complain about their slow progress, which he found rather odd. If he had been in her position, he would have been eager to complete the trip. Instead, she sat quietly in the Denford travel coach, reading her book, and occasionally lifting her head to glance out the window at the passing countryside.

Piers tried in vain to keep his own nose in a book, but he

found it difficult to concentrate. More than once, he caught himself staring at her. At her beautiful, sable locks, which he was pleased to see Maggie was now wearing in a simple pony-tail, finished off with a lilac ribbon. Whispers of hair kissed either side of her cheeks. Without a maid at her disposal, she was plainly just brushing her hair out each day and making do. He liked her "making do;" it framed her face perfectly.

The only thing he didn't appreciate was her manner of dress. Those dowdy grays and pale purples did nothing for her complexion.

I would love to see you in bright colors. You would look stunning in red.

Anything but the attire which constantly reminded him that she had almost once belonged to someone else. *Almost.*

"Piers?"

He blinked back to the now and their gazes met. She had caught him staring at her.

Blast.

A flush of heat raced to his cheeks. "Ah. Yes?"

"Was there something you wished to say? You were looking at me and your lips were moving, but nothing came out of your mouth."

He almost turned away, then a sudden thought struck him. Here was a perfect opportunity to engage Maggie in conversation. To find out a little more about her. Only a fool would let such a chance go to waste. "I was going to ask you about Robert. How did you meet?"

She shifted in her seat, and he silently cursed himself for having raised the subject. Now they were going to share the rest of the journey to Towcester in awkward silence.

But Maggie simply nodded. The lack of emotion in her eyes, tore at Piers. Joy had been stripped from this young woman's life.

"He was at the theater. Well, actually, standing outside in

the street. Our eyes met, and he boldly stepped up and introduced himself. My parents were talking to some other friends at the time and so they didn't notice. As you know, it is not the usual way that a gentleman approaches a lady, but he looked so smart in his uniform that I let the oversight go."

She bent and began to rummage around in her oversized travel bag, then pulled out a small notebook. "That reminds me. I would like you to read the letter I received when Robert died. Since you are in the army and likely have experience with these matters, it might be worthwhile for you to take a look."

Maggie opened the book and handed Piers a folded-up piece of paper. He opened it and quickly read the brief missive.

A horrid feeling sunk to the pit of his stomach. This was not an official letter from the commander of the regiment. The lack of letterhead was a tell-tale sign. As was the fact that it was signed from the Commander-in-Chief of the First Foot. The regiment had been granted a new title under royal proclamation as soon as the battle was over. The letter should have been from the Commander-in-Chief of the Grenadier Guards.

From what he could guess, someone had written this note with some idea of what was usually included in such correspondence, but they had omitted many of the obvious details such as Robert Taylor's muster roll number and the correct regiment. Important details that an army officer tasked with writing such a significant letter would normally take pains to include.

Maggie let out an anxious sob. "It's not real, is it? That letter didn't come from the British Army. I have been a bloody fool."

Piers folded the paper and handed it back to her. He

couldn't imagine why someone would pen such a letter unless they were unable to get their hands on the real one.

"No, I don't think it came from the war office, but that does not imply that the contents are false. It could have been sent from a friend seeking to do you a kindness. Robert's family would have received the official letter as his next of kin. You were only his fiancée."

Idiot, why did you have to frame it that way?

"I mean, you and he were not ..."

"I know what you mean, Piers. I was never his wife and so shouldn't expect to have been accorded the respect due of one. But I still feel that somehow, somewhere, this is all wrong. It's a suspicion that has been growing in my mind for some time now."

He hadn't expected to hear that from her lips. His own theory was that Robert Taylor, or whatever his real name was, had duped Maggie into falling in love with him. There was a strong doubt in his mind that the man had been a captain. But this poor girl had grieved for him, had put her life and happiness away while doing what she believed to be honoring his memory.

If he had lied to her, the blackguard hadn't deserved one minute of her time, let alone her promise to be with him forever.

Piers sat forward in his seat, offering her his hand. Maggie took it, giving him a faint smile when he placed his other hand over hers. "Let's assume for the time being that what you know of Robert is the truth. But we should keep an open mind. If it transpires that Robert was a fraud, then at least it will settle a great number of questions. Either way, that puts the power back in your hands. The choice to move on with your life can't be taken away from you. Let us see what we can find—only then should you decide. I am not trying to tell you what to do; I am simply asking that you don't leap to any conclusions. I have seen others do that, and the price that was paid was far too high."

Maggie nodded. "It's strange to think that coming out of grief could somehow be more painful than being in it. I spent so long in a fog of misery. But my vision is becoming clearer every day, and I am finding that the closer I look at what I know of Robert's life, the less it makes sense."

Piers caught the unmistakable note of sadness in Maggie's voice. It tore at him. If only he could wrap his arms around her and offer Maggie comfort. Hold her and give her reassurance that things would sort themselves out.

You could do that, but since you don't believe in happy endings yourself, it would be the height of hypocrisy to promise Maggie that she could have one.

"Thank you, Piers. We haven't known one another very long, but I value your advice. You speak plainly. I don't need someone who is trying to placate me with pretty words."

He let go of her hand and sat back in his seat. She had already placed her trust in him, and that was a mistake. Shame sat heavily on him; his intentions were not honorable when it came to Maggie Radley. The longer he spent in her company, the more convinced of that he became.

Maggie was bright. Alluring. Piers hadn't ever thought that it was possible for him to be so engaged by a woman, but there was no doubt it was happening. Every minute they spent together, she was, bit by bit, stealing his heart.

The thought of Robert Taylor had jealousy stirring within him. He wanted nothing more than to reveal the man to have been a fraud, a liar. Only when Maggie stopped thinking of him as being some sort of war hero might she decide that it was time to find love again.

And when she did, Piers would be waiting.

Chapter Fifteen

Their stay at the Saracen's Head was brief and uneventful. The food was good, the company in the main tavern lively and engaging. But Maggie was subdued and retired to her room early. Piers could imagine that her mind was a constant worry of what she might discover in Coventry. Or what she might not. There were no guarantees in life.

He didn't linger in the tavern late. Instead, he paid a quick social call to some cousins who lived nearby, then returned to the inn and went to bed. Spending all day sitting in a travel coach was a surprisingly tiring occupation. His fatigue was worsened by his constant worry about Maggie, about what she may be thinking. And also, how she would react to whatever they might uncover in Robert's hometown.

They were barely beyond the stage of being strangers, but he found himself thinking about her far more than he should. He kept reminding himself that this wasn't some country jaunt; he had a job to do, and when it was done, he had to return to London.

But even as they sat opposite one another in the travel coach the following morning, Piers couldn't stop from sneaking sly little glances at her. He silently chided himself. He was acting like an infatuated fool.

Why am I behaving this way around her? It doesn't make sense.

A slow, deep breath, followed by yet another concerted effort to read his book, failed to stop his mind from wandering. With an exasperated huff, he tossed the book onto the bench.

Maggie lifted her head and their gazes met. "A boring tome?"

"Something like that," he lied.

She snapped her own book closed and set it on her lap. "Perhaps we should talk. We have a long day ahead of us. There will be time to attempt more reading later."

Piers nodded. There were plenty of letters he could write but the roads in this part of the county were not particularly well maintained. Any attempts to put pen to paper were doomed to fail. His handwriting was poor enough without making it look like a drunken pigeon had walked across the page. The carriage bounced along well enough most of the time, but there had been several occasions when both he and Maggie had quickly grabbed a hold of their armrests and held on for dear life.

"What would you like to talk about?" he replied.

Please don't let it be about Robert.

"How long have you been in the army?"

Maggie prayed that it was a simple and innocuous enough question to begin their conversation. She had other things she wished to ask Piers, but her instincts told her to tread carefully. He knew more about her than she did him, and she suspected that was by design.

"I joined in eighteen fourteen, but to be honest, they

didn't actually expect me to see any real fighting. Becoming an officer was something that I felt obliged to do. If I had known what it would cost me, I would have said no. But there are some men in British society who you don't ever refuse."

Piers fell silent after that last remark. He had been pressured into joining the army and regretted it.

So much for an innocent question. A slow shake of his head was enough to let Maggie know she really ought to change the subject. Seek refuge in the calmer waters of small talk.

"Do you spend much time in town? I mean, socially. I ask because our paths have never crossed before, and I find that a little strange," she blurted out.

This is so awkward.

"How is that strange? I mean, you have been out of circulation for some time. How can you not be surprised that we haven't met before?"

Maggie bit down nervously on her bottom lip. Trying to conduct a conversation with Piers was harder than it really ought to be, and those dark brown eyes of his weren't making it any easier.

But she rallied. Radleys were not known for backing down in any situation.

"I'm twenty-six years old, so I had been 'out' for some time before ..."

She left the rest of it unsaid, not wishing to make mention of Robert in the current discussion. Until recently, he was all she could talk about. Now a shift was taking place—one which she couldn't muster the energy to fight.

"I know your cousin, Alex, the Marquis of Brooke. And I also know your brother James. We were all at school at Eton at the same time. And while James is a few years younger than me, the age difference didn't stop him from giving me a bloodied nose in a fight."

Maggie let out a gasp of surprise. Piers knew James? And they had fought. This was an unexpected revelation.

Her interest stirred to excitement; Maggie leaned forward. She was eager to hear what else Piers had to say about her brother. "Don't keep me in suspense—tell me everything. James was always saying how much of a saint he was at school. You must give me something to use against him," she replied gleefully.

A laughing Piers wagged a finger at her. "Oh, no. I have a horrid feeling I shouldn't have told you that. I expect I have just broken some ancient code of the school and will be struck down by lightning at any minute now."

"You tease! How can you possibly tempt me with such scandalous gossip and then refuse to say any more? I demand you reveal every single sordid thing that you know about my brother. James has given Claire and I plenty of stick over the years when it came to our misdeeds. Revenge is long overdue."

"And how will you pay for this information, Miss Radley? Gossip is the currency of the *ton*, so it's only fair that a trade should be made."

The glint of mischief in his eye, sent heat racing down her spine. Maggie stopped laughing, tearing her gaze away. When had flirting with Piers become part of their connection? This was dangerous.

By playing these games, they were stepping well outside the boundaries of social propriety. Far beyond what she should be doing with a betrothed man.

If you were mine, I would never allow you to travel to Coventry with another woman.

If Piers was hers, the minute he proposed, Maggie would

have made plans for them to be wed with all due haste. Snapped him up as fast as she could, and never let him go.

But he isn't married.

If her mother had been correct in her take on the situation, Piers had been engaged for well over a year—something which was almost unheard of within London high society. Maggie didn't know of any couples who'd waited so long to wed.

She would dearly love to ask him about his fiancée. About the woman he was yet to make his wife.

Small talk. Make small talk. Something safe to set things back on an even keel.

"It's funny when you consider who knows who in our social circle, even if you and I have only just become acquainted. You know James from school. And my mother knows Lady Denford from the Queen's court circle. But then again, Mama is on a first-name basis with just about everyone in the *ton*. I doubt there are few people she doesn't know."

"I expect that comes from being the wife of the Bishop of London. Social gatherings must be a day-to-day proposition for her. And like with my mother, those things are ingrained from birth," he replied.

Maggie shook her head. "Actually, my mother didn't come from polite society. Her father was a professor at Cambridge University. That's how my parents met. Papa was one of his theology students. But they didn't really fall in love until after my father had graduated."

The story of how Hugh Radley had saved Mary Gray from an almost penniless existence after Professor Gray's death was one, she had heard many times. The romance which had finally blossomed at Strathmore Castle was one she had hoped to replicate herself. She wanted to share forever with someone special.

Can love strike twice in a life? Or have I already had my one chance taken from me?

Piers raised an eyebrow. "I can imagine it would have been difficult for your parents if they had been in love while Lord Hugh was still at university. The various colleges have firm rules against students having wives."

She hadn't wanted to ask, but he'd just given her the perfect opportunity. Maggie bit the bullet. "And what about you, Piers? I understand you have a fiancée. Have the two of you set a date for your wedding?"

She was fishing, and if the odd expression which quickly flittered across his face was any indication, Piers was well aware of what she was doing.

He cleared his throat. "It's complicated. And since the lady in question is owed a degree of discretion, I can't discuss it. I'm sorry, Maggie; I don't mean to be evasive with my answer. I just have to make sure that the feelings of others and their situations are protected."

His words were polite, but they were clear. She should mind her own business and not pry into his affairs. If anyone could understand how difficult things could be for someone who should rightly be married by now, it was her. "I am the one who should be apologizing, Piers. I have no right to ask such personal questions. It was not my intention to cause offense," she replied.

"You didn't. I wish I could tell you, but Lady Dinah and I made a pact last summer. Neither of us would discuss the status of our betrothal with anyone else."

He was being guarded with his words, but there was a definite undercurrent of relief in the way he spoke. Maggie guessed that the betrothal had come to an end, and while Piers was waiting for Lady Dinah to make that public, he clearly wasn't disappointed that it was over. His behavior was understandable—a gentleman wouldn't ever be so crass as to speak of the end of an engagement, especially before the lady involved let it be known in her private circle.

She searched for another, safer topic for discussion. "Your brother, Jonathan. Is he your only sibling?"

Piers smiled at her, and the air between them cleared. "No. He is my younger brother; there are also three girls in the family. I was baby number four, and to the utter relief of my parents, a boy. My older sisters are all married, as is Jonathan."

Keen to move away from the subject of marriage, Maggie focused on their destination. "Whereabouts in Coventry, are we staying? I don't know the city; it's not somewhere that we have ever visited. My family tends to move around London, only leaving for Scotland when it is Christmas." She had travelled the Great North Road so many times, Maggie was certain she could find her way to Strathmore Castle without a map.

"Jonathan and Elizabeth live in St. Mary's Street, which is in central Coventry, not far from the churches of St. Michael's and Holy Trinity. It's convenient for our purposes as we should be able to visit both them and other nearby churches in order to look for Robert's baptism records. I will also have to check in with the barracks since I am visiting the city on army business. I could ask around there and see if anyone remembers Robert."

A strange sensation touched Maggie. She didn't want to hear Piers mention the name of her former fiancé. When it came to Robert, something had shifted in her heart.

The silence was deafening.

Chapter Sixteen

"I can't believe you arrived unannounced on my doorstep with the Bishop of London's daughter in tow. Brother dearest, you have some explaining to do," said Jonathan, closing the door of his study. His wife, Elizabeth, was busy showing Maggie upstairs to her room.

Piers rubbed his tired temple. Where was he to begin? "I am sorry. I should have written, but things happened all rather quickly. I was ordered to come north only a few days ago."

He gratefully accepted the generous glass of brandy his brother handed him, then took a seat in an old leather chair. Jonathan sat opposite Piers on the other side of his desk.

Elizabeth's stepfather was a major shareholder in the Coventry Canal Company, and Jonathan worked for them as a manager, liaising with the various mining companies which sent their coal down the canal to the English midlands and beyond.

Jonathan Denford had a good head for figures, and he had helped retrieve the fortunes of the company after the construction costs of the canal had threatened to send it bankrupt.

Silence hung in the room, only finally broken when Piers softly chuckled. "You are not going to give me an inch, are you?"

His brother shook his head. "No. Consider it punishment for not having been to visit for eleven months. We haven't seen you since Christmas, and then all of a sudden, you are knocking on the front door asking to stay. Just be grateful that Elizabeth is a pragmatic woman. Now talk."

Piers sipped at his brandy. It was a relief to finally be in Coventry and also to see a familiar face. Jonathan might well be giving him grief, but it was nothing compared to what Piers had endured almost every day in London.

Where to begin?

"Maggie Radley's fiancé died at Waterloo. And while that was tragic enough, she has recently discovered that he may not have been all that he claimed to be," he replied.

Jonathan's eyes went wide. "You mean, he was a fraud?"

"I am beginning to suspect he might have been. I can't find any record of him in the army files in London. He is not on the muster rolls. We came to Coventry because that is where he is supposed to have been born. I just want Maggie to get some answers. And perhaps be able to close that chapter of her life."

It was a relief to finally give voice to that horrid thought. Speaking ill of the dead didn't sit well with him, but from what he had discovered, or rather, *not* discovered about Robert Taylor, Piers was of the opinion that the captain had lied to Maggie.

Jonathan set his glass on the desk and clasped his hands together. "Speaking of answers, have you heard anything more regarding your own situation? I take it the British Army hasn't moved to formally charge you with anything. But that doesn't mean that they won't at some juncture. You need that letter of support from the Prince of Orange. He might well be the heir to the throne of the Netherlands, and as such a very important member of a foreign royal family, but even he cannot just leave you hanging like this. You helped save his life."

Piers sighed; he had been expecting this but had hoped his brother might at least have left it alone until he had finished his drink. "Yes, I know the prince is honor bound to support me, but I still haven't heard back from him. I have written to the Dutch royal family several times over the past year. But nothing has come of it."

"Too busy renovating the lavish toy palace his papa gave him for his heroic stupidity at Waterloo," huffed Jonathan.

King Willem I had gifted his son Soestdijk Palace in recognition of his efforts during the battle at Waterloo. And it was rumored that the prince was spending a fortune on expanding and upgrading the main building, adding two more wings to the already impressive structure.

Piers didn't want to get into a discussion about the role the Prince of Orange had played in both the skirmish at Quatre Bras and the bloody battle at Waterloo. Many people in Britain had labelled him a rash fool, and at the age of twenty-two, far too young to be in command. But the young prince Piers had witnessed during the campaign was anything but hot-headed. He was brave and fearless. A fool he was not.

None of this helped with Piers's personal situation. The Prince of Orange was back in Europe, while Piers was stuck serving under the command of a man who would love to see him hauled before a military court and destroyed. Jonathan might well be frustrated, but he had no idea what it was like for Piers to endure the taunts of his nemesis every day.

"I'm worried about you, dear brother. What are you going

to do if they decide to press charges against you?" Jonathan asked.

I dread to think. "They haven't done anything until now. At times, I wonder if they have any real evidence. It will be my word against that of Major Hall. He is a cunning bastard, which is probably why he is more than content to have me working through mounds of paperwork."

He didn't want to make mention of the rest of the mistreatment he suffered on an almost daily basis. His family shouldn't have to bear the burden of his troubles.

"What about the Prince Regent? Have you tried to approach him?" suggested Jonathan.

"Yes, but I didn't have much success. I couldn't get an audience. And now, with the death of Princess Charlotte, he is not likely to be answering any correspondence or seeing anyone for the foreseeable future. Poor Prinny. No one deserves to bury their child."

"No, it's a terrible business. He must feel so hopeless."

Piers took another long drink of his brandy. He understood only too well what it was to feel a lack of hope. Part of his reason for wanting to come to Coventry and help Maggie was that it gave him a sense of purpose. He might not be able to move on with his own life, but if he could help her, it would be something.

Where there is life, there is hope.

"Who else can you write to? There must be someone. You are the son of a viscount—not some private from the slums of St. Giles. I refuse to let you give up on getting justice," pressed Jonathan.

His brother was right. And it was good to hear someone speak in his defense. But none of this mess was as simple as others seemed to think. There were delicate layers to it. If one of them was disturbed, it could easily destroy not only Piers's chances of getting out of the army, but also his family's name. This never-ending purgatory was slowly but surely killing him.

"I understand your frustration. I have written a number of letters recently, seeking out support from other quarters, but they have either chosen not to reply or the response has been a guarded *no*," replied Piers.

The Denford family wasn't without friends or influence. Piers did, however, get a distinct impression that within the *ton*, people not only didn't want to get involved, but they were also doing their utmost to ensure their names were not connected in any way with his current situation. The mere sniff of a scandal had sent people scurrying away.

"And of course, you won't let Father get involved," said Jonathan.

Piers didn't reply. If they started in on this particular topic, there was every chance that he and Maggie would soon be decamping to the nearest hotel. It was better if he simply held his tongue. This was his fight—not his father's or Jonathan's.

His brother got to his feet and came around to the front of his desk. Piers rose. Jonathan took the glass from his hand and placed it on the desk. Then the two of them embraced— a reassuring, brotherly hug. When they finally broke apart, both were wiping tears away.

"I miss you," said Piers.

Jonathan nodded. "Same here, Piers. You have no idea. I just wish this whole army business was over and done with."

Piers gave a resigned sigh. "Some of it is my own fault. I foolishly assumed that I would receive swift justice over the accusations of that report from the battle. I was naïve. I kept writing to the Prince of Orange and when he didn't reply, I let the British Army bury me under a mountain of paperwork. I know I have to try another way to get this matter resolved. It's part of the reason why I wanted to come north. I need time to get my thoughts straight. To put a new strategy together. When I return to town, I'm going to ask to see both the Secretary at War and the Duke of Wellington."

Jonathan threw up his hands. "Finally. It's only taken you two years to give up your stubborn resistance and actually seek help from a higher authority."

That wasn't exactly true. Piers had tried a number of avenues, none of which had been successful. To his dismay, he had discovered that Major Hall also had friends in high places. Ones who shared his suspicions about anyone who had served with the Prince of Orange.

"You know I don't like having to ask for help. It's not in my nature."

"Yes, but you are more than willing to put yourself in harm's way, or at least significant inconvenience, to come to the aid of others. I am certain that this trip to Coventry wouldn't have happened if you weren't trying to rescue a damsel in distress," replied Jonathan.

He let that remark go. Jonathan had every right to vent his frustration.

"Speaking of damsels, have you heard from Lady Dinah?" Jonathan asked.

It was a subtle but no less painful change in subject. Jonathan was always one for dealing with problems head on. His success in business reflected his pragmatic disposition.

Piers slowly shook his head, his gaze dropping to the floor. "No, we agreed to let things fall silent for the time being. Though I expect she will wish to make things official after Christmas. I can't blame her."

Jonathan cleared his throat and Piers flinched. He didn't like the expression on his brother's face. It spoke of deep worry. And bad news.

"Elizabeth met Lady Dinah's brother, Lord Gibney, in town last week. He was here for the wool sales. Apparently, and don't quote me on this, she has become quite sweet on the son of a local magistrate. The chap in question has a good background, and the family has a magnificent estate not far from London."

Piers hadn't heard anything directly from his former fiancée, but he could understand why her brother had made mention of it to Elizabeth. It was a subtle but pointed nudge for him to do something about his situation, and therefore give Lady Dinah a way out of their betrothal.

At least that was one mess Piers could do something about. While he was here in Coventry, he would pen a letter to Lady Dinah, asking for a month's grace, at the end of which she could officially jilt him. In doing so, it would put a time limit on his own actions and free the ever-patient earl's daughter from their agreement.

She has been more than generous in holding off.

"I swear that between now and Christmas I will get this matter resolved. I'm tired of having the bloody Sword of Damocles hanging over my head. The army can't prove me guilty of anything because ... well, I didn't do anything wrong. If I had stayed where Major Hall wanted me, the Prince of Orange would be dead. As for the rest of the vile rumors, well they have no substance."

He had done his job as best he could. Brought the wounded prince to safety and helped save his life. And yet, all he had received in return was his name slandered in a scathing report from the battle and the army's continued refusal to let him resign.

Piers glanced at his empty glass, picked it up, and held it out to his brother. "I could do with another, and this time, don't hold back when you pour."

Chapter Seventeen

H e might well be in Coventry and a welcome hundred miles away from Major Hall, but the army still had its claws firmly stuck in Piers's skin. The first thing on his long list of things to do the morning after he and Maggie arrived in the city was to report to the barracks on Smithford Street and let the commanding officer know of his presence.

Before joining the army, Piers had enjoyed a life of freedom with few ties. Having to answer to the army when all he wanted to do was resign his commission was humiliating. But he was not going to give them any excuse to punish him further. He couldn't think of anything worse than spending his days filling in paperwork and answering letters, but he was certain that, given half the chance, Major Hall could come up with something.

The barracks themselves were mostly empty with only a few guards marching up and down the square. He made himself known at the gate and was quickly escorted to the main administrative building, where the clearly perplexed muster roll officer, Captain Ward, greeted him.

"Captain Denford. It's a pleasure to meet you. I didn't

realize we had troop movements coming up from London. Do you have your orders with you?" he asked.

Piers shook his head. "No soldiers; just me. I am under direct orders from Major Hall at the Horse Guards. He has sent me to deal with an outstanding matter."

The captain raised a single eyebrow in response to Piers's cryptic words but wisely said nothing. From the white and gray specks in his hair, coupled with the deep crow's feet at the corner of his eyes, he appeared to be a man who had already seen more than enough during his service in the army. Men like him understood the expression of being on a need-to-know basis only too well. "I see. Is there anything I can help you with, Captain Denford?"

Piers's conversation with Jonathan dropped into his thoughts. He had told his brother he was going start asking for more assistance. Stop being so stubbornly self-reliant and take back control of his life. That included seeking help from all levels of society. Not just the rich and powerful.

"Any assistance you can give me will be gratefully received. I am looking for an officer who was reportedly born in Coventry. He died at Waterloo. There appears to be an issue with his records, and Major Hall is most keen to have the matter set straight. I was hoping to be able to check the muster or payroll records here. The officer in question claimed to have been based in Coventry some time before shipping out for the final battle against Napoleon's forces. But my understanding is that there weren't any regiments coming out of Coventry. Were there any based here?"

His suspicions regarding Robert Taylor were well-formed; he just needed them to be confirmed.

"Apart from the guards and a few administrative officers, there isn't a permanent body of soldiers here. There hasn't been since the Seventeenth and then the Fourteenth Light Dragoons were stationed at the barracks, and that goes back some eight years. The Smithford Street Barracks are purely a stopping point for regiments moving from the north to the south and vice versa. This officer you seek wasn't stationed here. But, if you think he originated from Coventry, then you might have better luck searching the parish records of the local churches," replied Captain Ward.

Piers was disappointed, but not at all surprised. He hadn't expected to have luck with the barracks, but he owed it to Maggie to make sure he chased down all possible leads. To get to the truth of Robert Taylor.

The churches it is. I hope they have their records in order.

"Would you happen to know which of the major churches might keep the records of people baptized here in the city of Coventry? If I am going to see if I can find the elusive captain in them, I might as well start with the bigger ones."

"Ah, yes, I would. While St. Michael's is the larger church, it's actually Holy Trinity where most of the records of the city are kept. I would suggest you start there. It is on New Street at the top of the hill. Do you know where that is?"

Piers nodded. "Yes, my younger brother, Jonathan, lives in St. Mary's Street. He is a senior member of the company which owns and manages the Coventry canal."

A knowing smile appeared on the captain's lips. "I was wondering if you were Piers Denford, not just Captain Denford. I'm originally from Thrapston; my mother used to work in the kitchens at Denford Park."

"Ah, small world. I recall Mrs. Ward; she used to bake the most wonderful scones. She would put a slice of cheese inside them as soon as they came out of the oven. I burnt my tongue on them more than once in a greedy attempt to stuff a hot scone into my mouth. Tell me, is your mother still alive?"

Captain Ward gave a brief shake of his head. "No, we lost Mama a few years back. I was on service in the Canadian territories at the time. I am glad to hear that you enjoyed her cooking; I do miss her scones."

"I shall remind my mother of yours when I next visit Denford Park. Now I wish I had a hot scone in my hand," said Piers.

After a brief exchange of salutes, Piers headed toward the front door. In a matter of minutes, he was climbing the slight rise which led up to the Holy Trinity Church. His mission? To find the baptismal records of Robert Eustace Taylor.

Inside the towering medieval structure which dated back to the thirteenth century, he found a deacon who led him down into the dusty chamber of records. There were shelves full of scrolls and papers. In the middle of the room, a large oak table was covered in numerous piles of papers and books. The thought that all of them contained the parish records of births, marriages, and deaths had Piers wishing he had stopped for a cup of tea on his way up the hill.

Putting his hand into his coat pocket, Piers took out the last letter Maggie had written to him. In it, she had noted Robert's full name and the city of Coventry as being his place of birth, but nothing else.

He handed it to the deacon, who screwed up his nose at the paucity of information.

"Would you have any idea as to how old Robert Taylor was when he passed away?" he asked.

Piers frowned as he racked his brain trying to recall the date Maggie had penned in her notes. He hadn't made much of an effort to remember those sorts of details. He didn't want to think too much about Captain Taylor at all.

Was he born in 1790? I think that was what Maggie had written in her notes.

He couldn't be certain, but then again, Maggie had also not been sure of Robert's year of birth. A guess would have to suffice.

"I am assuming he was aged somewhere in his mid-twenties—thirty at the oldest. He was a captain, and most men are not at that rank in their younger years."

He was only guessing that would be the case, but they had to start somewhere.

The deacon nodded. "That brings the number of books we have to search down to a manageable number. Let's start with the yearbook of seventeen ninety; that would have made the man you seek twenty-five when he died. If we don't find anything in that book, we can always go back further."

"Good idea. I think his fiancée thought Captain Taylor had been born around that time, but she wasn't certain."

In a city the size of Coventry, there had to be a good number of births every year.

This might take quite some time.

Piers was keen to find some answers to Maggie's many questions. If it took all day, then so be it. To be able to give her at least some verified information would be well worth his effort.

It had been such a long time since he had held any tangible control over his own life that Piers was genuinely excited at the prospect of thumbing through dusty old books. Of successfully hunting down a clue.

The deacon retrieved a large blue leather-bound book from a nearby shelf and, pushing aside a pile of the papers, set it on the table in the middle of the room.

That looks like my desk at the Horse Guards.

To Piers's surprise, the book wasn't that thick. His hopes stirred at the prospect of this search not being too big a task. *If I can get through this quickly, I might be able to grab a bite to eat on the way home.*

"Now, let us see. Baptisms for the year of our Lord, seventeen ninety," said the deacon. He thumbed through a number of pages. "Here we are."

He ran his finger down the length of the page, then shook his head. "No. No Robert Taylor for that year. He may, in fact, have already been born at that time, as not all parents bring their children for baptism straight away. Not like they used to in the old days. It is not uncommon for us to see children of six months and older now being brought to the font."

"Does that mean he could be in the records for the following year?" replied Piers.

The deacon sighed. "Or not at all. There is a slow movement away from the Church of England. You would be surprised how many people don't go to the service on Sunday morning. Folks use the time to rest from their labors."

Piers didn't want to consider that awkward option. If Robert had been an army officer, there was every chance he came from a respectable family. One which went to church every week. And one which also had their children baptized in a timely fashion.

The deacon retrieved a second book from the shelves. "This is the book for seventeen ninety-one. He may be in here."

He flipped through the book, then bent and examined one of the pages. "This looks promising." The deacon tapped his finger on a spot two thirds of the way down the page.

Piers stirred from his musings and glanced at the place where the deacon was pointing.

Robert Eustace Taylor. Son of Thomas and Alice.
Abode. 84 Little Park Street, Coventry

His breath caught sharp. Robert had really existed.

Damn.

He'd been secretly hoping that Robert had been a false name, adopted by a lying knave who would forever remain an unsolved mystery. Shame over his conflicted emotions welled up inside Piers.

I am jealous of a man I have never met. Someone who died in battle. What sort of person does that make me?

"Little Park Street is close by. You never know—the Taylors may still be at that address. People don't tend to move unless it is necessary. And if Robert Taylor was still a young man when he died, then there is a good chance that someone in Little Park Street will know his family," said the deacon.

A reluctant Piers nodded his agreement. "You are probably right. It would be worth paying a visit to the house where he was born. Thank you."

To find out more about him. And whether the rest of what he told Maggie was indeed a lie. But if he really was an officer, why doesn't the army have any record of him?

Mission accomplished, Piers left the church and headed back to St. Mary's Street. He was sorely tempted to take a detour via Little Park Street, but he resisted. Much as he wanted to push forward and find out more, he was forced to acknowledge that this was Maggie's quest. She should be the one to make the decision about whether they would reach out to Robert's family. All he could do was accept and respect whatever she decided.

But there was one thing he wouldn't allow her to do, and that was to go and visit the Taylor family on her own. Piers was firm in that regard. Someone had to be there for Maggie when she finally confronted the truth of her fiancé's past.

He may well have existed, but Robert Taylor still had a lot of explaining to do. Even if it was from beyond the grave.

Chapter Eighteen

Maggie stared at her gowns laid out on the bed. They had been the staples of her wardrobe for the past two and a half years, and until today, she had worn them with a sense of pride and dignity. Her gaze took in the black, the dull grays, and the washed-out lilac. It was a palette of misery, the visual signs of her grief.

She was possessed with an overwhelming need to cast all the garments aside and never wear them again. They no longer represented who she was or her state of mind. Earlier, she had slipped the betrothal ring from her hand and put it in her travel bag. It was time to move on.

I feel a sense of change in me. And it's a good one.

Coventry was a large city. There were shops where she could purchase new gowns. One or two would be enough to see her through this trip. Maggie could just imagine the smile on her mother's face when she walked through the door at Fulham Palace wearing a dress of a colorful hue.

"You have served me well, but now it is time that we part ways," she whispered to her dresses.

Decision made, she donned her lilac gown for the last time, then went in search of Elizabeth.

~

The morning spent wandering the drapery stores and shops of Coventry yielded a whole new wardrobe for Maggie. At the back of the fitting room in Elizabeth's favorite modiste, she had uncovered a pale apple green and rose-striped ready-made gown. To her delight, the dress fitted. After trying it on, she decided to buy it. Further examination of the rest of the workroom wardrobes resulted in a pale pink, and a deep blue gown, which joined her growing collection. But the grand discovery of the day was a scarlet red dress, cinched at the waist, which fitted Maggie so perfectly that it could only have been destiny which brought the two of them together.

As soon as they returned home, Maggie gave all her other gowns to the lady's maid who Elizabeth had assigned to her. The maid was more than delighted to take the cast-off garments. Anything made by a top London modiste would fetch a pretty penny on the thriving secondhand clothes market.

Deciding to keep the red gown for a special occasion, Maggie changed into the blue dress. She instantly transformed from her dowdy-looking self to something faintly resembling the Maggie Radley of old. There was even a smile on her lips as she considered her reflection in the dressing mirror.

Stepping into Maggie's room, Elizabeth nodded her approval. "It suits you so much better than those other gowns. And it goes beautifully with your hair."

She took a hold of Maggie's hand. "I know we have known one another only a day or so, but I am proud of you. It takes strength to move on from loss. My mother was widowed young, and I can still remember the day four years after my father died when she came home with a new cream-colored gown. It wasn't the dress; it was the light which had returned to her eyes that gave me such joy."

"I think I know how she might have been feeling. The moment I put this dress on, a weight lifted off my shoulders. Tell me, did your mother ever remarry?" Maggie's gaze shifted from the mirror, and she met the tear-filled eyes of her hostess.

"Yes. To a lovely man who, after proposing to Mama, asked if I would consider calling him Papa. He honored the memory of my father with that simple request. And he has made my mother happy every day since."

A tide of emotion welled up inside Maggie—a sense of hope for the future. That someday she, too, might find a man who would bring her happiness. That love would once more grace her heart.

The sound of the front door being closed drifted upstairs. Elizabeth hurried out to the landing and called out, "Piers, we are up here."

"Ah, very good. Is Maggie with you?"

"Yes, I am," she replied.

The thrum of his boots echoed up the stairs, and he quickly appeared. He gave Elizabeth a brief hug, then turned to Maggie. A flush raced to her cheeks as his gaze settled on her gown and an approving smile formed on his lips.

"You look lovely, Maggie. Is that new?" he asked.

Her ears and cheeks burned. Piers had an effect on her, she couldn't control. It was sweet of him to have noticed the change in her attire. The glint in his eyes spoke of a deeper appreciation. She swallowed deeply, trying to keep her face from going up in flames.

I'm so pleased he likes the gown. And he thinks I look lovely.

"I bought it this morning. Elizabeth kindly took me shopping and I thought it might be nice to wear something with a little more color."

She put a hand to her face, praying it would cool down. Blushing like this was deeply embarrassing.

Change the subject. Ask him about his morning.

"How did your visit to the barracks go?" she asked.

Piers nodded. "Good. I discovered a few things. And then I paid a call to Holy Trinity Church, where they keep the parish registers. And that uncovered some interesting information."

Elizabeth brushed a hand on Maggie's arm. "I shall leave the two of you to talk. I had better go and check on the children. They are quiet, and that is never a good sign."

As soon as she was gone, Piers ushered Maggie into the drawing room and closed the door. "The captain at the barracks confirmed that no regiments have been permanently based here for quite a few years, and he has no recollection of a Captain Taylor. But I did find a Robert Eustace Taylor in the births and baptisms at Holy Trinity Church. While we suspect that he may not have been an army captain, he certainly existed."

Maggie wasn't sure how she felt about that piece of news. Or if she found it to be any sort of comfort. The man who had captured her heart had lied to her. She had never really known him.

"There is also an address where his family lived when he was born. Number eighty-four, Little Park Street. It's not too far from here, so I thought perhaps you and I could go for a walk. See if we can find anyone who might remember him, or even knock on the door and discover if the family still resides there. You did say you would like to meet Robert's relatives," said Piers.

She considered his offer for a moment. If the Taylor

family did live at number eighty-four, and she came knocking on their door, what would she say?

Pardon me for coming to your house, but at one time I was actually betrothed to your late son. And by the way, did you know he pretended to be an army officer?

Maggie shook her head. There had to be another way to find out about his family. "Could we walk the street, and then you go and knock on the door? You could say you were an old army friend who just happened to be passing through Coventry."

Her light mood of the morning was quickly dissipating, replaced by fear. Fear of what she might discover. Confronting the truth had her nerves on edge.

It was foolish to allow her emotions to sway back and forth. To let them feed on her insecurity.

When she met Piers's gaze, he grimly nodded. "Alright, let's do that. There is nothing to say that we cannot go back and visit the house again if you change your mind when we get there. I will be led by your needs."

"Thank you. I know it all sounds rather silly, but I'm not sure how I would react if I happened to meet a member of the Taylor family. I might need a day or two to summon up the courage if they are indeed at that address. But yes, it cannot hurt to take a stroll past the house."

His gaze drifted to the door. "How do you feel about us going now? I mean, strike while the iron is hot."

Maggie could understand Piers's reasons for wanting to follow through on his efforts of the morning. The sooner they knew, the sooner she could begin to deal with the truth. And then he could return to London.

"That's a sensible idea. I shall go and get my cloak," she said.

As she headed up to her room, Maggie's heart was beating at

a clip. Her mouth was dry. She had thought about this day for such a long time, practiced what she might say to Robert's family, so it was surprising to discover she was more than a little anxious.

She stopped at the entrance to her room and clutched the wooden door jamb for support.

"Thank you, Lord, for sending me Piers. I don't know if I could do this on my own."

~

A few minutes later, they left the house and made their way down the hill. Turning right, they stepped into Earl Street, then walked over onto Little Park. At the corner, Maggie slowed her steps. She placed her hand flat on her chest, praying that her heart would stop beating so hard.

Oh no, please not today.

Piers brushed his hand over the back of her neck. While his fingers were warm, their touch still made her shiver.

She turned to face him. "There is something I should tell you. For a time, I suffered from strange nervous attacks where my breathing became labored, and I would feel giddy. The doctor called them widow's wails, which I suppose fitted my mental state."

"I've heard of similar things happening to soldiers on the battlefield. Of course, the military don't openly discuss it. They regard a man affected in such a way to be a coward," he said, placing a hand on her arm. "Thank you for telling me; I suspect that wasn't an easy thing to do. I am here for you, Maggie. If there is any moment when you feel that this is all too much, you just have to say the word and we will go home."

Maggie hadn't wanted to confess her secret, but Piers deserved to know, just in case one of those attacks suddenly occurred. It had been more than a year since her last episode, brought on by stress. Right now, she couldn't think of anything more stressful than possibly meeting the family of her dead fiancé.

No matter how much I don't want to do this, I know I must. I have to face the past.

If she didn't, she couldn't ever be fully ready to move forward.

After taking a deep breath, Maggie straightened her shoulders. She gave Piers a tight smile. "Lead on."

It was just his luck. There was nothing little about Little Park Street. From the way the houses were numbered, eighty-four was situated a long way down.

Poor Maggie. Piers couldn't begin to imagine how hard every single step must have been for her. But to her credit, she held her head high and kept going. After hearing her confession about the attacks of nerves, he was keeping a close eye on her, ready to escort her back to St. Mary's Street the second she began to falter.

When they reached number seventy, Piers caught sight of an elderly gentleman standing in the front yard, casually leaning over the fence. He sensed an opportunity.

"Good afternoon," Piers said.

The old man took one look at Piers's officers' uniform and raised a weathered hand to his head, giving a stiff salute. "Sir."

"You look like a chap who knows everyone in this street. I would bet a shilling that you have lived here for a great many years." *And seen everything that has happened.*

His remark was greeted with a gruff, grumbling chuckle. "Try fifty-three years. This was my wife's family home; I moved here when we were first married. Been here ever since."

Capital. Just the sort of man I need.

Piers nodded toward Maggie. "We are seeking the family of an old friend. Robert Taylor. We understand they used to live in this street at number eighty-four. Would you happen to know if the Taylor family is still in residence at that address?"

The old man screwed up his already lined and craggy face. "The rest of the Taylor family moved away a few years back, but Robert didn't. His house is around the corner. But, if you don't mind me saying so, you don't seem the type of people who would mix with the likes of Robert Taylor. You are quality, and he is far from that."

From the look on his face, it was clear the old man hadn't thought much of Robert. The hairs on the back of Piers's neck shifted.

What else had that blackguard done before heading off to London and charming Maggie into falling in love with him?

Concern was now building into deep suspicion. Had Maggie given her heart to an utter cad? One who had lied about everything?

Maggie gave the man a tight smile. "No. It was a different sort of friendship. I was hoping to maybe commission a statue in his honor. To recognize his sacrifice for his country."

"Why? He hasn't done anything of note. The only thing he has sacrificed is that shambles of a front garden. And the house needs painting. I'd give him a medal if he got off his arse and did more than drink and gamble."

He is talking of Robert in the present tense, as if he were still alive. But why?

Doing his best to shake off his growing unease, Piers chanced a glance at Maggie. While she shifted a little on her feet, her eyes were focused firmly on the old man, taking in everything he said. She was an intelligent woman, so there was every chance that her mind was also putting two and two together. And coming up with a horrible outcome.

"You say Robert Taylor moved around the corner—to where, exactly?" asked Piers.

The old man nodded his head in the direction of the opposite side of the street. Piers's gaze followed. At that part of the street, a narrow lane way with houses on one side of it intersected with Little Park Street.

"He and his wife moved into Cow Lane. Number fifteen, I think. With a growing brood, they needed more room."

No. He—no!

Even Piers hadn't seen that one coming.

Chapter Nineteen

Maggie's mind was a swirl of confusion. The old man must be wrong. He had to have his Taylors mixed up. It was a common enough surname. And there were likely dozens of men called Robert.

He must be mistaken. He has to be.

The other option was all too awful to even consider.

Grabbing a hold of Piers's sleeve, she tugged hard, desperate to get his attention. When he turned, their gazes met. She silently pleaded with him for them to leave. Her nerves were already starting to unravel.

I don't want to have an attack in the middle of the street.

He glanced down at her gloved hand gripping tightly to his coat and gave a brief nod.

Message received and understood.

"Thank you for your valuable information, kind sir. We shall go and see if there is anyone home at number fifteen. Good day to you," said Piers.

"You are welcome. And if Robert is home, tell him he needs to get his hands dirty and pull up some weeds. His garden is an utter disgrace."

Crossing the street, Maggie kept a firm hold of Piers's arm, too afraid to let go.

Please. Please let the old man be mistaken.

Piers stopped and turned to face her. "Are you alright Maggie? If you want us to go home, we can. I will understand if that is your decision."

Maggie was tempted but she had come to Coventry seeking answers. No matter how painful, she was determined to discover the truth.

"I have to do this, Piers. I have to know."

Cow Lane was mercifully short, with only a handful of houses situated along the right-hand side of the street. They walked past the first few before Piers suddenly stopped in front of a dilapidated house. He deftly placed a hand around her waist, steadying Maggie as she stumbled to a halt.

"It's alright. I'm here. I will protect you," he said.

She sensed he was referring to more than just her anxiety attacks. Whatever they discovered at the Taylor residence, he would be there for her.

It was strange, but in the short time that she and Piers had spent in each other's company, an easy connection of minds had somehow been established. Both seemed able to perceive what the other was thinking without the need for words. She had never before shared such a close bond with another person, not even Robert.

"I could come back here on my own if you like," he offered.

It would be all too easy to say yes, to spare herself from what she might find, but Maggie had learned enough about herself over the past few years to know that fear had to be faced. It was the only way to conquer it.

She drew out of Piers's hold. Straightening her shoulders,

she took a deep breath, determined that fear wouldn't get the better of her.

"I have come this far to get answers. I am not going to take a step back at the last," she replied. She cursed the tremble in her voice.

They entered in through the front gate, passing the tangled knots of weeds which had overtaken much of the garden. The front of the house was as the old man had described—poorly maintained and badly in need of a coat of paint. A nail or two also wouldn't go astray.

Piers rapped politely on the door.

No answer.

He tried again but still, no one came. "They must be out. We could leave a note, but I think it better that we come back later."

Cow Lane wasn't all that far from Jonathan and Elizabeth's house. It would be easy enough for them to pay the Taylors another visit.

Besides, if they did leave a note, what on earth would they write?

Pardon the intrusion, but we came looking for a person whose life was apparently a lie. We will call again when it is convenient.

Maggie was secretly relieved that the Taylor family wasn't at home. Going back to St. Mary's Street meant she would have time to gather the reserves of her courage. To compose her response if ... no, she wouldn't even consider that as being any sort of possibility.

Because if it was, then her life for the better part of the last three years would have been a tragic farce.

"Piers let's leave. It's clear that no one is at home, so we shouldn't waste any more of our time. I would dearly love a cup of tea and some peaceful solitude," she said.

They headed back the way they had come. At the crossroad, they turned left once more into Little Park Street. Soon they would be back at Jonathan and Elizabeth's home.

Thank heavens.

A sense of relief slowly settled in her mind.

"We could wait until tomorrow to come back. Perhaps visit earlier in the day," suggested Piers.

Maggie nodded absentmindedly. Her gaze had drifted to the other side of the street, settling on a young couple approaching down the hill.

They were walking side by side. A small child was held in the man's arms, while two older children trailed behind them. The heavily pregnant woman leaned in and spoke to her partner. The man laughed. There was a comforting familiarity about the exchange. It spoke of a long, loving relationship.

As they drew closer, Maggie narrowed her eyes. Her whole focus was now on the man. On the familiar features. On that winning, charming smile. She could hear his laughter carrying on the light wind.

Maggie stopped dead in the street, unable to take another step.

"What is it? What is wrong? Maggie?" said Piers, reaching for her arm.

"It's Robert."

Her legs buckled from under her.

Chapter Twenty

✦✦✦

When she came to, Maggie found herself staring up into Piers's dark brown eyes. They were two pools of deep worry.

"Thank God. For a moment there I thought you had expired on the spot."

She tried to sit up, but her woozy head quickly put paid to those plans, and she settled back carefully onto the pavement.

"Steady. Just rest for a minute longer. Let yourself come fully awake."

Blinking, she tried to recall what had been going through her mind the moment before everything went black. "What happened?"

"You fainted, Maggie. I managed to catch you as you fell."

I fainted.

She had never passed out before. The anxiety attacks had always made her giddy and light-headed, but not enough to lose consciousness. "I don't understand," she murmured.

And then it all came rushing back. The couple. The gaggle of happy children.

Him.

Piers had dropped to the stone pavement beside her and was cradling Maggie in his arms. A small crowd was gathered around them, strangers all staring down at her. No doubt they were wondering why the well-dressed young woman was lying on her back in the middle of the footpath.

"Please make them go away. This is all too embarrassing," she whispered, clutching the lapel of his coat. She needed something, someone steady to hold onto.

He lifted his head and nodded at the onlookers. "Thank you for your kind concern, but please — give my wife and me a moment to handle this matter in private. She will soon be well enough for us to continue on our way home."

Maggie hid her face in the front of Piers's coat waiting until the last of the gathering had dispersed. The only concession to her public embarrassment was the fact that she was in Coventry, and no one apart from Piers and his family knew her. Or her family.

That's not true. Robert knows who you are.

He had to have seen her fall. To have heard the small cry she let out as she collapsed.

Piers shifted his weight and struggled to his feet. He hauled Maggie upright, staggering back as he took her weight. She fell against him. Her legs felt like they were made of jelly.

"You saw him, didn't you? I mean, he wasn't a ghost," she said.

"I heard you say Robert just before you dropped. But I was too busy stopping you from dashing your head against the stone path to have time to look around."

The crowd of onlookers had moved on, going about their business. No doubt they were all talking about the lady in the blue gown who had collapsed in the street, giving their own opinions as to what could have been the cause of her distress.

Robert and his family were nowhere to be seen.

A gust of icy wind raced up the street, and a shivering Maggie pressed herself against Piers. "I can't believe he is still alive. That he would fake his own death. How could a man do such a dishonorable thing?"

"I don't know, but I swear I will get to the bottom of this. The blackguard will pay for what he has done to you. There is nothing he could possibly say that would make any of this right. You have suffered the worst of torture at the hands of that selfish cad."

"Can we please keep going? My head is clearer now," she said.

She was torn between marching straight up to the front door of the Taylor home and putting a bullet in her former fiancé's brain and running home and seeking refuge in her room. The desire to bury herself under the bedclothes was, fortunately for Robert, the stronger one.

"Alright. But if you feel faint again, please let me know. I can carry you the rest of the way if needs be; lord knows, hackney cabs are few and far between in Coventry," replied Piers.

With Piers's arm about her waist, and Maggie leaning against him for support, they started for home. It was slow-going up the hill, but they finally made it to the crossroads at Earl Street. The sound of boots approaching at a fast rate had them both looking back the way they had just come.

Maggie sighed. "It's him. Robert."

The swine should thank his lucky stars. If he hadn't been holding tightly onto Maggie, Piers would have dropped Robert Taylor where he stood. Instead, he continued to make her his highest priority. To ensure he was doing everything in his power to protect her. Until she was back at his brother's house, Maggie was Piers's only concern.

He was, however, reserving the right to come back later and throttle Robert Taylor. Piers wanted nothing more than to take to the lying fiend with his fists and inflict a solid dose of rough justice.

When Robert stopped a little too close to Maggie for his liking, Piers growled. "If you know what's good for you, you will keep your distance."

His fingers were itching to wrap themselves around the bastard's throat. It would give him great pleasure to watch the man who had hurt Maggie, suffer some pain of his own.

Robert casually held his hands up, a smarmy grin sat on his lips. "We should talk. Sort this little misunderstanding between Maggie and me. But not here. And not now."

The nerve of the man. He had lied to Maggie, ruined her life, and now he had the gall to try and dictate terms.

I bet your wife doesn't know you are here. Or who Maggie is.

To Piers's surprise, Maggie pulled out of his protective embrace and faced her former paramour down. "When?"

The smile on Robert's face widened. "You always were a little too forward, Maggie, my love. Itching to give me what I wanted. Does your army beau know the sort of girl you are? I would guess, from the clueless look on his face, he doesn't."

I would dearly love to wipe that smug grin off your chops with my fists.

Maggie narrowed her eyes. "I might be many things, Robert, but I am most certainly not your love. You are a deceitful swine. Does that poor woman know what sort of man you are?"

That's my girl. Don't let him try and sweet talk you. I am sure that smile might have worked on you before, but not anymore.

Robert glanced back over his shoulder. For the first time since his arrival, he appeared less sure of himself. It was obvious he didn't wish to be seen talking to them. "Tomorrow morning at nine o'clock. My wife, Catherine, and her mother will be at the market. We can meet at the Kings Head Hotel on the corner of High and Smithfield Streets. It's a bit more graceful than a public house. I'm sure Maggie would prefer that. She has always liked the finer things in life."

Condescending cur. More like you want somewhere far enough away from home that your wife won't find out.

Maggie nodded her agreement, but Piers wasn't finished yet. "I am warning you—if you don't make an appearance tomorrow morning, I shall make it my personal quest to tell everyone in your street that you tried to ruin a young woman. I doubt they will want to have anything to do with you once they discover that you offered to marry her when you already happened to have a wife. And when that is done, I shall go and find a magistrate and have you arrested. Impersonating an officer of His Majesty's British Army carries severe criminal penalties."

The smarmy Robert flinched at Piers' words. He was clearly a man not used to being challenged. He turned his attention back to Maggie, taking a step forward. A gentle expression rested comfortably on his face. The charmer.

"Your soldier boy here thinks himself high and mighty. But I know you, Maggie—your family is all about forgiveness. I ask you to please think of my children, and my unborn babe. Of the high price they would pay for my little indiscretion. They shouldn't be separated from their dearest papa just because I indulged in a trifling dalliance. You had to know it was all a bit of a lark."

With that, he turned on his heel and raced off back down Little Park Street.

"Trifling? I would hate to see what he considers to be a serious matter," grumbled Piers. Maggie only had to give the word and he would chase after Robert and set to him. He couldn't think of another man in all of Christendom who needed to be pummeled into submission as badly as Robert Taylor did.

Maggie slipped her hand in his, and in a voice barely above a whisper, said, "Piers, can we please go home? I need to be away from here."

Chapter Twenty-One

Elizabeth and Jonathan stood waiting in the foyer of their home when Maggie and Piers returned. Maggie gritted her teeth, steeling herself for the inevitable questions. She wasn't sure if she could give them any kind of sensible answer, having none herself.

"How did things go? Did you find out anything?" asked Jonathan.

"Terribly. And yes, we discovered a great deal more than either of us expected," replied Piers. He motioned toward the doorway of the nearby sitting room. "Could we please talk in there? I don't think the foyer is the appropriate place for this conversation."

The four of them gathered in the room. Maggie refused the offer of a seat on the sofa next to Elizabeth. She wanted this over and done with, after which, she planned to immediately head upstairs and take to her bed. To hide from the world. Only then could she begin to absorb the shock.

"Robert Taylor is alive. He has a wife, and a growing brood of children," announced Piers.

Elizabeth gasped. "Dear Lord, that is awful. I mean, he's

alive, which I suppose is good news. But the rest of it, oh, Maggie—you poor girl."

She rose from her chair, but Maggie waved her away. Comfort and condolences were the last thing she needed right this minute. She was determined to be as cold as stone —not to give in to her emotions and most certainly not cry. The friendly warmth that Elizabeth would surely offer might well shatter Maggie's resolve.

Jonathan slowly shook his head. "That dirty rotten cad. Why would he do such a heinous thing?"

Maggie suspected she knew the answer. Money. If she and Robert had gone ahead and married, then he would have had access to her dowry. To more wealth than he would have ever known in his life.

I can't believe he would have been so blind as to think his past wouldn't catch up with him.

Putting a hand to her mouth, she swallowed down a lump of bile. If they had married, she would have become the unlawful wife of a bigamist. At some point, the truth would surely have come to light, and once exposed, their marriage would have been stripped of all dignity and legal standing.

She would have been forever ruined in the eyes of polite society. Any children they may have been blessed with, condemned as the illegitimate offspring of a wicked union.

The shocking scandal would likely have seen her father forced to relinquish his post as Bishop of London. The Church of England couldn't have its third-most powerful member being the sire of a fallen woman.

And poor Claire. No respectable man would want to marry a girl whose family was so badly tainted by disgrace.

Her sister's prospects for a good marriage would have disappeared in an instant. The scandal would have destroyed both Maggie and her family.

Had Robert got cold feet? Was that why he had gone

through with the elaborate ruse of going off to war and dying? The letter she had received was probably penned by his own hand.

"I expect Robert Taylor had his sights set firmly on the money and power that being connected to the Radley family would have brought him. He got a taste of a better life, but couldn't go through with it," Piers said.

Nausea rose fast in Maggie's stomach and her throat. "Perhaps we shall be granted more of an insight into Robert and his sordid motivations tomorrow. He has agreed to meet with Piers and me at the King's Head. Now, if you would please excuse me, I must go and lie down," she said.

On her way to the door, Maggie stopped at Piers's side. She reached out and took his hand, giving it a gentle squeeze "Thank you. I don't know what I would have done without you," she whispered.

She wanted to say more, but the presence of his relatives had her holding back the words. As long as Piers knew she was grateful, the rest of the conversation could wait until they were alone and able to talk privately.

He leaned in close. "If it is alright, I will come and check on you a little later. I'm worried about you, Maggie."

Her heart gave a little pitter-patter as she took in the earnest expression of concern on Piers's face. There was a tender warmth in his regard which suggested he was more than just concerned about the state of her health. And she certainly wasn't unaware of the change in a man's countenance when his mind shifted from polite interest in a woman to the early stages of attraction.

"I shall be fine. But yes, please, come and see me in an hour or so. Hopefully, I will feel better once I have had a short nap."

Captain Piers Denford was fast becoming her hero. He cared about her—that much was obvious. They had moved past the point of being merely acquaintances and travelling companions. The bond between them was strong.

In Piers, Maggie had found the one person who truly understood her predicament. The one in whom she could place her trust.

What she couldn't trust, however, were her growing feelings for him.

~

Piers met with his brother a short time later in Jonathan's study. His pangs of guilt over not including Elizabeth were tempered by the knowledge that she would understand that the tone of the conversation might not be socially polite.

Jonathan closed the door behind him. "Bloody hell. How did you keep from throttling the filthy dog? If it were me, I don't think I could have stayed my hand."

"Maggie fainted when she saw him the first time. All I wanted to do was get her safely back here. We were partway home when he caught up with us. To say he was cocksure of himself, and condescending would be an understatement," replied Piers.

"I would have punched him there and then," said Jonathan.

If Maggie hadn't been in such a precarious state, Piers most certainly would have hit Robert. "I'm still in two minds as to whether I should go around to his house right now and have it out with him. He needs a bloody good thrashing. But I can't do that—especially not in front of his wife and children," replied Piers.

Catherine Taylor might well be clueless as to the sort of man her husband was, and if she was oblivious to his duplicity, she certainly didn't deserve to find out the truth from an angry stranger. Her children and delicate condition had to be considered. There were other innocents aside from Maggie involved in this whole saga.

"What are the chances that Taylor will show his face tomorrow? Who is to say he won't undertake a midnight flit out of the city?" said Jonathan.

The very same notion had crossed Piers's mind. But he had moved on from that point, from thoughts of bloody revenge to worrying about Maggie and how she was feeling right now. He wanted her to know he would do everything he could to help her get through the rest of today, as well as be standing by her side tomorrow when she met with her former love.

Robert Taylor's slimy grin dropped into his mind. That was the look of a man unafraid of repercussions. A man capable of carelessly, needlessly hurting an innocent woman wasn't about to give up the comforts of home.

"From the state of his house and garden, Taylor doesn't look like a chap who has too many coins to rub together. He won't be going anywhere. Besides, I got the distinct impression that he fancies his chances of talking his way out of the whole mess. He still thinks he holds sway over Maggie."

Robert had labelled the connection between him and Maggie as being trifling, an indulgence. The words were carefully crafted in a deliberate attempt to convince her that she was the one who was being too emotional. That she had placed more weight upon their so-called relationship than had ever existed.

If you tell someone something enough times, they will eventually begin to believe it.

But the betrothal had been real. He had seen the ring on Maggie's finger.

Though it wasn't there when I held her hand earlier.

Maggie had given up her mourning clothes, along with the engagement ring.

My brave girl.

She had stood up to Robert. Even after the shock of having seen him, and then the embarrassment of collapsing in the street, she had rallied.

It had been heartbreaking to see the scales finally fall from her eyes—for her to have her supposed war hero revealed as nothing more than a lying fraud.

"What do you intend to do if Taylor does front up tomorrow?" asked Jonathan.

"I'm not sure. Much as I might want to be Maggie's knight in shining armor, this isn't my fight. I will go with her if she wants me to, but I am not going to press my opinions on her."

Jonathan nodded. "Good. That's exactly what I was hoping you would say. Protect but not dictate. In my opinion, it is the best thing you can do for her. Elizabeth and I have only known her for a day or so, but I think it is obvious that Maggie is an intelligent lady. She is not going to let Taylor get the better of her a second time."

"No."

And if Robert Taylor tried to sweet talk his way out of things, Piers would be ready to set him straight.

He hated seeing Maggie in pain, but he could also privately admit to having an awkward sense of relief over her reaction to Robert. Whatever love she may have still held for him had hopefully died on the streets of Coventry this afternoon.

Thank goodness it had.

But the relief he felt made him no better a man than Robert.

What sort of cad takes pleasure in seeing a woman suffer heart break?

There was no avoiding the obvious answer. He wanted Robert Taylor gone from Maggie's affections, Every ounce of warmth she had once felt for him obliterated from her heart.

Because only when she had purged Robert from her soul could Piers stand any chance of claiming Maggie's love for himself. It was wrong to want her, but his heart was beating its own fierce demand.

"I think I might go for a short walk up the hill, just to burn off some of my anger. Then, when I return, I will check in on Maggie and see how she is doing."

Jonathan met his gaze. The look on his brother's face was one of deep concern. "Just be careful, will you? Maggie has already had to deal with one man who hurt her deeply; don't let yourself become another."

"You mean, I shouldn't allow myself to fall for Maggie when I may not be in a position to offer her marriage? Thank you, brother. I respect your words of caution."

Piers left the house a short time later, his temper still not fully under control. Robert Taylor stood in the way of Maggie finding a bright future. While, he had the whole of the British Army to contend with when it came to his own.

Chapter Twenty-Two

I t was late when Piers finally made his way to Maggie's room. His conflicted mind had seen him take a long walk up the hill to the church, then down to the army barracks, around the block back up Warwick Lane, and then, finally, home. He had passed close by the Taylor house but had managed to resist the temptation to go and confront the man who had caused Maggie such grief and pain.

He was saving his rage for the morning, readying himself to go to war on her behalf.

After tapping lightly on the door of her bedroom, he listened. A faint "Come in," came from within. Pushing the door open, he was greeted with a heartbreaking sight.

Maggie was seated on the bed with her knees drawn up. Her head rested on her folded arms. She greeted him with a sad smile.

Piers could have wept as he took in her sad, red-rimmed eyes, the clear evidence of her heartache.

That bastard made her suffer, and he is still hurting her.

He took two hesitant, faltering steps into the room. Coming in here was crossing one of the immutable boundaries of polite society's hard and fast rules. Unwed couples did not spend time together in private rooms—not unless they were prepared to accept the consequences.

If the Bishop of London had the slightest notion that his daughter had been travelling for days with Piers in his private coach, he would be on the doorstep of Denford House the second Piers returned to London, demanding that he offer for Maggie's hand in marriage. The fact that he supposedly had a fiancée waiting in the wings wouldn't matter.

Maggie Denford—now there is an appealing name.

It took a great deal of effort for him to push the enticing thought away. If the day ever came that he could freely consider marriage, Maggie would be at the top of his list of potential brides.

But now that she knows the truth, Maggie won't remain in her mourning any longer. Which means she will rejoin society. And a beautiful woman like her will be a prized catch for any man.

She shifted on the bed, breaking him out of his daze. Before he could register what was happening, she had crossed the floor and thrown herself into his arms. Piers wrapped her up in his embrace, not caring if anyone saw them or what they might think.

"Maggie." He brushed his hand over her long dark tresses, smoothing out the crinkles. Over her head, he spied the rumpled bed covers. She must have cried herself to sleep sometime earlier.

"Thank you for being here. I wasn't sure whether you were going to come or not," she said.

"I went for a walk; it ended up being longer than planned. Needed to clear my head somewhat. It's been quite a day."

She drew out of his embrace and headed to the door. To Piers's surprise, Maggie closed and locked it.

"The maid Elizabeth assigned to me is a lovely girl, but she does have an annoying habit of barely knocking before she comes into the room. I would hate to have to explain this to her or her mistress."

Piers scowled, unsure of what she meant. He had deliberately left the door open for the sake of respectability; but it was Maggie who had closed it. "I don't understand."

She returned to where he was, coming to a halt barely half a foot away. Lifting her head, she met his gaze. "I could explain with words, but I'd rather you just hold me."

This isn't wise. It could bring me a world of trouble.

Maggie took a hold of the front of his jacket and pulled herself hard against him, sweeping Piers's brief moment of self-doubt and hesitancy aside, "Please, just hold me," she breathed.

A more honorable man would protest. Cite his fiancée as being reason enough not to touch another woman.

Who are you kidding? You have wanted this from the first moment you met her.

Piers silently thanked Lady Dinah Gibney for having taken the initiative and found someone else. He couldn't feel guilty over being alone with Maggie if his former fiancée had fallen in love with another man.

But he didn't want to just hold her. And from the way her fingers rested against his chest, he suspected he wasn't alone in this moment of wavering strength.

When he met Maggie's stunning blue eyes, Piers knew the energy between them had shifted. "Piers," she whispered.

A man only had so much power over himself. A finite length to the tether of his self-control. His was badly frayed at the end and ready to snap.

Days of being close to Maggie, of constant temptation, slipped away as Piers cupped his hand under her nape and lowered his head. Their lips brushed for a mere second, then he drew back. Today had been enough of a trial for them both; the last thing he wanted was for her to suddenly pull out of his embrace and tell him it had all been a terrible mistake. That she had only been seeking comfort.

To his bone-deep relief, Maggie kissed him back.

Her soft, pliant lips brushed against his over and over. He groaned when she opened her mouth, inviting him to deepen the encounter.

Her response informed him that Maggie had been thoroughly kissed before by someone else. Piers fought against the surge of jealousy that came with knowing he wasn't her first. Even as their tongues danced elegantly together, he wrestled with his hatred of Robert.

And himself.

He was alone in the bedroom of a vulnerable young woman, taking advantage of her. Kissing her when he had no right. Taking what she offered when, to all the world, and especially her, he still had a fiancée.

You are little better than him. A liar and a cad. Stealing kisses under false pretenses.

That thought had him breaking the kiss. Pulling away.

"I am sorry. I shouldn't have done that. I beg your forgiveness," he said.

Maggie shook her head. "Piers, I—".

"No." He backed away. "I have overstepped both our friendship and the mission to which I was tasked. Forgive me. You deserve better."

His fingers were on the door handle, and the key turned before she caught up with him. For a brief moment, they both stood silent, staring deep into one another's eyes.

If only you could be mine. Destiny can be so cruel.

"Piers, you must know that we are more than friends. I don't think that kiss was wrong. My only regret is that I had no right to it. You, like Robert, belong to someone else." She lay her hand over his and opened the door. "I seem fated to fall for men who I cannot have. Good night, Piers."

He stepped out into the hallway. He was still in two minds as to whether he should throw all caution to the wind and go back and kiss Maggie for a second time when the door closed behind him. The click of the latch gave him the answer he needed.

It had been a mistake. And he was a selfish fool.

Chapter Twenty-Three

Maggie was relieved that she had given her black and pale lilac gowns to the maid the previous day. By having them out of reach, it took away the temptation of wearing them to meet with Robert. To show him with more than just words what he had done to her.

But she understood only too well that while she had invested her heart and soul in their love affair, he had been merely toying with her. She would not give him the satisfaction of knowing that she had put her life on hold for over two years, thinking he was dead.

No. You no longer have that power over me.

The smirk he had so effortlessly offered the previous day had been like a knife to her heart, killing any and all tenderness she may have once held for him.

Robert may not be in his grave, but today, Maggie was determined to bury him deep in her past. She would keep shoveling the dirt over the mound until he finally fell silent in her heart and mind.

Stepping confidently into the pale apple and rose-striped gown that she had bought from Elizabeth's modiste, she considered her reflection in the mirror. What she saw looking back at her was a young woman unafraid of her past, one who now looked forward to a brighter future. This was the Maggie Radley she so desperately wanted Robert to see.

Not the Maggie who had collapsed in the street. Nor the Maggie who had cried herself to exhaustion on the bed yesterday afternoon. And most certainly not the Maggie who had been taken for a fool, the one who had wasted all those days grieving for a scoundrel. She closed her eyes and took a deep, calming breath. Whatever she might still feel inside, she was determined to project this happy version of herself to the world.

At least for this morning. Until I am sure he is gone from my life.

"I do so love this gown on you, Miss Radley," said her maid.

Opening her eyes, Maggie glanced at her reflection in the mirror once more and smiled. She had almost forgotten the wonder of cheerful colors and what they did to her complexion. The change in color palette was welcome. An appointment with her modiste would be high on the list of things she would have to attend to once she returned to London.

Ridding herself of the rest of her mourning gowns, and any correspondence relating to Robert, were at the very top of that list.

"It's a pity I don't have any boots to match the gown, but these black ones will have to do. I don't expect we shall remain much longer in Coventry. Captain Denford has already completed the work he came here to do," she said.

Under other circumstances, she would have loved to stay on and see more of the city and the surrounding countryside, but she doubted Piers would want to linger. He had many other pressing commitments in London, and it wouldn't be fair to ask him to indulge her any further.

Her fingers found their way to her lips, touching the place

where Piers had kissed her the previous evening. The memory of his arms around her, the heady scent of his gentleman's cologne. His long, lingering kiss . . . She shivered, recalling how much she wished him to do it again.

You know that is impossible. He has a fiancée, and you shouldn't be the cause of heartbreak to another woman. Not after what you have been through.

What she had done was wrong.

The maid finished lacing up the back of the gown, then handed Maggie her cloak.

"Thank you. Would you please let Captain Denford know that I will meet him downstairs shortly?"

Maggie needed time alone to put her emotional armor firmly into place. To prepare herself for meeting Robert.

And to spend more time with Piers.

A calm and composed Maggie met Piers in the foyer some fifteen minutes later. She couldn't hold back her smile when she caught sight of him. He was clad in his long army coat, his red officer's coatee peeking out from between the open lapels. Talk about handsome. Her tall, dark protector was still determined to accompany her today.

Thank you, Piers.

She was grateful that last night's passionate kiss followed by its awkward conclusion had been temporarily set aside while they dealt with the matter of Robert. Piers would be with her. His strength would be hers.

The hero every woman needs.

He gave her a sheepish grin, then dipped into a low bow. He was still clearly uncomfortable over the previous evening's encounter, and therefore, overcompensating for it. Hopefully, they would have time later to discuss things and come to some sort of resolution. One which she wished would allow for them to remain friends.

Piers stepped closer to her but maintained a socially acceptable distance. It was disappointing but not unexpected. "Are you still wishing to go and meet with him? I mean, you don't have to do this; Robert isn't dead and that's probably all that really matters," he said.

Maggie straightened her spine. She was a Radley, and that meant she wasn't going to hide from the truth of the situation. Robert Taylor had questions to answer, and she was determined he was going to sit in the King's Head and talk until she had got her fill of them.

And if he is stupid enough to try and tell me lies, I might just make his death a reality.

"Thank you, Piers. I must see Robert today. I'm not dreading the encounter; in fact, I think meeting him will be a good thing. Facing down that lying toad is something I am quite looking forward to doing."

Piers scowled. She could understand his reaction. There were plenty of women of her acquaintance who wouldn't do it. They wouldn't be able to find the courage to meet Robert —to look him in the eye. Instead, they would have headed out of Coventry at first light and been well on their way back to London, never again to venture to the outer limits of the home counties.

"Alright. But have you thought how you will approach this meeting? Yesterday you collapsed in the street. And last night, you were . . . well . . ."

It was rather sweet to see Piers less than sure of himself; it was an obvious point of difference between him and her former fiancé. A vulnerability that Robert had never once displayed.

"I am fine, Piers. And as for last night, can we talk about it later? While I am sure that neither of us wants it hanging over us, now is probably not the time."

"Of course." He held out his hand, and Maggie passed her cloak to him. Piers came to stand behind her, draping the fine woolen garment over her shoulders. While Maggie secured the ties at the front, he leaned in close. "You are a very brave lady. But just remember, I will be with you all the way."

Her knight in shining armor would be beside her as she went to face down the dragon. Robert should thank his lucky stars that Piers didn't have a sword. From the way he held himself, if he did have a sharp weapon, he would have been more than happy to slay the beast.

Chapter Twenty-Four

W hile the King's Head called itself a hotel, it wasn't much more than a well-to-do coaching inn. It had a proper lounge and public area for dining, which set it a step above the usual.

It also had an assembly room. Maggie noted a sign on the main door advertising a forthcoming musical performance by a boy aged seven and a girl aged five. Tickets were two shillings, children half-price.

"Someone must have proud parents," said Piers.

The moment they stepped into the public dining area; Maggie scanned the room for Robert. Her heart pumped at a furious rate. She held her hands tightly together. It was all she could do to stop them from shaking.

"There he is." Piers pointed toward the table in the farthest corner of the room. Robert got to his feet as they approached.

He held out his hand to Piers, who glanced disapprovingly at it, then said, "You must be in jest."

Maggie also ignored Robert's stilted bow.

She and Piers both took a seat on the opposite side of the table from Robert.

Robert cleared his throat. "Thank you for coming. And I am pleased to see that you are recovered from yesterday, Maggie. There has been plenty of gossip around the neighborhood about the lady of quality who collapsed in the street yesterday."

Listening to a voice she had never thought to hear ever again was most peculiar. He had come to her in dreams many times during those first few months following his supposed death, but those moments were brief snatches in time, mixed up memories. The man seated across from her was very much alive.

"As one can imagine, seeing you walking down the street, a man of flesh and blood, came as somewhat of a shock. And while I had reconciled myself to the reality that you hadn't been an officer in the army, the fact that you had then faked your own death, leaving me to wallow in grief all that time, was a bit too much for my mind to comprehend. Hence, my body's physical reaction. I promise it won't happen again."

"Would you believe that it all began as a bit of a lark? I won the uniform from an officer in a game of cards. He must have had a spare as he didn't seem to mind handing it over. My friends and I then had a wager on who could manage to secure an invitation to a grand ball," said Robert.

Under the table Maggie rested her hands in her lap.

He can't hurt me anymore. The damage is done.

"Go on," she replied, grateful that Piers was holding his tongue.

Robert slowly shook his head. "I didn't initially mean to take things as far as I did. But you offered me a way out of this life. And I found myself torn. You are an enchanting woman, Maggie."

But you didn't ever love me.

All his little tricks and sweet endearments had been lies. He hadn't ever given a damn about her. A man capable of such villainy didn't know the first thing of what it meant to care for another.

What sort of man steals a woman's love for a lark?

A hotel waiter appeared at Piers's shoulder. "May I take your orders for some refreshments? We have a freshly baked lemon cake available this morning."

Maggie quickly nodded. Anything to make the attendant go away. She chanced a look at Piers, silently pleading for him to deal with the pressing matter of cake and tea.

"The lady and I shall have a pot of tea. And a slice of cake each, thank you. The other gentleman will pay the bill," he said.

As soon as the waiter had disappeared, Maggie turned her attention back to Robert. "Go on. And just stick to the bare facts; I am not interested in anything else you might feel you need to say."

"Of course. I had been with Catherine, my wife, before I came to London. She had been in love with me for many years and was heartbroken when I left. I treated her poorly. I probably still do."

That actually sounds like the truth.

"Unlike Maggie?" Piers asked. She reached for his hand and gave it a squeeze.

"I was ready to walk away from my old life to be with you, but then a letter came from Coventry. Catherine was pregnant again. It pulled me up short. Made me realize what a cad I had become. I had lied to two women. And was about to ruin both their lives."

"So, you decided to come back here and do the right thing?" she replied.

Robert winced. "To be honest, I was still unsure. But it

was your father who convinced me of what I should do. He sealed things for me."

"My father? You told him?"

"No. But the last time you and I sat through one of His Grace's sermons at St. Paul's, he talked about loyalty. Responsibility. Of what being a man truly involved. It meant making the right choices. After listening to him, I knew I had to return to Catherine. Try to be some sort of husband."

This revelation made clear something which had always puzzled Maggie. On the night before Robert was meant to ship out, she had offered herself to him. They had shared enough kisses and touches for her to know he desired her, yet he had refused.

At the time, she had been hurt. Viewed it as rejection. Now she understood why. The last thing he'd have wanted was for her to carry his baby. She should be grateful for such luck.

"But why lie? Why not just call things off? You didn't have to go through with the whole charade of going to war and pretending to be dead. A simple letter telling me you were not going through with our wedding would have sufficed."

Robert nodded. "I panicked. I had lied about being an officer. Your father was asking which clubs he should nominate me for; I knew I would be asked to prove my army rank in order to join them. I was also worried about your family."

"My family?"

"When I first met you, I didn't realize how well-connected they were, how powerful. Upon my return to Coventry, I figured that if I ended things with you and you took it badly, your family would come looking for me. But if I was dead, all my problems would be solved."

The waiter arrived, carrying a tray. He set a pot of tea, two cups, and some plates on the table. When no one paid him any attention, he had the good sense not to linger. The air around the table was thick with tension.

"But you didn't reckon on Maggie's steadfast loyalty. Nor do you seem to care about the fact that she has wasted over two years of her life grieving for a thoughtless, heartless, dirty fraud." Trust Piers to be able to take her pain and put it so succinctly into words. That was exactly what she had lived through, what this liar had done to her.

She gave a tired laugh. "I was going to have a statue erected for you. It was going to be unveiled during a service with local dignitaries in attendance. I even sketched a memorial garden that it would be placed within. You have no idea what your little deception, your trifling affair, has done to me. And even now, I think you couldn't care less."

Robert finally met her gaze. "Oh, Maggie, that's harsh. I do care."

"You only care that this is coming home to bite you," she replied.

His faced hardened. His eyes lost all their gentleness. It was as if a mask had suddenly been removed and she was now seeing the real Robert. "Alright. Yes, I haven't thought about you more than once or twice over the past couple of years. But you have my full attention now. What are you going to do?"

Those were the words of a man who'd suddenly realized his whole world was in peril. It wouldn't take much for Maggie to destroy Robert's life.

She had sat up late in the night thinking what she would say to Robert this morning. It was ironic that while her father's sermon had influenced him, helping Robert to make the decision to return to Coventry and his wife, it was also Hugh's teachings that had guided Maggie as to how she would respond to her former fiancé's betrayal.

What am I going to do?

Last night, she had toyed with the idea of getting dressed and heading to the nearby church to pray. To seek spiritual guidance. In the end, she hadn't needed it. The thought of Robert's young family, his wife, and children, was enough.

The decision to grasp tightly to some notion of revenge or simply walk away was a surprisingly easy one for her to make. Maggie got to her feet. She rested a hand on Piers's shoulder as he attempted to rise.

This was her moment.

"I wasted over two years of my life weeping for you. Likely thrown away countless opportunities to be happy. Who knows? The love of my life may have passed me by while I was busy grieving. And all because you are a selfish coward. I should report you to the authorities, but where would that leave your wife and family?"

Much as she wished it were otherwise, two wrongs did not make a right. She would not be the cause of Robert being taken from his family. For his crimes, there was every chance that he would be flogged and then transported to the far-flung colony of New South Wales, never to return to England.

"My father might not agree with my sentiments, but I can never forgive you for what you did. For forcing me to live your lie. And you are despicable for trying to blacken the name of my family. We would never have sought to harm you. All you had to do was be honest with me. Be a man."

She pushed back her chair and stepped away. After tucking it back under the table, Maggie leaned on its upright and glared down at Robert. "I am done. You don't deserve another minute of my time. Oh, and this is yours."

She pulled the betrothal ring from out of her skirt pocket and tossed it onto the table. Robert quickly scooped it up.

Maggie turned and headed for the door. Piers got to his feet and followed, hot on her heels. He finally caught up with her as she set foot onto the pavement, wrapping an arm protectively around her waist.

"Are you alright?" he asked.

"I'm fine. You can let go; I promise I am not going to faint."

She was so light, she positively bounced on her feet. Piers released her from his hold.

"Can we go somewhere? I mean, anywhere but here. To be honest, I'm annoyed at having to leave that delicious-looking cake behind at the hotel. I have no doubt *he* will be stuffing his face with it. I hope he chokes," she said.

She was in urgent need of a strong pot of tea and something sticky and sweet. Or, better still, a hot pie.

"Do you happen to know of any places around here where they make good meat pies?" she asked.

Piers nodded. "Actually, I do. And the perfect bakery is close by. Are you sure that is what you want to do?"

"Absolutely. And the sooner, the better."

It seemed odd, but instead of being sad, Maggie wanted to celebrate. Seeing Robert alive had finally set her free. He had moved on with his life, putting her in the past. Today, she was going to do the same.

"It's a Radley family tradition to stop in the town of Falkirk, Scotland, when we are on our way to Strathmore Castle and feast on the local pastries. And while I don't expect the offerings in Coventry will come to up to scratch against those of the Falkirk pie shop, I am still willing to give them a try."

She grinned as a chuckling Piers offered her his arm. "I hear a challenge in those words, Miss Radley. As a nobleman born in this part of England, I feel it is my duty to defend the honor of the region. There are four excellent bakers in the city, and if you feel up to it, then we shall visit them all."

Placing her arm in his, Maggie laughed. "Four. Oh, dear."

Chapter Twenty-Five

"Do you yield?"

Piers closed the door behind him, following Maggie into the foyer of his brother's house. He held up his hands in surrender. "Yes. I yield. I can't believe you ate four pies, and then managed to polish off a slice of lemon cake."

He had never met a woman who could eat that much food. His own efforts had included two full pies and a small bite of one other. The cake was well beyond him.

If the price of him losing the beef pie battle was the happy grin on Maggie's face, it was well worth it. It was wonderful to see her relaxed and enjoying the simple pleasures of life. Perhaps she really had put *him* in the past.

"I am just going upstairs to freshen up," said Maggie.

Piers waited until she had gone, then went in search of Elizabeth. Jonathan would still be at the offices of the canal company until later in the day.

His sister-in-law was in the drawing room on the second floor. As Piers stepped into the room, Elizabeth set the shirt she was stitching onto the side table and rose.

"How did the day with Maggie go? And, more importantly, did the blackguard show? I was expecting you home hours ago. I've barely gotten two buttons sewn on that shirt worrying over what might have happened."

Piers could have kicked himself. Of course, Elizabeth would have been concerned. They should have stopped by the house before heading off to indulge their stomachs. His thoughts had only been of Maggie and how she had responded to the morning's events.

"My apologies for keeping you in suspense, Elizabeth; it was not done deliberately. Robert Taylor came. Told a pack of lies about why he felt the need to fake his demise, after which Maggie gave him short shrift. We then left the King's Head and she said she wanted to find some food. We've spent the past few hours on a slow tour of Much Park Street, visiting the pie shops. We ate so much that I can barely breathe."

The expression on Elizabeth's face didn't soften. She was clearly worried. "So, it was Maggie's idea to go and eat half a hundred-weight of baked pastries? Oh dear, that is not good."

"Why would you say that? We had a lovely time."

Elizabeth rolled her eyes. Piers recognized that look—it was her "I don't believe it" face. One she was very good at using around both her husband and children.

"Because Maggie is clearly still in denial over everything. She is overcompensating. And when a woman does that, I can tell you it is never a good thing. Was she light and gay all day? Laughing at your jests?"

He pondered his response for a moment. Maggie had been bright and cheery, but he had seen that as having been a positive sign of her getting over Robert. She had been brave and strong in the hotel.

"She made it a fun outing. And yes, she did laugh at my pathetic attempts at humor," he replied.

The kindhearted Elizabeth graciously didn't give him her thoughts on that matter. She didn't need to; the signs of

Maggie's odd behavior had all been there all along. He had just chosen not to see them.

Maggie had been effusive at every shop they visited, over friendly with the staff. And had purchased far too much food.

Denford, you dolt. Only small children and polite old ladies ever laugh at your jests.

Maggie was still in a world of pain.

How can she not be? It's been barely a day since she discovered that her long-dead fiancé was, in fact, alive. Married. And the father of numerous children.

"What am I to do? I haven't a clue as to how I can help her," he said.

Elizabeth met his eyes. He was relieved to catch the kind smile on her lips. "You like Maggie, don't you? In fact, I would go so far as to say you have a soft spot for her. That much has been apparent since you arrived. If you are open to my advice, I would suggest that now is a very good time to take a step back. Be her friend. That is what she needs from you. As for any other sort of connection between the two of you, let Maggie take the reins."

Wise words indeed. If he pushed things with Maggie, she might well retreat further into herself. She had enough to contend with at present without him being selfish and asking for more.

And what in all honesty can I offer her?

The brief kiss they had shared had been nothing short of folly. Reckless and ungentlemanlike conduct on his part.

"Thank you for your counsel, dear sister. As always, it is most welcome. I shall do as you suggest."

A tap at the door announced the arrival of Maggie. Piers and Elizabeth exchanged a silent look of agreement. He could only hope she hadn't overhead their conversation.

Elizabeth welcomed Maggie with open arms as she stepped into the room. They were about to embrace when she stopped. Her gaze dropped to Maggie's stomach. "Perhaps I shouldn't hug you. Piers informs me that between the two of you, a temporary pie shortage now exists in the city of Coventry."

Maggie gave a laugh. "Yes, more than likely. I am ashamed to say I also managed a slice of lemon cake from the last shop." She shot a grin in Piers's direction. "I don't think either of us will be rushing to the supper table this evening. In fact, I don't plan to go anywhere."

"Speaking of plans, have you had any time to give thought as to what you will do now? I mean, will you stay in Coventry or go straight home?" Elizabeth asked.

Maggie shrugged. "I'm not sure. To be honest, I consider my travel plans to be in the hands of your brother-in-law. Piers is the one who is expected back in London. I have no pressing commitments. And my family won't be headed to Scotland until the week before Christmas."

Hope flared in Piers's heart. Maggie wasn't demanding that he immediately make arrangements to leave. Could she perhaps be open to other options?

Like spending time with me?

Elizabeth and Jonathan's eldest son made an appearance in the doorway. He clutched a piece of paper in his hand, upon which his many attempts to write the letters of the alphabet was evident. "Mama, I need more paper," he said.

"Excuse me. I had better go and help in the schoolroom. I shall leave the two of you to talk about travel plans. But whatever you decide, I want you both to know that you are more than welcome to stay here with Jonathan and me. It's nice to have family around." She turned to Maggie. "And I include you in that. Any friend of Piers is family to us."

Piers had always had a soft spot for his sister-in-law, never more than right at that minute. Elizabeth had just cleared away one of the largest obstacles that might have stood in the way of Maggie agreeing to stay on in Coventry.

"Thank you," said Maggie.

Elizabeth followed her son out the room, leaving Piers and Maggie alone. They may have spent the day together, but this was the first time they had actually been somewhere private. Somewhere they could talk. He badly needed to know how Maggie was really feeling. For her to lower her guard and trust him. And for him to share the things he was keeping from her.

But here inside the house felt like the wrong place for this sort of conversation. "Would you care to take a walk in the garden? I would like for us to sit and talk," he offered.

She shook her head. "I am still so uncomfortable after all that food. Perhaps we could take a stroll up the hill to the church? I found a lovely, sunny spot there yesterday."

This was an even better suggestion, to his way of thinking. It would take them away from the house and prying ears and eyes.

It was a short walk from the house, through the nearby Bayley Lane, up to St. Michael's. When they reached the grounds of the church, Maggie pointed to a wooden garden bench that sat in the middle of a grassy area. To one side of it was the open cemetery, with its aged and tilted headstones. Not exactly the spot for a romantic chat, but it would have to do.

She took a seat at one end of the bench, and Piers politely sat at the other.

"We are in a public place, so I don't think you have to keep four feet between us," she said, patting the seat next to her. "Come and sit here."

"Are you sure?"

He was treading carefully, worried that any false step on his part might see her collapse into a heap of tears. Maggie was being all too self-confident and calm, and it set Piers's nerves on edge.

Shifting, he came to sit beside her, ready to offer assistance at the first sign of Maggie's bubbly façade finally cracking.

"Thank you for today. I really appreciated your support. I know I could have faced him on my own, but it was nice to have a friend with me."

Piers noted the deliberate use of the word *him* rather than Robert. Maggie was already trying to forget the blackguard who had hurt her.

Good.

But it also brought his own behavior of the previous night into sharp focus. He, too, had not behaved honorably. Guilt sat heavily in Piers's heart. Maggie was owed another apology and an explanation.

"I don't think I am worthy of the term friend. Last night, I took advantage of you when you were vulnerable. That makes me no better than him. And I went along with the pie shop expedition when perhaps it would have been better that I brought you home."

She fell silent, and Piers sensed she was composing her response. Searching for the right words. He could understand why. It would be awkward to call him to task over that kiss especially knowing that they were going to have to travel back to London together at some point.

Maggie stared at the ground. While her fingers were lightly curved over the edge of the wooden bench, there was a definite stiffness to her posture.

She let out a heavy sigh and, lifting her head, turned to meet his gaze. "If we are being honest with one another, Piers, I was as much to blame for that kiss as you. I not only wanted it, but I craved it more than a respectable woman should. And considering the fact that you are betrothed, it makes me a terrible human being as well as an utter hypocrite," she said.

"That's not true."

"No? Robert used me for his own devices, and I have done the same to you."

Tell her. Get it out in the open.

"I don't have a fiancée, Maggie. Lady Dinah Gibney and I are no longer betrothed."

Chapter Twenty-Six

H ad she heard him correctly? He wasn't engaged. Maggie tightened the grip of her fingers so hard on the seat that her knuckles turned white. "What did you say?"

Piers slowly nodded. "I said, I am not engaged. Lady Dinah and I broke off our betrothal early in the summer. We agreed to keep things quiet until the time was right to make it public. The day that we arrived in Coventry, I was made aware that Lady Dinah has found someone else. I was planning to write to her and ask that she wait until after Christmas to make the news of our break official. It would save us both having to answer awkward questions during the festivities."

So, he hadn't been a cheating swine when he kissed her. But it still didn't explain why he and his former fiancée were keeping the end of their long engagement a tightly held secret.

Her head was still spinning after this morning. Maggie wasn't sure if she could deal with another dramatic event.

It would take some time before she would be able to reconcile the depth of Robert's indifference to her. His softly whispered words of love hadn't stopped him from condemning her to abject misery.

Him. Do not ever speak his name again. You must think of him as him.

"Would you grant me a boon, Piers?"

"Of course. Anything. Name it."

"Let's agree not to make any mention of former loves for the rest of the day. I know you want to explain what happened between you and her, but I . . ." She sighed.

Her efforts at being light and cheerful had taken their toll. Maggie had little left to give.

The warmth of his hand on hers had her fighting back tears. There were times when Piers appeared to have strong instincts when it came to what she was feeling, but in other moments, he seemed to flounder.

But at least he was trying. At least he cared.

They sat in silence, gazing at the city which spread out before them at the bottom of the hill. If only it could be this way between them always. Friends who could share quiet moments.

She lay her head back against the upright of the bench and closed her eyes.

But what if it could be more? Would you dare to risk your heart again?

There was only one way to find out the answer to that question. It would mean having to open herself once more to the possibility of another crushing heartache.

I'm not sure if I would survive it a second time.

Chapter Twenty-Seven

T he fire was burning low when Maggie woke in the dark of the night. Piers was asleep in the chair opposite to her, his hands folded on his stomach. She grinned as he twitched in his sleep—he was clearly lost deep in a dream. A glance at the clock on the mantelpiece showed it was just after the hour of midnight. Bed beckoned, but she resisted the call.

After returning to the house, and both politely declining any supper, they had set themselves up in the small sitting room at the end of the second-floor hallway. A warm fire created a cozy nook for the two of them.

While Piers went through his military paperwork, filing reports and writing letters, Maggie penned some of her own correspondence.

She wrote letters to her family, including one to her new sister-in-law, Leah, in Cornwall. Her missives included the highlights of her journey north. She made note of the wonderful food and the interesting sights but didn't include anything of real substance.

Informing her family of the outcome of her trip wasn't going to be easy. She didn't make mention of the discovery that Robert was still alive, her rationale being that some things were better said face to face. Or perhaps not at all. What she was actually going to tell her family, she hadn't yet decided.

Did I mention that the man I grieved over all those years isn't actually dead? Oh, and that he already had a wife and family when he met me. But it's not a problem because he says that my love for him was nothing more than trifling.

Burning shame and embarrassment sat continually at the corner of her conscious thoughts. While her parents and Piers could be trusted to keep it all a secret, she wasn't sure if living a lie was the right thing to do.

But if it protects the innocent, then perhaps that is the greater good.

Her mind continued to wander, now settling on the man who slept but a foot or two away. Maggie was certain that his dark locks whispered for her to touch them. In repose, Piers was even more handsome than when he was awake. She hadn't thought that possible, but sleep softened the worry lines which often sat deep on his brow.

Piers clearly had his own problems, and yet here he was, doing his utmost best to help her.

Why didn't the two of you marry? And why did Lady Dinah hold off on letting the world know you were free? Was she hedging her bets?

Piers stirred in his sleep. Maggie was in two minds as to whether she should wake him and insist he go to bed. But her long experience with both her father and brother had taught her to leave slumbering males well alone. They tended to be grumpy creatures when woken.

She left him snoozing in the chair and went back to her

bedroom; there, she collected her heavy woolen cloak and made her way downstairs and out into the night garden. Piers was right about fresh air and the healing effect it had on one's mind.

It was a crisp November night. The air was clear, but it held the promise of a frosty morning. Maggie loved this time of year.

This year, she would look forward to Christmas at Strathmore Castle—to snowball fights with her cousins and the gigantic bonfire which Ewan always commissioned the estate workers to build for the eve of Hogmanay. The annual march up to the castle by the local villagers, where the First Foot ceremony would take place just after the stroke of the new year, was her particular favorite moment on the entire calendar.

There was just under a month until the family gathered at the ancestral seat—time in which she could put her thoughts to her plans for the fresh year which lay ahead.

To new beginnings.

Her gaze lifted to the tall spire of the nearby St. Michael's church. A swirl of snow danced around the cross at the very top. The wind was strong up high, and the white icy flakes didn't make it all the way to the ground. Instead, they disappeared into the night sky.

The scene above seemed to mirror her own emotions. Her anger had cleared and now only a faint, dull ache remained. In time, that too would hopefully fade.

For a while, Maggie was simply content to stand and stare at the high stone wall of St. Michael's. She had spent her entire life around the community of the Church of England, and its familiarity brought her comfort.

At the rear of the garden was a small gate, which she assumed led out into the lane way behind the house. She hadn't noticed it earlier. On the other side of the lane was the church grounds and cemetery.

She was tempted to head up to the church through this shortcut and seek solace in prayer or even speak to someone. But Maggie wouldn't risk her personal safety just to seek counsel.

"It's late, and you are in a strange city," she whispered to the night sky.

Yesterday had already given her plenty to think about. The subject of Piers and what she was going to do with regard to her growing affections for him could wait until the morning.

At least I finally have answers about Robert, horrid though they might be.

All those worries. The endless letters. She could finally put them aside.

One of her first tasks when she returned to Fulham Palace would be to burn every scrap of correspondence, note, and memorial garden plan that she could find. Erase every physical reminder of Robert from her life.

Heavy boots crunched across the ice ground. She turned. Piers approached, carrying a large mug. Steam drifted up from inside it.

"I'm afraid it's only one cup. We shall have to share. I didn't think it fair to wake the household servants in order to get an extra spot of tea."

He offered her the mug, and Maggie took it. "Thank you." After a tentative sip, she handed it back. "It's hot; that's all that matters. Though next time, you might want to find the caddy and put two lumps of sugar in it."

Piers shuddered. "Urgh. I hate sugar in my tea. It makes it too sweet."

Maggie couldn't hold back her smile. "Well, we shall have

to find a compromise. How about next time you make us tea, you add one lump of sugar?"

He gave her a devilish grin and her heart skipped a beat. "Alright, but it has to be a small lump."

"If it tastes like lukewarm dishwater, you are going back to the kitchen," she replied.

His features softened. A kind regard sat on his face. In the dull light, she could just make out the glint in his eyes. "How are you feeling?" he asked.

"I'm a lot better than I was when we got home. I must confess, I was quite drained. An hour or so of sleep in the chair by the fire has done me the world of good. I didn't wake you because you were snoozing so deeply."

And because she wanted time to be alone, to put the strange new emotions which Piers had stirred within her into some semblance of order. That was still very much a work in progress.

"Piers?" she asked.

"Yes."

"Do you remember when we sat on the bench outside St. Michael's and talked, and I said I didn't want to discuss old loves for the rest of the day?"

"Yes, of course, I do."

"Well, it's past midnight. It's a new day."

He sipped at the tea, then slowly nodded. "You want to know about Lady Dinah. Why she and I broke things off?"

"Only if it is not too painful. I mean, I am the last person who should be trying to push anyone into talking about their broken heart."

Was Piers nursing a shattered heart? Or had the end of the betrothal been a blessed relief for him? The only thing which she was certain of was the emotion he had put into that kiss.

There had been passion in his embrace. He might have

been trying to hold back, but he'd been close to losing control.

She would give anything to experience Piers unleashed. And if there was even the slightest of chances that they could deepen their bond before they returned to London, she would be a fool not to take it.

Chapter Twenty-Eight

Hᵉ had been disappointed to wake alone in the sitting room and find Maggie gone. Piers had initially assumed she had retired to bed, but upon passing her bedroom, he saw that the door was open, and she was nowhere to be seen. Worried, he had searched the house, looking for her.

Only when he finally spied her out of a ground-floor window, standing in the garden and staring up at the nearby church, had his racing heart calmed.

Piers had thought to share a late-night cup of tea and a social chat, but it was clear Maggie was in the mood to talk about more personal matters. When she asked about Lady Dinah, there was a definite spark of life about her.

Explaining the truth about his broken betrothal wasn't, however, going to be easy.

She was honest with you. Perhaps now it is time to tell her some of the truth. Let her decide what she makes of it.

He cleared his throat, and plunged in. "Lady Dinah and I have known one another since we were children. Our parents had arranged our betrothal many years ago. I grew up assuming I would marry her."

They had met occasionally over the years and been on friendly enough terms. Neither found the other repulsive enough to call things off. Though love matches were on the increase, arranged marriages were still very much the norm amongst the English noble class.

"After I got back from Europe and the war was over, Lady Dinah's family pressed to go ahead with the wedding. We officially announced our engagement last year, but a number of things happened, and we kept putting it off."

Maggie met his gaze. "What sort of things?"

Deuce, how do I explain this?

"Well, for a start, I was still in the army. Lady Dinah wasn't happy with that and demanded that I resign my commission before we were wed."

That had been the first real sign of trouble between him and his former fiancée. Dinah was firmly against marrying Piers while he remained in the military. She had made it plain that she was to marry a future viscount, not a captain.

"Her family came to Denford Park earlier this year for a week-long stay. The idea was that settlements would be finalized and a date for the wedding set." He gulped down a large mouthful of the rapidly cooling tea, shuddering as it went down.

Maggie remained silent.

There was nothing else to do but for him to press on. "During that week, Lady Dinah and I spent some time together. The two of us walked around the house gardens at Denford Park."

His hopes had been that Dinah would begin to envisage a happy future at the Denford family estate. Picture herself settled and raising a brood of children with him.

He couldn't have been more wrong.

She'd refused his offer to go tramping in the woods and pick bluebells. Nor had she shown the slightest of interest in the bubbling brook he had planned for them to picnic beside. That was where Piers had thought they would share their first real kiss.

Then he had asked if she would like to go out into the field and do a spot of late-night stargazing. The summer evenings were warm enough that a light coat would do. Again, it was the perfect place for a young, betrothed couple to spend some time alone.

Lady Dinah had turned him down flat on that suggestion. She didn't want to go anywhere with him.

"Suffice to say, Lady Dinah and I quickly concluded that there were major points of difference between us. We agreed that we didn't suit."

Piers wasn't going to make mention that Lady Dinah had made it patently clear that their union was going to be very much based on him toeing the line. Her family was far wealthier than his, her father, an earl. She considered her future husband to be beneath her.

The only saving grace had been the fact that both his and Lady Dinah's mother had also come to the same conclusion. They'd jointly voiced their concerns about the union and the engagement was finally put to an end.

"I'm sorry things didn't work out between the two of you. But that doesn't explain why you have kept up the pretense of still being betrothed," replied Maggie.

He knew all her darkest secrets, her pain—it was only fair that he shared something of his own troubles. If he wanted to be her friend, he had to learn to confide in Maggie.

Where to begin?

"Firstly, let me address the issue of why I am still in the army. I haven't stayed because I enjoy dealing with mountains of paperwork. Believe me—I hate it. The best I can say is that there is some unfinished business which resulted from my time serving with the Prince of Orange. Until that is cleared up, I cannot resign my commission."

He pulled at the cuffs of his coat, growing uneasy at having to give voice to his problems. Apart from Jonathan and his parents, few people had any real understanding of his difficult predicament. Maggie was the last person he wanted to drag into his nightmare.

"Lady Dinah is aware that there is an issue. And that little progress has been made over the past year to resolve it. We agreed to keep the end of our betrothal a secret so as not to make other people think that she had passed judgment on me."

Piers wasn't going to mention any more of the situation to Maggie. She didn't need to hear the true depth of his problems or what he might be facing if he couldn't resolve them.

I just wish the prince would reply to my letters. Tell the Commander-in-Chief that I was trying to save his life that day. I was doing my duty.

"What did you do that would make Lady Dinah judge you?" she asked.

Piers was annoyed with himself for having framed his words so poorly. "Nothing. I didn't do anything. Could we please leave that topic of conversation where it is for the time being? I didn't come out here to burden you with my problems. I wanted to see how you were and if perhaps you might have had time to consider what you will do next," he said.

He handed her back the cup of tea and Maggie took a sip. She screwed up her face. "It still needs sugar."

Maggie turned away; her back was now to him. She pointed to the high stone edifice of St. Michael's church. Piers had always liked how it loomed over the garden—a giant protective wall against the winds of the world.

"I was just thinking about making time to go and speak to the minister at the church. Tell him something of my problems. I wasn't actually going to make mention to him as to who I am. I know that would be a little dishonest of me, but if I am to confide in someone and receive their counsel, I can't do that if they know I am the daughter of the Bishop of London," she said.

That was a sudden and unexpected emotional punch to the gut for Piers. Maggie didn't trust him enough to ask for his advice. Had he read their friendship wrong?

Doing his best to hide his wounded pride, he came to stand alongside her. "You could always speak to me. I would be more than happy to listen."

She gifted him with such a sad smile, he had to briefly turn away. "I'm sorry, Piers. I didn't mean to cause offense. I hadn't thought to ask for your opinion because some of my questions directly involve you."

For the second time in as many minutes, Maggie's words took Piers by surprise. "What do you mean?"

Her hand touched his, and their fingers entwined. "I was interested to know someone else's opinion as to what I should do if I found myself falling in love with a man who was meant to marry someone else. Even if his betrothal was at an end, he might not be open to the idea of finding love again so soon. I expect the answer would have been for me to pack my things and get on board the first available coach headed toward London."

Oh, Maggie.

Thank heavens she hadn't done that. He would have been forced to leap on the back of the nearest horse and chase after the coach, flagging it down like a good old-fashioned highwayman. Anything to stop her from leaving.

Piers gently pulled her into his embrace. "I am glad you didn't seek that counsel. I am hoping that now we have cleared the air somewhat between us, you might reconsider your plans."

She lifted her face and met his gaze. "If you are referring to my travel plans, at this juncture, I don't really have any. I am content to go anywhere as long as it is with you."

Those words were what Piers had longed to hear Maggie say. As long as they were together—that was all that mattered.

I will never let you go. I have to find a way to keep you—forever.

"Well, that sounds like the best plan of all, so I suggest we stick to it," said Piers. He lowered his lips to hers, and sealed their agreement with a long, lingering kiss.

Chapter Twenty-Nine

The revelation that Piers was not engaged to be married immediately changed the nature of their relationship. The kiss they shared in the night garden signaled a new direction for Maggie and Piers.

By rights, they should have been on their way back to London late the following morning. Instead, the Denford coach was headed six miles west of Coventry to the town of Kenilworth and the beautiful red sandstone ruins of Kenilworth Castle.

And rather than their luggage being onboard, a picnic basket, freshly prepared by the Denford family cook, rested on the seat opposite to where Piers and Maggie sat, hand in hand.

After their late night, Maggie had risen before the dawn. She had chosen the pale pink gown for today's outing. Her maid had offered to fashion Maggie's hair into French braids, then pin it into the hat Elizabeth had kindly lent her, but she had demurred, preferring to wear it in a soft chignon.

If she wore the hat low enough, it might help to hide the

dark circles under her eyes. There was nothing she could do about her drawn appearance but hope Piers didn't notice.

"You look lovely, Maggie. That shade of pink suits your fine complexion," said Piers.

Her gaze dropped to the wide-brimmed hat on her lap. Piers's charming words had set her heart running at a pitter-patter. She smiled; her heart was once more filled with the joy of the first heady days of romance.

"How are you this morning, Maggie. A little tired perhaps? I'll admit that getting out of bed was a bit of a struggle for me."

"No, I am fine, thank you. I shall manage."

The prospect of spending time alone with Piers was more than enough motivation to get Maggie out of bed. She loved how he had speared his fingers into her hair while he held her in his arms and kissed her in the early hours of the morning. Her hopes for the day included him slipping the hat from her head and ruffling her hair once more.

And if he is kissing me, then he won't notice how tired I really am.

"Thank you. I hope this gown and cloak will be warm enough for a day out in the country," she replied.

"If the weather turns poorly, we can always stop for a meal at the Sign of the Two Virgins inn. It's an old pub close by the castle."

"Do you know every tavern, inn, and pub in England?" she asked. Piers seemed to have a guide's map in his head detailing places where food and drink could be readily found.

He gave a half-shrug. "I like my food. And I enjoy finding the best of it. The restaurants and private clubs of London might think they serve the top nosh, but it's out here in the small English towns where the real flavors of this country can be found."

Maggie pointed to the picnic basket. "Did you have a hand in selecting our provisions for the day?"

"Yes."

A laugh burst from her lips. Elizabeth had been at great pains to explain how much time Piers had spent in the kitchen this morning, overseeing the preparations for their day trip. The Denford family cook had been muttering foul oaths under her breath the whole time.

"My apologies. I hear you gave the kitchen servants detailed instructions as to how they should slice the bread for our sandwiches. Tell me, Piers, where do you stand on the important argument between slicing on the diagonal or straight down the middle?"

She pretended not to see his sly side eye or hear his obvious *tsk* of disapproval.

"The diagonal if the bread is sliced and flat; across the middle if it is a rounded roll. And as for a French stick . . ."

With her lips sucked tightly together, Maggie looked away. She was doing her best to stop from laughing too hard, but her shaking torso betrayed her mirth.

A strong hand cupped her chin, gently turning her to face him. She found herself looking into the warm brown eyes of the man who had changed her life. "You are quite the tease, Miss Radley. I think today will be fun."

Kiss me.

When he went to draw back, she leaned forward, placing her hand over his. "It doesn't have to be a tease, Captain Denford. I am willing to make good on my promise."

He studied for her a moment, and Maggie wondered. *What are you thinking?*

"Let's not rush this. We should let things develop slowly. You have been through a lot in the past day or two. Despite what you have told me, I can see that there are rings under your eyes. I will be happier when I know you have gotten some sleep," he said.

His words of caution stung, but she could understand his reasoning. She *had* been through a lot in the last few days. Many truths that she had held tightly onto had been revealed as lies. Added to that was Piers's announcement that he was no longer betrothed.

"Just promise me one thing, will you? I want no secrets between us. I can accept many things, but I don't think I could ever be with someone who is not open with me. Not after *him*," she said.

There was another long moment of silence from Piers. "So, you are admitting that you are not sleeping?" he finally asked.

Fair was fair. If she was going to demand that he be honest with her, she had to do the same. "Yes. I am not getting much rest. My nerves are still not settled. Like all good things, sleep will come in time. Is there anything more which you would like to tell me about your own situation?"

Fair was definitely fair. One confession deserved another. She had caught him in his own game. Piers sighed. "I have told you what I can at the moment regarding my situation with the army. It is complicated, and I don't have much control over it. Until it is resolved, I am stuck at being an army captain."

"What would happen if you tried to resign your commission? They can't force you to remain in the army, can they?"

From what she had heard from her cousin Will Saunders, the army had discharged most of its troops and stood down the rest. Apart from pushing papers around, she couldn't understand why they would have much use for Piers.

"It has been made patently clear to me that if I try to leave the army it will be with a dishonorable discharge. My family name will be tarnished forever. I won't do that to my father, Jonathan, or my future children."

Maggie released her hold on him, and Piers's hand fell away. It was clear he wasn't telling her the whole truth of his predicament but her knowing what the army was holding over his head was enough for the moment. She could understand why Piers wanted to let their relationship develop slowly. "I understand. A dishonorable discharge would be a heavy burden to bear for our children," she replied.

Piers turned his head and gazed out the window. If he had heard her deliberate remark about their future children, he was making an obvious effort not to show it.

Maggie wisely let it go. She followed his lead and turned to gaze at the passing countryside, nodding her acknowledgment whenever Piers pointed out something of interest. There wasn't a great deal to see, just green fields and the occasional farm.

Eventually, the carriage slowed, and they took a detour off the main Coventry-to- Warwick Road and through the town of Kenilworth. When they reached the High Street, they turned left. Piers leaned forward in his seat and pointed out the window. Maggie caught sight of an old, white-washed building with a sign hanging out the front. A black and white image of two women dressed in medieval clothes had been painted on it.

"Is that the Sign of the Two Virgins? The tavern you mentioned earlier?" she asked.

"Well spotted. Yes, it's been serving patrons since the year fifteen sixty-three. Can you imagine the people it has seen through its front doors? I mean, Lord Robert Dudley, lived only a half mile up the road, so it must have been a watering hole for many of England's most powerful and wealthy in its heyday."

A historian as well as a lover of fine food. Piers Denford

was a man of many talents. In some ways he reminded her of her brother, James.

The thought of her family sent a pang of homesickness to her heart. She had been gone from home for less than a week, but it was the longest Maggie had ever been apart from her family.

A few more yards up the road, and Maggie got her first glimpse of Kenilworth Castle. Behind it the mid-morning sun framed its silhouette beautifully. Shattered towers of red sandstone reached into the sky.

What remained of the main castle was situated across a meadow, surrounded by green fields. There were many plump and wooly sheep grazing in and around what looked to have once been a moat. It was not how she had expected it to be—ruined and abandoned.

"You can understand why so many artists have painted that scene over the years," Piers said.

Maggie nodded. She could just imagine James seated on a stool, sketchbook in hand, feverishly attempting to capture a likeness on paper. "I would love to see it at sunset. The fiery red of the dying sun would look spectacular on the walls."

The coach drew up outside the front of the castle's main entrance. Piers pointed out a nearby building. "That's Leicester's building. The local authority still uses it for town meetings. It's about the only part of the castle the Parliamentarians didn't slight during the civil war."

"I have always found the term a touch peculiar. A slight is meant to be a small insult or snub. Taking a canon or explosives and reducing something almost to rubble really should be referred to by a different term, such as a levelling," she replied.

"You have a valid point. A levelling or a destruction actually describes what happens. A slight, sounds more like someone marched up to the castle and gave it a slap," he said.

Such a thought should have been amusing, but it was sad to see, what had once been a magnificent palace, now reduced to an empty ruined shell. The English Civil War had seen a great deal of the country's heritage laid to ruin.

The coachman opened the door, and Piers climbed out. He helped Maggie down from the step, then reached in and collected the picnic basket. With a blanket draped over his arm, Piers bowed to her. He looked for all the world like a lord welcoming a lady to his humble palace. "Welcome to Kenilworth, Miss Radley."

"Thank you, kind sir."

Maggie glanced down at her boots, silently congratulating herself on packing such sensible footwear. The grounds were not well kept, and if they intended to have a picnic among the ruins, they would need to traipse across the wet grass.

I hope Elizabeth's housemaid will forgive me if I get a stain or two on these pale pink skirts. They will require some scrubbing if I do.

They followed the narrow path which ran around the left side of the castle grounds and away from the main entrance. Piers pointed to the low, wide expanse which circled the site.

"When this was still a pleasure palace, there was a great mere full of water in the south-west of the grounds. It was deep enough for sailing boats. It's all long gone now, but in the spring, the area still floods. That's why the grass is lush and green, and why the sheep are so content to graze here."

Maggie's gaze traced the line of the red brick wall which circled the lower part of the castle grounds. In her mind's eye, she could see the waters lapping against it. "From what I recall, this was once one of the premier castles in England. Queen Elizabeth visited on numerous occasions."

"Yes, she did. The castle's owner, Lord Robert Dudley, was one of Queen Elizabeth's favorites for a long time. But when his wife died under suspicious circumstances, there were all manner of rumors of her having met with foul play. Dudley likely thought to marry the queen and being already in possession of a wife was an inconvenience. Nothing was ever proven, but the notion of him becoming royal consort pretty much ended at that point."

They made for an area higher up toward the great hall which towered over the landscape. Maggie politely waited for Piers to deliver the next part of his guided tour.

"John of Gaunt extended much of the castle and the inner bailey during an eight-year period from thirteen seventy-two to thirteen eighty. He also built the great hall, which is the building we are standing under," he announced.

There was a glint of pride shining in his eyes as he spoke. Piers truly loved this place. Kenilworth might well be a ruin, but it was still stunning—perhaps even more lovely in its shattered state than it might have been when it was a fully functioning castle.

Maggie lifted her gaze, taking in the massive structure. The stone frames of its soaring windows remained intact in many places.

"The great hall is almost one hundred feet high," added Piers.

She pointed at the outer walls, counting the lines on the bricks which marked where the original floors had once been. "That's at least four levels. There must have been hundreds of people living here in Dudley's day."

Piers nodded. "If we have time, I shall take you around to the other side of the castle and show you where the formal Elizabethan gardens once stood. It's all just an overgrown patch of weeds these days, but you can still get a good idea of the scale of what the Earl of Leicester did to the place and how much it must have cost him."

And all to woo a queen who decided that as much as she

loved him, Dudley was too great a risk for Elizabeth to ever marry.

But if you don't take a chance on love, you can never know how wonderful it can be.

Or how heartbreaking.

Maggie pushed that thought away. She had spent too long in the dark. Today was a day for sunshine and light. For spending precious time with a dashing army captain.

"For someone who is not actually from this part of England, you know an awful lot about Kenilworth," she observed.

Piers cleared his throat. "When I went up to Oxford University, I couldn't decide what I wanted to study. Theology bored me." He gave Maggie a nervous grin.

She waved it away. "Papa knows the church is not for everyone. As a second son, he had the usual options. Military. Church. Or spending his days in Scotland trying to stay out of the way of his father. He felt a calling for the church."

"My apologies. I didn't mean to sound like I was belittling your father's illustrious career. As the heir to the title of Viscount Denford, the church wasn't really something I would have seriously considered. And I had no real interest in the army, either. I only eventually joined because it was meant to be for a short spell."

She caught the bitterness in his words. Likely, someone had convinced Piers to take on the role of an officer, promising him that he was doing the right thing for his country and the war in Europe would soon be over.

But it isn't over for him.

"When I arrived at Oxford, I decided to study something which held my interest, and that was the English Civil War. I got an education as well as a splendid opportunity to travel the countryside and visit many of the sites of the major battles. The fact that a number of them were close to home was a bonus."

"I haven't visited many places outside of London. Papa is always so busy with church business. When we do travel, it's usually straight from London to Strathmore Castle, and then back again. I'm happy to admit I am envious of you," she said.

He set the basket down and came to her side. When he slipped a hand about her waist, she stepped into his embrace, relieved that the earlier awkwardness in the carriage appeared to have passed. Piers bent under her hat and brushed a kiss on her cheek. He whispered, "Don't worry about the envy part; just be happy. That's all any of us should do."

She lifted her head and smiled up at him. "You do say the loveliest of things. Perhaps that's why I think you are the nicest man I have ever met."

When Piers's brows knitted together, Maggie could guess what he was thinking. He wanted her to think of him as being more than just nice. "Nice and rather dashing. Is that better?" she offered.

His low growl of need sent a frisson of heat racing down her spine. With a deft flick of her fingers, Maggie's hat disappeared from her head. She rose up on her toes. "Or would you rather be a touch nice and naughty?"

The deep, toe-curling kiss he gave her was all the answer she could ever need.

Chapter Thirty

Piers and Maggie found a small, protected spot out of the wind at the base of the Strong Tower. A cluster of low shrubs added further protection from the elements.

He produced two bottles of ginger ale from the seemingly bottomless basket and handed one to Maggie. To his surprise, she promptly pulled the cork out with her teeth.

"I was going to open it for you," he said.

"Old Scottish custom. Never stand on ceremony when it comes to food and drink. It's best to have everyone watered and fed before the dancing," she replied.

He hadn't heard that saying before, but he couldn't find fault with the logic. Piers was always on the hunt for his next meal.

Maggie lay the blanket out on a patch of dry ground. She then set to rummaging through the picnic basket. "Oh, cake! And those sandwiches look delicious."

Piers leaned over the basket, scanning its contents. Had they packed the pickled pork and apple slices?

They better have packed them. Jonathan will eat them all if they have been left in the kitchen.

He breathed a sigh of relief as Maggie produced a square dish wrapped in a blue tea towel from the bottom of the basket. She lifted the cloth and peeked inside. "That looks interesting."

Taking it from her hands, Piers removed the cover. He couldn't help himself. He picked up a piece of the pork and apple with his fingers and swiftly stuffed it into his mouth.

"Piers Denford, where are your manners?" cried Maggie with a laugh.

She handed him a fork and a suitably admonished Piers slid it into the dish. He finished his mouthful, and they emptied the basket and laid two dinner plates on the blanket.

"The pork and apple spiced slices are a specialty of Jonathan and Elizabeth's household cook. She prepares them every time I visit," he explained.

"It looks a veritable feast. I don't know if we are going to be able to eat it all," replied Maggie. She held up her hand and pointed a finger in his direction. "Then again, we may succeed. My cousin Alex made mention of you at supper the night before we left London. He said you had quite the reputation at school when it came to food. Could finish a whole plate and still be sniffing around for more."

He bit back a laugh. The bloody Marquis of Brooke. Trust him to tell Maggie all the good gossip from his time at Eton.

Settling on the blanket, next to her, he accepted the plate Maggie passed to him. Soon, sandwiches and cold meats were piled high on it.

"Eat up. I promise not to tell anyone how much you ate. It's good to have a healthy appetite. And this picnic is the best I have enjoyed in a long time," she said.

They sat in companionable silence for a while. They ate, observing the nearby sheep as they grazed in the old mere below the castle. Occasionally, a fellow tourist or local farmer waved to them from the other side of the Great Hall, but the rest of the time it was just the two of them.

With bellies full, they finally packed up the basket and put it to one side of the blanket. Piers yawned. He was badly in need of a post-feast snooze. "I might just lie down here for a short while if that's alright with you."

Maggie nodded. "I feel the same. Two days running I have eaten a huge midday meal. I shall need to walk all the way back to Coventry to work this food off or my new clothes won't fit."

"You would look lovely at any size, Maggie. I on the other hand might need to start cutting back on supper. Military uniforms don't have much give in them, especially the buttons," replied Piers.

His heavy eyes closed. He wanted to rest, but not sleep. These moments alone with Maggie were something to be savored.

"Have you had a chance to think any more about the future? I mean, what will you do when you finally return to London?" he asked.

He didn't want to push Maggie, but Piers was keen for her to consider what her life might look like after this trip. She could stay away for as long as she liked, but eventually, she would have to return to her family.

"I gave it some thought last night. I couldn't sleep. My mind was too busy. I suppose the obvious is to try and pick up the pieces of my life. To put this awful business behind me."

You are right; this has been an awful business. And that scoundrel has made you suffer needlessly.

"Easier said than done," he replied.

"Yes. It's going to be difficult to talk to my family, but it is what it is. I've also come to some decisions regarding him. I think it is best that I leave all of it in the past. He has a wife and children. They shouldn't have to suffer because of his selfish stupidity."

Piers opened his eyes. "That's very magnanimous of you, Maggie. Plenty of other people wouldn't see it that way. They would want him punished."

He wanted nothing more than to wrap Maggie up in his arms and offer her comfort, but the moment he moved toward her, she held up a trembling hand.

"Please don't. I need to be able to deal with this without other people having to continually offer me their sympathy."

"I hate to see you upset."

The meek smile she gave him in return struck at his heart. "I know, but I've got very good at accepting bad news. It will just take me a little time to be able to get this all straight in my head. And some of it, I fear, I may never be able to understand."

The thought of her going home and trying to explain things to her family filled him with empty sadness. Hadn't Maggie suffered enough already? There had to be something he could do. A way to ease her burden.

What if she doesn't go back to town straight away? Time and distance could be what she needs. Get her out of Coventry. Away from the worry of running into that blackguard.

But would she agree to come with him? And was he being completely honest with himself when it came to his motives? To the plans that were evolving in his mind.

Nothing ventured, nothing gained.

"Maggie, you said before that you hadn't had much of an opportunity to see the rest of England. That your family travels the well-worn path back and forth to Scotland each year."

"Hmm. Yes, that's what we do."

"Well, I was thinking we might take the long road back to London. We could do a spot of sightseeing on the way. My parents are in residence at Denford Park, which is a couple of days easy coach ride east of Coventry. I haven't been allowed home since the summer, and I would dearly love to see my parents."

And to introduce you to them.

Firstly, as his friend, but in time, hopefully as something else. His mother and Maggie's were acquainted. They came from similar backgrounds. Good families. They were the sort of people who he could count upon not to judge Maggie for her misfortune.

"We can travel through Naseby on the way to Denford Park. Continue our tour of battle scenes from the English civil wars. Naseby is the site of the major turning point of the first English Civil War; Kenilworth's destruction came at the end of the second."

"And the invasion of Scotland took place during the third war," she replied, giving him a nod. Piers wasn't the only one who knew his British history. Maggie Radley was clearly an intelligent, well-read woman. Perfect material for his future viscountess.

And the mother of your children.

Maggie finished the last of her ginger beer and put the empty bottle back into the basket. Piers held his tongue, not wishing to press her for an answer. It didn't need saying that him arriving home at the family estate with the Bishop of London's unwed daughter would bring with it more than one or two questions.

Expectations would no doubt also arise. And at that moment, Piers wasn't certain he had a firm hold on anything. He had no answers.

This is an imprudent idea.

"I'm sorry, Maggie. It wasn't fair of me to ask you to go to Denford Park. We can travel directly back to London when you are ready to leave Coventry."

"I would rather that we travelled to Denford Park. It would be nice to meet your family and see your home. And, if I am being honest, the thought of going back to my own home fills me with trepidation. I will of course have to deal with my parents at some juncture, but I'm not ready for that. Not yet."

She got to her feet, dusting breadcrumbs from her cloak and gown. Leaning against the sandstone wall, she closed her eyes. A soft sigh escaped her lips.

Maggie Radley was an exquisite woman, possessed with both beauty and a bright mind. Any man who could hold her heart would consider himself most fortunate.

"If you and I are travelling together, then you are still technically on army business, aren't you, Piers?" she asked.

"I suppose so. My job was to go to Coventry and follow up your case. Until I set foot back in the Horse Guards, I am still in your service."

"Well then, I think that answers your question. I am perfectly happy to go anywhere, as long as you and I are together, Captain Denford." She pushed off the wall. Bending, Maggie began to pick up the various dishes from the picnic, packing them back into the basket. A decision had been made, and she clearly didn't wish to discuss it any further.

Denford Park it is.

Chapter Thirty-One

M aggie noticed the familiar signs of a full-blown anxiety attack long before they reached the entrance to the castle grounds. Her breathing grew labored and shallow, her head felt light. She slowed her steps, desperately fighting against the rising tide of fear.

In the first few days after receiving the letter informing of her Robert's supposed death, she had been swept up in the maelstrom of grief. She had endured long hours of crying, lamenting the future that had been so cruelly stolen from them.

She had naively thought that when the tears finally did dry it was the end of her physical reaction to the shock of losing her love. But as sadness became her constant companion, she'd fought to find sleep.

A vicious cycle of restless nights and fatigue-filled days had taken her to the brink of a breakdown. And then, when she didn't think it could get any worse, the attacks began. At times, she would hyperventilate so much that she would come close to actually blacking out.

Piers, the picnic basket, slung leisurely over his arm

walked ahead of her on the path. He was oblivious to her growing distress.

She struggled to control her breathing. To calm the rapid intake of air. It didn't make sense. Why was this happening?

I thought all this was behind me.

Maggie stopped dead in her tracks; her hand was held to her chest. Her heart thumped hard. Forcing herself to take a slow, deep breath, she managed one word: "Piers."

He whirled round, and his expression flashed with worry. Piers dropped the basket and rushed to her side. "What's wrong? You look as pale as a ghost."

How do I explain this? He will think me gone mad.

"I can't control my breathing. My heart is racing at a gallop." Maggie slumped against Piers as he put an arm around her, taking her weight.

"Are you going to faint?" he asked.

"I hope not, but please don't let go."

"Never."

It was so frustrating to think that Robert could still have this sort of hold over her. Would she ever be free of him?

"Did you want me to carry you? It's not far to the coach. I can get the driver to come back for the basket," said Piers.

Maggie shook her head. "No. I think I am better off trying to walk; it forces me to take deep breaths. I thought I was past all this, but my mind and body are still fighting one another."

All she wanted to do was curl up in a tight ball and sleep. To go back to hiding away from the world.

"You have been through a lot, and you are not sleeping. I'm not surprised that your nerves are giving out on you."

"Yes, I know," she replied, failing to hide the disappointment in her voice.

She stood still for a time, her gaze roaming over the nearby fields and farms as she tried to calm herself. Eventually, her breathing grew steadier. "If it is alright with you, could we forget about going to see the site of the Elizabethan gardens, and instead just head back to the carriage?"

"Of course. I think the best place for you to be is safely at my brother's home where you can rest," he replied.

With Piers gently holding an arm around her waist, the basket in his other hand, they slowly made their way back to the entrance of the castle grounds.

"We will be heading straight to Coventry and my brother's house," Piers instructed the coachman.

He helped her onboard, and Maggie sank into the seat. "I'm sorry I don't feel up to the rest of your guided tour. I was so looking forward to visiting the town and the tavern. And I know you probably have plenty of interesting historical tidbits to share. Perhaps another time."

With her cloak wrapped about herself, and the blanket covering her legs, Maggie settled into the corner of the carriage. Piers produced another folded-up blanket from the storage box under the other seat and gave it to Maggie to use as a pillow.

"It will take an hour or so to return to Jonathan and Elizabeth's house. Maybe close your eyes and see if you can take a short nap."

"Any sleep would be good," she replied.

She closed her eyes, and the gentle, swaying motion of the coach soon had her drifting off to sleep.

When she woke a little while later, she found herself wrapped in Piers's arms. He dropped a tender kiss on her forehead. "Sleep. You are safe with me."

Chapter Thirty-Two

Piers woke in the middle of the night to the sound of voices in the hallway outside his bedroom. He recognized Elizabeth and Jonathan, but there was a third unknown person.

Climbing out of bed, he grabbed his jacket and quickly pulled on a pair of trousers. Opening the door, he was greeted with the sight of his brother and sister-in-law. They were having a heated conversation with a gentleman carrying a doctor's bag.

"She really needs to either be somewhere for the mentally unstable or at least sedated. If not, I fear she might well harm herself," said the stranger.

"I don't think we should be sending her anywhere. Maggie is safe here," said Elizabeth.

Piers stepped out into the hall. "What's going on?"

Elizabeth greeted him with reddened eyes. "It's Maggie; she has had some sort of mental breakdown. I didn't know what to do so I summoned Doctor Hewson."

Piers couldn't believe what he was hearing. Maggie was in

trouble but instead of waking him, they had sent for a physician. "Where is she?"

"I have sedated her, and we managed to put her back to bed. The young lady was most distressed," replied the doctor. His gaze flittered over Piers's army coat. "And you are?"

Jonathan cleared his throat. "Doctor Hewson, this is my older brother, the Honorable Piers Denford."

The doctor's demeanor changed in an instant. He bowed to Piers. "My lord."

Piers was more concerned about Maggie's well-being than bothering to correct the gentleman on the proper form of address for a viscount's heir. "What sort of medicine did you give her?"

"A good dose of laudanum, with a prescription to have it given to her twice daily. If she is calm, she cannot come to harm."

Nor will she be able to think straight. Bloody quacks, why is keeping a patient silent always the first option?

He was barely keeping his temper under control. While he had been fast asleep, others had been making decisions on Maggie's behalf. That wouldn't do. He was her protector, self-appointed or not.

He turned to Jonathan. "Could you please escort Doctor Hewson to the front door?"

It didn't matter that this wasn't his house; Piers's tone brooked no argument. His younger brother would know that he was beyond angry.

Jonathan nodded. "Of course. Doctor Hewson, would you please follow me?"

"I should take another look at the patient before I leave," the doctor protested.

Piers took a step forward and loomed over the shorter man. Doctor Hewson winced at this less-than-subtle attempt at intimidation. "Perhaps it can wait until morning," said the doctor.

"I appreciate that your time is precious. And thank you for coming out at this ungodly hour, but we shouldn't keep you from your bed a minute longer. My family and I will check on the condition of the young lady at regular intervals over the rest of the night. Then, in the morning we can decide what, if any, further medical intervention is required," replied Piers.

Jonathan showed the doctor out before returning to where Piers and a subdued Elizabeth waited.

"Now, tell me what happened, and why you didn't wake me?" demanded Piers.

"I found Maggie outside in the garden, dressed in nothing more than her nightgown. She was pacing back and forth, barefoot, and muttering under her breath. I thought she might have gone mad. I'm sorry, Piers. I panicked and sent for the doctor. I realize now we should have woken you," Jonathan said.

Piers sighed. "Maggie has been suffering from panic attacks. She had them quite severely two years ago when she first found out about Robert Taylor being dead. When we were leaving from Kenilworth Castle, she began to have difficulty breathing and her heart was racing. She told me she hasn't been sleeping. I'm sorry if I was curt with you just now. This is your home, so it was an oversight on my part not to have privately mentioned Maggie's health to the both of you as soon as we returned here this afternoon."

Elizabeth dabbed at her eyes with a handkerchief. "I take it you don't agree with Doctor Hewson's plans to treat Maggie, but we can't just leave her to suffer."

No, they couldn't. But he would be damned if they were going to keep her heavily sedated, or worse—send her somewhere.

"She was in a terrible state, and it took quite some time for us to finally convince her to come inside," Jonathan added.

Piers's mind was made up. Elizabeth was right; he didn't hold with the doctor's plans, but neither did he think it fair to impose an emotionally distressed young woman on his brother and sister-in-law. They had their own family to consider.

He had intended to stay in Coventry for a few more days and show Maggie the local sights, but tonight's developments had scuttled those plans. When Maggie woke, he would talk to her. Seek her opinion on a way forward.

"I'm sorry to have brought this trouble to your door. We will leave Coventry as soon as we can in the morning," said Piers.

"Will you head back to London? Maggie might feel better once she is at home with her own family," said Jonathan.

"I will talk to Maggie when she is fully awake." It was late and Piers wasn't in the mood to start an argument. He would go and sit with Maggie and wait for the laudanum to wear off.

His offer for them to travel onto Denford Park still stood. But Maggie's health was of paramount importance.

Where they went was her decision. As long as they were together, Piers didn't care. If she wished to be with her family, they would leave for London at first light. If she wanted to be with him, he would find a way to make it work.

I just want her to be somewhere she feels safe.

Chapter Thirty-Three

The drugs had knocked Maggie out cold. It was midmorning before she'd finally cracked open her eyes. The first thing she'd seen was Piers seated in a nearby chair, his chin pressed to his chest. He'd been snoring softly, only stirring when she shifted in the bed and sat up.

"How are you feeling this morning?" he asked.

She pulled the bedclothes up around her. It wasn't socially acceptable for a man to be in the bedroom of an unmarried woman while she was awake, let alone while she was asleep.

Vague memories of the night prior crept into her mind. She had broken recollections of a stranger peering down at her, then being forced to drink something bitter. Then nothing. "I am feeling lethargic and quite drained. What happened?"

He bit on his bottom lip as she waited for his answer. "You had a bit of a turn. They found you barefoot and wandering about the garden. Do you remember anything that happened after you went to bed?"

Maggie's mouth dropped open. *Oh, sweet lord, no. I didn't sleepwalk, did I?*

"No. I retired just after supper. I was tired after the trip to Kenilworth, even with sleeping on the way home."

Sometime during the night, she must have stirred in her sleep and gone downstairs, the lure of the garden capturing her unconscious mind.

Maggie covered her face with her hands. How was she ever going to face Elizabeth and Jonathan again?

"They called for a doctor. When he came, he prescribed you a dose of laudanum."

They? Where was Piers?

He rose from the chair and began to pace slowly up and down. His shirt was creased, and his cravat and waistcoat were both missing.

"I was asleep while all of this was happening. If I had known the doctor was going to force a draught down your throat, I would have stopped him. From all accounts, you were in a state of distress, but I, for one, don't hold with drugging people."

Piers returned to his seat, leaning forward, hands clasped together. There was a decided amount of discomfort in his stiffly held posture. "I think we should leave Coventry today. This city is not good for you."

"Do you think that perhaps my mind is continuing to relive the moment when I saw him again? The emotional shock is somehow still fresh? It would go a long way towards explaining why my nerves are in such a delicate state."

"Possibly. There is also the ongoing risk of you accidentally running into him at some point while you are out and about in town. I wouldn't be the least surprised if your nerves were still on edge knowing that threat still exists."

Maggie hadn't actually considered that she may encounter Robert or his family again. As far as she was concerned, the moment she had walked out the door of the King's Head he'd been as good as dead to her.

But Robert still lived only a few streets away from the Denford's' home. He probably passed by the end of their lane every day. *Why hasn't this crossed my mind before now?*

"You might be right on both counts. Which means getting away from Coventry is the best thing to do. I'm just not sure where I should go," she replied.

She didn't want to remain at the house, especially not if a laudanum-dispensing physician had decided he knew what was best for her. For physical maladies she was prepared to trust to a doctor, but not her mental well-being. Sedation didn't solve her problems; it only masked them.

"The offer to go to Denford Park still stands. You could take some time to let things settle. Eat good food, tramp over the wide fields. It would be just like you were in Scotland, except for the lack of a castle and deep snowdrifts," replied Piers.

Maggie softly smiled. There was nowhere in all of England that was anything like Strathmore Castle.

You are one of only a few people who seem to understand me

"What will your parents say when you arrive home with me? I mean, won't it seem a little odd? And my strange behavior may well continue." The thought of further embarrassing Piers filled her with worry. The sensible thing would be to ask him to take her home. To go back to hiding out at Fulham Palace until she was over this latest bout of instability.

"If I bring the daughter of the Bishop of London to my family home, it is going to raise plenty of questions. But I promise that I will consult you before I answer any of them. You are not under obligation to me, Maggie. I'm your friend firstly and . . ."

What harm could a little adventure to Northamptonshire do? It could also bring her the relief that Piers suggested it might.

And if he was with her at Denford Park, it would give them the opportunity to delve deeper into their connection. For them to explore their feelings for one another more fully.

To move on to more than just kissing.

All it would take would be for her to throw back the blankets, climb out of bed, and come to him. She could run her fingers through his thick, dark mane. Plant butterfly kisses on his furrowed brow. Flick open the top of her gown and whisper to him,

"Piers I want us to be more than friends."

What am I doing? The laudanum must have addled my brain.

Pushing aside all thoughts of seduction, Maggie came to a decision. She would go with Piers to Denford Park, and what happened after that was up to fate. If they were meant to be together then love would surely blossom.

There was, of course, a degree of danger in heading off into the wilds of England with him. What if she did have another episode while they were on the road? If in a dazed state she went wandering the streets of some distant town, she could well come to harm.

"How many days would it take us to reach Denford Park? I mean if we left early tomorrow morning," she asked. Maggie needed a day in bed to recover from the heavy dose of laudanum. She wanted her head and stomach to be settled when they left Coventry.

"It's fifty miles from here. So, if we left just after first light, spent tomorrow night at the Fitzgerald Arms tavern in Naseby, then pushed on early, we would reach my family's estate by late afternoon. We could be at Denford Park the day after tomorrow." The way the whole itinerary rolled off his tongue, it was clear Piers had undertaken the trip on numerous occasions.

Once they reached Denford Park, she could relax. There

would be family and servants about the place, and she would be safe.

"I would like to go with you, my only concern being this sudden onset of dream-walking. If we stay at the Fitzgerald Arms tomorrow night, I will take a sleeping draught. That should be enough to keep me in a deep state of slumber, so I don't stir from my bed," she said.

The lines on his face softened. "Good. I am glad that you have made that choice. We can leave in the morning once you are dressed and have had breakfast. I shall go and speak with my brother."

As soon as Piers had left the room, Maggie slipped out of bed and retrieved her dressing gown. She was still a little woozy and unsteady on her feet, but she had a pressing task which demanded her attention. Only after she had dealt with it would she be able to go back to bed and sleep.

While Piers was dealing with his brother, she, in turn, was eager to speak to Elizabeth. To thank her for being such a generous hostess, but mostly to apologize.

Chapter Thirty-Four

Doctor Hewson was in the foyer talking to Jonathan when Piers made his way down the stairs. His brother wore a worried expression on his face.

"The doctor would like to examine Miss Radley this morning," he said.

At least someone was asking this time, rather than just assuming. But it still set Piers on edge. As far as he was concerned, and judging by their recent conversation, Maggie was of the same opinion as him—she didn't need a doctor. What she did need however, was fresh air and time to get her thoughts back into order.

"Maggie doesn't want or need visitors this morning. I am heading out shortly to get some travel provisions as she and I are heading to Denford Park tomorrow. Coventry no longer agrees with us," replied Piers.

He ignored the respective frowns from both his brother and the doctor at his use of her first name. Yes, it spoke of a personal familiarity, but he didn't give a damn what anyone thought of it.

"Lord Denford—I mean, Captain Denford, I must

protest. Miss Radley should be kept sedated and confined to bed. Her mental state is not that of someone who should be undertaking any sort of journey," said the doctor.

Piers fixed Doctor Hewson with a hard glare. "I have spoken to the young lady this morning and she has made her position clear. She is coming with me. I thank you for your concern and wish to reassure you that I shall do everything to ensure that she continues to make a full recovery."

No. They were not going to treat her like an invalid. Maggie wasn't suffering from some terrible affliction. She needed privacy and a place to heal. That was exactly what his family home could provide.

The doctor cleared his throat once more. "I must protest."

Piers held up his hand. "Protest heard, noted, and dismissed." He turned to his brother. "When the good doctor has left, could you please spare me a few minutes in your study?"

After a moment's hesitation, Jonathan nodded. "Yes, of course."

Piers headed back upstairs to wait in Jonathan's study. He wasn't interested in conducting a long discussion with Doctor Hewson. If Maggie felt she was well enough to make the journey to Denford Park, that was all he needed to know.

A few minutes later, Jonathan appeared. He closed the door a little more firmly than was required. Piers readied himself for a showdown.

"Was it really necessary for you to be so bloody rude to him? The man graciously made a house call in the middle of the night to assist Maggie, and then this morning, you treated him like he was a beggar at the door," Jonathan said.

"I have just spoken to Maggie. She is not feeble of mind. That poor girl has suffered a recent shock. Little wonder she is finding things difficult. But the last thing she needs is to be drugged."

Jonathan fixed him with a look that spoke of deep concern, and also, suspicion. More than likely, he and Elizabeth had spoken and shared their opinions on the subject of what may actually lay between Maggie and Piers. "You are protective of her. More than I think you realize."

No, actually I am fully aware of how protective I am.

Piers had every reason to have Maggie's welfare as his top priority. She meant a great deal to him. Seeing her suffer because of that selfish bastard of a former fiancé had cut him to the quick.

"Can I share something with you? And I would appreciate it if you waited until I was finished before you respond," said Piers.

Jonathan crossed his arms. "If you think telling me that you might be in love with Miss Radley is going to be some sort of surprise, you are gravely mistaken. And no, I am not going to stand here in my own house and have you lecture me. Piers, you are taking a risk with her. If your feelings are of the romantic kind, then you should be very careful about your next move with Maggie."

Piers hadn't expected that sort of response. Jonathan's words tore all the wind out of his sails. "What do you mean?"

"I mean, if you do care for her, you should be honest about your own situation. Taking Maggie home to meet Mama and Papa when you are not in a position to offer for her hand places her reputation at grave risk."

Trust Jonathan to put things into sharp perspective. And for him to be right.

His own situation was still in a state of flux. Until he could get support from the King of the Netherlands or the Prince of Orange, he was stuck.

Talk about a rock and a hard place.

It was selfish of him, but he wasn't prepared to give her up.

"Maggie knows enough. I have told her that if I try to resign my commission, I will receive a dishonorable discharge. I've also made mention that I have some unfinished business with the army."

"But not the rest of it? So, what you have told her is a few vague bits and pieces, but nothing of real substance."

"I don't think it would be fair to tell her the rest. At least, not yet."

Jonathan slowly shook his head. "And you think lying to her is being fair?"

Piers didn't have an answer for that. Lying by omission was still lying. He didn't want to tell Maggie everything because he didn't honestly know what to say.

But if he could get her to Denford Park, if they could build on their fledgling romance then maybe, just maybe, he might be able to find a way to explain things.

"I don't want to lose her. Maggie Radley is the best thing that has come into my life in a very long time."

His brother sighed. "If you take her home, you must understand that it will create expectations. Not just on her part, but that of our parents. I know you are concerned about your heart and finding a way to keep the woman you are clearly in love with, but don't let that be at the expense of the Denford family."

"They are not going to try to court martial me without having a fight on their hands. I've decided that when I get back to London, I am going to call on every person in a position of power who can help me. I'm not going to write any more letters. I am done with that. Instead, I will be knocking on doors. And if that fails, I am quite prepared to get on a boat and sail all the way to Ostend and then head to Amsterdam. The time for waiting for the Prince of Orange to get off his pampered arse and write me a letter of support is well past."

Jonathan unfurled his arms and slowly clapped. "About bloody time. And if the British Army come after you and try to charge you with desertion, Elizabeth and I will stand out the front of Westminster Palace every day with large placards in our hands protesting your innocence."

Piers grinned. He could just imagine his brother and sister-in-law doing something like that; they weren't the type of people to back down from a fight for justice. He could only pray that if it did come to that, Maggie would be standing right alongside them.

Chapter Thirty-Five

❧❀❧

"I cannot thank you enough for allowing me to stay. And I am so sorry for all the trouble I have caused," said Maggie.

Elizabeth brushed a kiss on her cheek. "It was a pleasure to meet you. I'm just sad that your journey here ended with more heartache and disappointment."

Maggie met her eyes. As she expected, they were full of deep concern. Instead of heading back to London and into the loving arms of her family, Maggie was venturing into the wilds of Northamptonshire with Piers.

"I want you know that it was my decision to go with Piers to Denford Park. He didn't do anything to compel me into agreeing," she said.

"I know. Just take care. You are both in a vulnerable state at the moment. I would just hate for either of you to make a mistake," replied Elizabeth.

Elizabeth stepped away as Piers came to Maggie's side. "Are you ready to leave?" he asked.

"Yes."

After another round of hugs, farewells, and giving her

solemn promise that Maggie would one day return, she climbed aboard the coach. As soon as Maggie had taken her seat, Piers had a blanket wrapped around her shoulders and another one placed across her lap.

"Can't have you getting cold. My mother would never forgive me."

When Maggie and Jonathan exchanged a look, Jonathan simply shook his head. Piers was fussing, and only a fool would get in the way.

While Piers was saying his final farewells to the Denford children, Jonathan leaned into the coach. "Take care, Maggie. I am sincere when I say that I hope to see you again. And a small piece of advice: don't let my brother remain his own worst enemy. He is a good stick, but sometimes he forgets to ask for help."

"Thank you. And yes, I can see he tends to let things lie rather than confront them. This army business—Piers hasn't told me much, but I was wondering if perhaps my cousin Will might be able to help. He is well regarded, and he has powerful connections in the war office. Do you think it might be worthwhile me raising Piers's case with him?"

Jonathan glanced at his brother. "Perhaps. But first, you have to get Piers to tell you the whole story of what happened in the lead up to and during the battle of Waterloo. There are people in the army who would gladly stand back and let him fall. Your cousin might have friends, but my brother has enemies. Some of those are unseen."

He stepped aside as Piers came to the door. "Safe travels, brother. I hope to see you in London and out of uniform very soon."

They embraced in a final hug, then Piers climbed aboard. He and Maggie both waved to the Denford children as the coach pulled out of St. Mary's Street and headed toward Gosford Street. A short time later, they reached Far Gosford

Street before finally leaving the city of Coventry behind them. Wide green fields slowly replaced the houses, and the stone streets fell away to gravel roads.

"Well, that was Coventry. I think we managed to survive our stay," said Piers.

"Thanks to you. I don't know what I would have done if I had arrived by myself and then discovered Robert was still alive."

The mere thought of travelling all the way back to London on her own in a state of distress and shock made Maggie shudder. With Piers by her side, she had made it through some of the worst days of her life.

And now, he is taking me to his family estate.

That raised a whole new set of questions in her mind. What would Lord and Lady Denford make of their son bringing the daughter of the Bishop of London home with him? Would they think it strange? Or would they accept it, but then demand that he offer for her?

Maggie could think of a million things worse than being compelled to marry Piers. Hopefully, he felt the same.

At least I know he won't fake his death to avoid marrying me.

Chapter Thirty-Six

The rest of the day's journey was mostly uneventful. The Denford coach drew up outside the Fitzgerald Arms in the early evening. Unfortunately for Piers, his hopes for him and Maggie to share a rustic supper ended not long after they arrived.

As soon as they reached the top of the stairs which led to the tavern's guest rooms, she drew him aside. "I am going to go to bed to try and get some sleep. I'm exhausted, and I suspect I might be coming down with a cold." She was pale and drawn.

"I expect standing out in the garden in your nightgown probably has something to do with you feeling unwell. How about you get into bed, and I will arrange for a bowl of soup to be brought up to you? A good night's sleep is probably what you need," he replied.

"That sounds like a perfect plan. I'm sorry I am not being sociable tonight, but I'm wrung out. It hurts to swallow and that is never a good sign."

While Maggie took her bag and got herself set up in her room, Piers went back downstairs and had a word with the innkeeper. A short time later, he knocked on Maggie's door. When she opened it, his happy pride at bringing her a tray of hot soup and bread vanished.

She was wrapped up in a blanket, her arms hugging her trembling body. "I am definitely coming down with something."

After closing the door, Piers placed the tray on a nearby small table. He drew Maggie into the warmth of his embrace, rubbing his hands up and down her back. "You need to be in bed."

Her gaze fell on the steaming bowl of soup. "But you went to all that effort to go and get me soup."

"And soup you shall have. Go on. Climb in under the blankets. I will bring the soup to you."

She gave him a quizzical look but did as he instructed. As soon as Maggie was seated in bed, the blankets all tucked up around her, Piers lifted the table and brought it over, setting it down beside the bed. After making himself comfortable on the edge of the mattress, he picked up the spoon and dipped it into the soup. Maggie shuffled a little closer as Piers turned and moved the spoon toward her mouth.

"Are you really going to feed me like a small child?" she asked.

He grinned. "Yes, I am. You are poorly and must be taken care of properly."

She sipped the soup, nodding her approval. "That is good. I need something hot to ward off the chills. Another please, Piers."

I like it when you say my name like that.

For the next short while, they settled into a quiet ritual of Piers scooping up chicken soup and Maggie drinking it down. When he scraped the last spoonful from the bottom of the bowl, she sat back in the bed and sighed. "That was delicious."

"Did you want some more? I could go downstairs and fetch you another bowl," he replied.

She waved his offer away. "Thank you, but no. My belly is comfortably full, and I want to try and get some sleep. Besides, you should go and eat."

Piers shook his head. "Perhaps later. I am more concerned with you at the moment. If it's alright with you, I might just sit over by the fire for a little while."

He was worried. Maggie was unwell, but the specter of her dream-walking also lurked in the back of his mind despite the sleeping draught she'd decided to take. The Fitzgerald Arms didn't have many patrons in the tavern, and he and Maggie were the only travelers lodging tonight, but Piers was still anxious as to what might happen if Maggie did happen to wander from her room.

"I don't want you going hungry," she said.

If she is worried about me, she won't sleep. "How is this for a compromise? I will take the tray and empty bowl back to the kitchen. While I am there, I shall ask them to make me up a plate of leftovers. I will bring that back here and eat my supper by the fire. You can go to sleep knowing that I have been fed and watered."

Her timid smile was all the answer he needed. Piers leaned over and planted a soft kiss on Maggie's forehead. The poor girl was burning with fever. "I shall arrange for a maid to bring up a fresh jug of water and some clean flannels so you can cool your face."

"Thank you. That would be lovely. You do spoil me, Piers Denford."

Their gazes met. Maggie's clear blue eyes lacked their usual shine. He brushed his hand on her warm cheek. "A woman such as you, Maggie, deserves to be spoiled. In fact, you should be worshiped."

He picked up the tray and headed for the door. "I will be back shortly."

As he made his way down the narrow staircase a little voice whispered in Piers's mind.

You have to find a way to be able to keep her. To be able to freely offer Maggie a life by your side.

First, he had to get Maggie to Denford Park and see her well again. Once his mind was free of worry over her health, he could start to plan his campaign to finally take on his enemies within the British Army. It was time to bring the fight to them—and win.

Only then would he be finally free and able to make Maggie his wife.

Chapter Thirty-Seven

As soon as they arrived at Denford Park late the following day, Piers swept Maggie up into his arms and carried her upstairs to his sister Annabel's old bedroom. Her protests at being treated like a feeble patient had gone unheard. He was determined that she was going to endure all the fussing he could muster.

He wanted her restored to full health. To see the light dance once more in her eyes. Seeing her so ill had his nerves on edge.

His surprised mother followed him up the stairs, handing out orders left and right to any member of the household staff who happened to be within earshot. Servants went scurrying to-and-fro, making hurried arrangements for the unexpected guests.

Meals were to be prepared. More blankets to be found. And someone had better hurry to the village and fetch the doctor.

That last order had Piers pausing at the top of the first set of risers. He glanced back over his shoulder at his mother.

"Hold off on the doctor for the moment, please. Maggie has a bad cold. Nothing else. She needs rest and chicken soup."

If her fever grew worse, then he would send for a physician.

After leaving his mother and some housemaids to help Maggie change into her nightclothes and get settled into bed, Piers went in search of his father.

Lord Denford was in his usual place—his study. "Piers. Thank heavens. It's been an eternity since you were home."

It had only been a matter of three months, but it did feel like forever.

A short while later, Piers and his father were seated comfortably in front of the fireplace. A glass of French brandy sat in Piers's hand. His teetotaler of a sire was nursing a cup of strong black tea.

"So, Lady Dinah Gibney has found someone else? I am not surprised; she is a good catch. Pity the two of you couldn't find a way to make it up the aisle, but it is what it is," observed Lord Denford.

Piers sipped at his drink and considered his response. "I know you are disappointed that she and I agreed to break off our betrothal, but it was for the best. There was no point in us marrying and then spending the rest of our days regretting it."

"And what about Miss Margaret Radley? You are not seriously expecting your mother and I to believe that she is here purely due to your altruistic nature? You are a kind- hearted man, Piers, but even that doesn't go all the way to fully explaining what you are doing. Please tell me this is not something you have done on impulse."

Piers shook his head. "No, it is not. In fact, I have given it a great deal of consideration. I am serious with my intentions toward Maggie. The main reason why I brought her here was so that she could have a place to get her own thoughts settled."

He didn't want to discuss the subject of Lady Dinah any further. It was old ground which, as far as Piers was concerned, had been thoroughly raked over.

"And what about this unfinished business with the army? What are you going to do about that?" pressed his father.

The last time he and Lord Denford had discussed the issue, Piers hadn't had a solid plan. He had been patiently waiting for the letters of support from the Dutch royal family —letters he now accepted he may never see.

"What I am going to do is to stop waiting for the wheels of justice to turn. I've already started preparing a list of people who I will visit once I get back to London. The time for writing polite letters is over."

If he had to shame the hierarchy of the British Army into giving him a fair hearing, or even better, dropping the matter entirely, then that was what he would do.

"I'm going to demand that all reports from the battle of Waterloo be made available to me. There must be other documents which support my version of the events of the day. And if they won't hand them over, I am going to petition parliament."

"Thank heavens," Lord Denford whispered.

The Piers Denford who had departed the offices of the Horse Guards was not the same Piers who would be walking back through the front door.

Let his enemies show themselves. He would rather face them in the open than continue fighting in the shadows.

His plan was not, however, without risk. If he stirred the hornets' nest, the army may well decide to come after him.

But the prospect of facing a court-martial no longer held the same potency it once had.

"I spoke to Jonathan when we were in Coventry. He offered to stage a protest outside the Houses of Parliament. Hopefully, it won't come to that."

His father set his cup on a side table. "What does Miss Radley know of all this? How much of it have you told her?"

"She knows I have some issues to deal with before I am able to leave the army. I haven't told her the rest," replied Piers.

"You have to, Piers. If you are remotely serious about making her your future viscountess, she has to know it all."

"The report said I was incompetent. Dereliction of duty is a serious crime. I am not sure how she would take to hearing that news. As for the rest of the ugly rumors, I haven't the foggiest notion as to how I could possibly discuss them with Maggie," he replied.

Lord Denford fixed him with a hard stare. Piers couldn't hold his father's gaze for more than a moment. He stared at his brandy.

"Piers, I know it will be difficult, but you need to broach the subject of the Prince of Orange with her. The last thing you want is for the woman whom you have in mind to marry finding out about those rumors from other parties."

After downing the last of his brandy, Piers kept his gaze focused on the empty glass. He might have a plan to deal with the army, but when it came to openly discussing what he had seen while serving under the prince, he was at a loss.

His father leaned forward and placed a hand firmly on his shoulder. "All you are doing by not challenging those rumors is giving your enemies more power. Your loyalty to the prince has not been rewarded with his support. He has the King of the Netherlands at his back; it's time to put you and your own family first."

It wasn't anything Piers hadn't already thought himself. "You are right. And that is what I am trying to do."

But courting Maggie, convincing her to become his wife, while at the same time having to reveal the dark rumors about him and the prince having once been lovers was not going to be easy. It didn't matter that there wasn't an ounce of truth to any of it. Piers had learned that while truth was the first casualty of war, lies never seemed to die.

Chapter Thirty-Eight

Maggie woke late the following morning feeling rested and somewhat recovered. The cold had been a minor one, successfully seen off by copious bowls of chicken soup and bed rest. After dressing warmly, and with a hearty breakfast in her belly, she was keen to explore Denford Park.

Stepping out from the front entrance of the main manor house, she was greeted with a vision of bucolic delight. Green fields stretched for miles in all directions. Sheep and cows grazed in the meadows. All seemed well in God's good country.

"Ah, she is risen!"

Maggie turned at the cheery greeting, smiling as Piers approached. Her gaze settled on his attire; he wasn't wearing his officer's uniform. It was first time she had seen him in civilian clothes. His traditional garb of black jacket, greatcoat, and tan trousers had her looking twice and blinking hard.

And I thought you were handsome in the red coat. You look even more dashing dressed in civilian attire.

"How are you this morning?" he asked.

"Better, thank you. I think my cold might just have been a nasty chill. Though the soup your cook made for me was so delicious that I must confess, I did consider feigning a cough just to get some more."

She didn't want to mention that she had missed him being part of her convalescence. The soup had been most welcome, but it wasn't the same as when Piers had sat on her bed in the inn and spoon-fed her.

He laughed. "Maggie, you may have soup for every meal if you wish. You only have to ask."

A moment of awkward silence descended upon them. They hadn't seen much of each other since their arrival the day before. She suspected Piers was as unsure of how they should behave toward one another as was she. This was his home. His parents were here.

And Lady Denford knows Mama. News of whatever happens at Denford Park is surely going to get back to London.

Changing the subject, she pointed toward the estate grounds. "You have a lovely home, Piers. Everywhere is so lush and green. I can understand why you were keen to bring me here."

"Thank you. And yes, it is a beautiful place. London might be exciting and full of life, but nothing is better than being here. If I could leave the army, I would be back home as much as possible."

There was a great deal left unsaid in that last remark. Maggie couldn't quite understand why Piers was still an army officer. A man such as himself, a future viscount, shouldn't have any problems in resigning his commission. She hadn't ever heard of a captain being forced to stay in the military. His unfinished business couldn't be all that important, could it?

There is something he is afraid to tell me.

This time at Denford Park might well provide her with

the opportunity to delve deeper into Piers's problems. To get to the bottom of them.

"Would you care for a stroll around the gardens? Only if you feel up to it, of course," he offered.

She had her cloak and gloves on, rugged up against the chill of a late November morning. The thought of stretching her legs and getting some fresh air was most appealing.

"I would love that. Your mother mentioned that she is a keen gardener. Though I can't say the same for myself."

"Really? The gardens at Fulham Palace are legendary. I assumed you would have a green thumb."

Maggie slowly shook her head. "The gardens at home are magnificent, but we have a whole retinue of gardeners to keep them looking as wonderful as they do. My sister, Claire, foolishly bought me a small potted plant for my birthday one year, hoping that I would take care of it. I'm ashamed to say it didn't survive very long."

"I shall make a note not to buy you plants as gifts. Speaking of birthdays, when is yours?"

Heat raced to Maggie's cheeks. She hadn't been hinting about presents—just making conversation. "December the second," she replied.

"That is soon."

"Yes. I had originally intended to be home by then, but it looks like I might be here. I shall have to write to my parents and make note of the occasion."

Piers clasped his hands together. "And we shall have a cake."

A cake? "Why a cake?"

"My grandmother was German, and it's a tradition in her old country for young children to have a cake baked on their birthday. Birthday cakes were so popular when Jonathan, Annabel, and I were children that we demanded that the tradition be kept going even when we were all grown up," he replied.

"Oh. That sounds delightful." She wasn't going to protest if someone was kind enough to bake a cake in her honor. "And Annabel is your sister, the one whose old bedroom I am staying in?"

"Yes. She married a local gentleman, Edward Monk." Piers pointed to a large manor house some way in the distance. "That gray monstrosity is their home. Lovely couple. Edward is a bit of a clod, but Annabel was always one for the numbers, so when it comes to money, he lets her make most of the major decisions."

He leaned in close and whispered, "Truth be told, he is madly in love with her, so Annabel always gets her way no matter what. She is also a giddy miss when it comes to him, which is probably why they have managed to have four children in the space of five years."

Maggie smiled. She loved children. Her greatest wish was to have a brood of her own. She secretly envied Piers's sister. The thought of being with someone who loved you as much as Edward appeared to love Annabel had her blinking back tears.

I wonder what sort of husband you will make, Piers.

An image of Piers bouncing a small child on his knee popped into her mind. He had a warm nature about him, reminiscent of her father. And if the sort of loving papa Hugh Radley had always been, was any indication, then Piers would make a wonderful parent.

I think you would also be a magnificent lover. You have a generous nature.

"A farthing for your thoughts, Miss Radley."

Maggie swallowed deep. Whenever Piers stood this close, she could barely think straight. And the thoughts that did manage to find their way into her mind were usually not the sort that an unwed woman should share with a man. *Wicked and delicious thoughts.*

She wasn't completely naïve when it came to desire. To what Piers did to her. Of what she secretly wished would happen between them.

"What sort of birthday cake do you recommend?" she replied.

The sly grin on Piers's face told her he wasn't buying her attempt at an innocent question in the slightest. When he gave a low hum in response, it sent a shiver down her spine.

"I like all things sweet. Though it's always good to mix it up with a bit of spice."

Maggie was sure she had just melted on the spot. She was throbbing in all the right places. Places that she touched when she was alone in her bed.

"We could ask cook to bake you a lemon and cream cake," he purred.

She swallowed deep once more at hearing the sensual tone in his voice. When had food become so arousing?

"That would be . . ." She licked her lips. "Delectable."

Piers gave a low groan as he turned away. He fussed with the buttons on the front of his long coat.

"I shall speak to cook this afternoon," he said.

Maggie's fever had gone, and her brow was cool, but if the burning red of Piers's cheeks was any indication, it was now his body which was on fire.

Chapter Thirty-Nine

T he conversation about cake had started out innocently enough, but when Maggie had mentioned the word delectable and licked her lips, Piers had sensed he was in serious trouble. His mind had instantly filled with the image of a naked Maggie laying beneath him. Her groans of pleasure as he sunk deep into her wet heat echoed in his mind. He burned to make love to her, to make her his.

No. Now is not the time to be thinking those sorts of thoughts about Maggie. Save it for when you are alone in bed. Then you can indulge.

Thank heavens for large greatcoats and their ability to hide a burgeoning erection.

He let out a slow, calming breath.

Change the bloody subject. Talk about anything else. And don't look at her lips.

If he didn't control his lust, he would be limping around the grounds in an uncomfortable state. Not the sort of thing a man wished to be dealing with, while he was trying to make polite conversation with a young lady.

"Could you ever see yourself living in the country, Maggie?

Away from the hustle and bustle of London?" That was a safe topic with enough room for discussion to take up most of the time while they walked.

"I haven't really given it much thought. When I was betrothed to Robert, he said we would remain in London." She let out a mocking laugh. "But of course, he would say that. It's rather difficult to take your new wife home to Coventry if you already have a family."

Piers watched her, carefully looking for signs of distress. Maggie, however, appeared relaxed and calm. Her former fiancé's name slipped easily from her tongue.

"It's alright, Piers. I have decided I can say his name. If I continue to dance around the subject, it only gives him power over me. Robert Taylor was and will always be a major misstep in my life. But I am not going to wallow in grief or regret. What's done is done."

He touched a hand to her arm. "I am proud of you."

She shrugged. "Thank you. But in answer to your question, yes, I would consider a life in the country. If I had a husband like your sister, who loved me, and we wanted to raise a family together outside of London, then I wouldn't hesitate to embrace that change in my life."

Jonathan's words of warning rang loudly in Piers's mind. He wasn't in a position to make any sort of plans with a woman, especially not with someone like Maggie. She had suffered enough already. To bring her into his complicated life would be most unfair.

But the thought of losing her, the fear of it, was much more powerful.

Say something. Make her at least think of it being a possibility.

"Of course, if you married a peer, you could have the best of both worlds. A life in the country and then be in town when parliament sits."

He wanted to say more, but Piers held back. If he had

succeeded in planting the seed of an idea in Maggie's mind, then that would have to be enough for now. She deserved time to get settled in at Denford Park and to recover from her recent trials. Only a cad would seek to push for more so soon. Maggie Radley had endured her fair share of misery at the hands of a blackguard.

"Does your mother go up to London with your father for each session of the House of Lords, or does she remain here?" Maggie asked.

It was a reasonable enough question. Not all noble families decamped to town for the various long sittings. Some wives and children remained in the country. "My mother goes everywhere with my father. He wouldn't dream of leaving her at home. And I am of the same mind. When I marry, I will expect my wife to travel with me."

The parliamentary sitting periods often ran for months at a time. Earlier in the year, his parents had been compelled to stay in London for almost six months while parliament dragged on. "I couldn't imagine being apart from my wife for any length of time," he added.

Maggie smiled up at him. "Why Piers, you sound like a man who is set on marrying for love."

I wouldn't have it any other way.

Piers nodded. "I am. I realized the grave mistake I would have made had I gone through with marrying Lady Dinah. The girl I make my wife will be someone who I want to be with and who wants to be with me."

He glanced quickly around, checking that there was no one in sight. Then in one deft move, he slipped a hand about her waist, and pulled Maggie to him. He leaned in and quickly brushed a kiss on her cheek. "You are cool. I am glad that you are better." A second kiss touched her forehead. "Yes, definitely well again."

Maggie rested her hands gently on his chest. "Piers. Why

did you bring me here? I know you said you wanted me to have a place where I could recover from everything in private, and I am grateful for your generosity. But I could have gone somewhere else. My Cousin David and his wife live at Sharn-brook, which is less than half a day from here."

He forced down his disappointment. "Is that what you want? To go and stay with your family? I was hoping you would like to visit here, but of course I won't force you."

"No. I want to be here with you. I'm sorry; I was just trying to tease you, and I clearly failed at it. I'm not very experienced or skillful when it comes to flirting."

"You don't need to play any games with me, Maggie. Just be honest."

"Alright. Then yes, I want to stay here. I think there is the beginning of something between us—a spark, perhaps. It could become more. And I know you are dealing with a diffi-cult situation with the army. But . . . oh, never mind." She went to pull away, but he took hold of her hand, and raised it to his lips. It was his fault that she was unsure of herself. He had only told her part of the story. His father was right. If he wanted Maggie to be honest with him, he had to do the same with her.

Can't I just have a little time to spend with her without worrying whether she believes me?

"I want to be candid with you regarding the problems I am facing, I really do. But I think we should wait. In the meantime, I can show you the estate and you can enjoy the beauty of this part of the country. If you discover that this place speaks to your heart, and you can see your future being here, then, Maggie, we should talk."

"And what about us, Piers? Do my feelings for you come into this?"

He hadn't expected that. They had kissed, and shared tender moments, but Piers had thought Maggie's affections would take time for him to win. "Your feelings are very much involved. I just didn't want to push. You have been through a lot. And then you were ill."

Maggie drew closer, pressing herself against him. "I am not a weak little bird. Yes, I've experienced a few difficult days, and that short fever certainly didn't help. But I'm a lot stronger than you think." She tugged gently on the front of his coat, forcing him to bend. "And just as determined."

Piers grinned. "Only a fool gets in the way of a strong-minded woman." He grabbed a hold of her hand and towed her toward the gate, which led into the top field of the Denford estate. "Come on. I am going to show you, my home."

And hopefully, Maggie would fall for it as hard as he had fallen for her.

Chapter Forty

Late that night, Maggie dressed in her warmest gown, then put on her cloak and gloves. November in England could be chilly enough during the day, but at night, it was positively freezing. Closing her bedroom door slowly so that it barely made a click, she quietly made her way downstairs.

As she reached the ground floor, a figure stepped out of the shadows. Piers beckoned her over. In his arms he held a heavy coat and scarf. "Your cloak won't keep you warm enough for where we are going. Put these on."

He handed her the coat. It was a gentleman's greatcoat made of fine wool. Maggie rid herself of her cloak, dropping it onto a nearby chair. She slipped her arms into the coat and buttoned it up, leaving the top open.

Piers wrapped the scarf around her neck, then tucked it inside the lapels. Maggie fastened the last of the buttons.

The coat was long, heavy, and reached right to her ankles. She held her arms out while Piers rolled the cuffs up. It was like being a small child and having your maid adjust your clothing—except her family maid had been nothing like the handsome male who was currently attending to her attire.

This is the sort of night walking I like—dressed warmly and fully awake.

"There. How is that?" he asked.

She moved her body inside the enormous coat. There was plenty of room. As her nose brushed up against the lapel, she caught the trace of his manly scent. She took a deep breath in. It was unmistakably Piers.

"Is this your coat? The one you have been wearing while on our trip?" she asked.

"Yes, it is." He pointed to Maggie's coat and then to the one he was wearing. "I bought two of them when I went first went into the army. It's not part of the official uniform, but they are a lot warmer than the coat they expected us to wear."

She couldn't fail to notice the edge of annoyance in his voice. Piers hadn't been made for the army, for taking orders. That much was clear. He was a man with his own opinions, and Maggie could just imagine how being under someone else's command would chafe at him.

The whole question of why he was still in the military was one he had not fully answered. There was more to it than mere unfinished business. He was unhappy. Frustrated with his life.

"I expect you got into a spot of trouble from some of the other senior officers for refusing to wear the army-issued uniform," she said.

He snorted. "There is nothing issued about it. Officers are expected to purchase their own clothing. The logic, of course, being that if a man has the blunt to buy a commission into the British Army, he can certainly afford a woolen coat."

And Piers being Piers, had settled on something that wasn't quite the standard offering for a captain.

Well, done. Don't let anyone ever try to stop you from being you.

"Are you ready to go?" he asked.

She nodded and followed him to the front door, a bubble of excitement bouncing around in her stomach. Sneaking out of the house while their parents were fast asleep upstairs was something her siblings and Radley family cousins had done many a Christmas at Strathmore Castle.

Piers stopped at the door. There was a rucksack, lit lantern, and blanket sitting on the floor. He bent and picked up the bag, then collected the lantern. Maggie recognized the blanket. It was the same one they had taken with them on their outing to Kenilworth Castle.

She scooped it up in her arms, determined that Piers was not going to carry everything.

Outside, he hoisted the rucksack on his back, then glanced up at the sky. It was mostly clear, with only a half moon shining its light on the formal garden which sat at the front of the main house. Maggie appreciated the colorful shrubs and carefully edged paths. It reminded her of home.

She missed her family, but these moments alone with Piers held a special significance of their own. They were full of promise. Her heart whispered all manner of sweet imaginings whenever they were close. *I wouldn't want to be anywhere else right this minute.*

A bank of dark gray clouds hung in the sky a little way off. Hopefully, they were distant enough not to spoil their evening expedition.

"Are those clouds going to cause us any problems?" she said, pointing at them.

"Not if we leave now. Though I must warn you that the weather in this part of the country can change quite quickly. And the last thing we need is to get caught in a rainstorm. There is a barn partway to the clearing, so if it does start to rain, we can shelter there."

A secluded barn. How convenient.

Maggie silently began to pray for rain.

Piers patted the bag slung over his shoulder. An excited grin sat on his lips; he was like a small child on Christmas morning. His enthusiasm was charming. "I have a telescope and the latest copy of the Nautical Almanac in here. The guidebook has all the calendars and star maps we will need. I spent some of this afternoon studying it."

Keen and intelligent. Maggie couldn't think of a better combination to have in a stargazing companion.

"My Uncle Ewan is a member of the Royal Society, and he always brings a copy of the almanac up to Scotland with him. On the nights when it is clear over Strathmore Mountain, you can see thousands of stars," she said. Lying on her back and staring up at the dazzling display was always a special delight. The six layers of clothing that were required on those freezing nights were less enjoyable, but necessary.

"I'm applying for membership, though they don't give as much attention to astronomy as I would like. It's not as exciting as sending expeditions off into the unknown places of the world. To be honest, I wouldn't be surprised if someone eventually decided to start their own astronomical society. If they do, I will be one of the first to put their hand up to join," said Piers.

"You would make a perfect candidate, Piers. Then again, any society would be honored to have you as a member." she replied.

The look which appeared on Piers's face was one which Maggie couldn't quite find the right word to describe. Surprise, mixed with happy gratitude, was the best she could manage.

"I've never met a woman like you before, Maggie Radley. So many other female members of the *haute ton* are all about themselves and the impression that they give, whereas you are open to new experiences and also refreshingly honest. Those are two rare gifts. Promise me you won't ever change."

It was her turn to struggle with accepting praise. She glanced down at her boots, to where they peeked out from under the hem of the coat.

Piers's breath warmed her cheek. "You are a like a colorful, precious stone. Diamonds might shine brightly, but only you capture and hold the eye so completely, Maggie."

His sweet words. His proximity. They did things to her, made her want and need everything he could possibly ever give.

She lifted her head and their gazes met. When Piers brushed his thumb over her lips, Maggie shivered.

Please kiss me. Let tonight be the night when we finally share our hearts.

But instead of taking her lips with his, he dropped his hand and moved away.

"We had better get going. It's a good half mile over the fields to the viewing place. And while the night might be clear now, we really do not want to get caught out in the open if it rains. My mother will have my guts for garters if you catch a second chill."

"Yes, and I wouldn't want to get your coat wet or ruined. You will need it once you go back to London and the Horse Guards," she replied.

"Probably. Though I would much prefer to leave it here."

Before she could stop herself, Maggie's fingers were on Piers's coat sleeve.

"Why don't you resign your commission? Surely, the army can find someone else to reply to all those letters."

He gave her a look which said that they both knew his problems extended well beyond some misguided sense of honor.

"That is true, Maggie, but just think on this: if I had left the army, no one would have followed up your case. You would have spent the rest of your life grieving over a man who didn't deserve it."

Maggie released her hold on Piers's coat. That thought hadn't occurred to her before. If someone else had received her letter, they might never have bothered to follow it up. Piers had been thorough in his efforts to trace Robert. Another officer may not have gone to all the trouble of making the trip to Coventry.

"I'm sorry. I didn't mean to push. You don't answer to me."

An all too familiar guarded smile sat on his lips. "Let's go and watch the night sky. I've been looking forward to this all day."

She shoved her disappointment deep inside and followed Piers toward the gate, which opened onto the top field. They had visited the viewing spot earlier in the day during their walk around the grounds. Piers's invitation to sneak out of the house and go stargazing had been a delightful surprise.

He wanted her; of that much, she was sure. But why he continually pulled back whenever they reached a point where matters might progress further between them, she couldn't understand. The only thing of which she was certain was that Piers was a reluctant member of the military. That given half a chance, he would resign.

I just wish you would trust me enough to share your problems.

The need for them to talk, for Piers to finally reveal his secrets and let them come into the light, was the only way they could move forward. Until then, she was left guessing at shadows.

Maggie had promised to let things lie, but she found it difficult. Patience wasn't a Radley family trait. With a soft sigh, Maggie stuffed her hands in her pockets and followed in Piers's wake.

She had never thought love could be this testing.

Chapter Forty-One

It was a mistake. He should never have asked Maggie to come stargazing. Piers blamed his impetuous nature; he could only pray he wouldn't come to regret extending the invitation.

Behind him, Maggie trudged through the grass. Her silence gnawed at Piers. He could just imagine her trying to find ways to broach the subject of him still being in the army. Of the truth behind why the military were keeping him.

Maggie wasn't blind to his discomfort; nor did he suspect she was going to leave things well alone for any length of time. He hadn't known her all that long, but patience was definitely not one of her strengths. In this situation, however, he couldn't fault her. They were both paying the price for Piers having waited too long for the Prince of Orange to put pen to paper.

I just don't know how much of it I should tell her. Or if, indeed, I should say anything.

He slowed his steps, allowing Maggie to catch up. If she fell too far behind, she would be out of range of the light from the lantern and not be able to see where her feet were about to tread.

"You said the skies over Scotland are stunning when it comes to stargazing," he said.

"Yes, they are," she replied.

Please can we just talk about the stars?

"Sometimes we go up my uncle's old hunting lodge. It's a wonderful place. You have to traverse a path which runs through a narrow gap in the side of Strathmore Mountain. It has high rock walls on either side. At the end, it eventually opens up into a natural amphitheater surrounded by more high stone walls. There is a lake in the middle of it. We call it the Key because if you were an eagle flying over, it would look like a keyhole."

"Sounds fascinating."

"That's the best place for watching the sky. The rock walls protect you from the winds on the mountain, and on summer nights, you can lay out for hours watching the heavens."

A pang of guilt stabbed at Piers. He was avoiding the difficult conversation and instead investing his energies in something which he hoped would keep Maggie from asking him any more questions.

They crossed the field and climbed the low rise to the clearing they had visited earlier in the day. Piers set the lantern down while Maggie spread the blanket out on the grass. He took the brass Dollond telescope and tripod from out of the rucksack and set them up on a flat piece of ground.

"What constellations have you been able to spot from here?" she asked.

"Quite a few. Tonight, I am hoping we will find the Winter Hexagon. It might be a little early for it, but you never know."

"Ah, yes. So, for that, we need Orion's Belt," she replied. Maggie lifted her gaze to the heavens and slowly turned.

"There is Orion." She pointed upward and toward the southeast.

He followed where her hand was directed, nodding when he spied the hourglass shape of Orion. "Come and have a look through the telescope. You should be able to see the three stars of Orion's Belt. They will point you to Sirius, which is the first star in the hexagon."

"And also, one point in the Winter Triangle," she replied.

He swiveled the telescope to face toward the southeastern sky and began searching for Sirius. Maggie came and stood next to him. Piers stepped aside and let her look through the lens.

She shifted the telescope barely an inch, then exclaimed. "I have you!"

The fact that she was able to find the star within a matter of seconds shouldn't have come as any surprise. Maggie waved her hand, beckoning Piers closer. "That is Sirius. And if you look around it, you can see all those other faint stars which comprise this part of the Milky Way."

She drew back, allowing Piers to take her place at the telescope. Through the lens, he could make out the bright star. "It's fascinating to think that we are looking up at the same constellations that the ancients did," he observed.

"Yes, and they really believed that the gods were living in the stars. And while I'm particularly fond of Greek mythology, you have to go a long way to beat the Norse gods. They were fierce creatures."

"I'm rather partial to the nine realms. I could imagine myself living quite happily in Asgard," replied Piers.

Next to him, Maggie softly chuckled. "Yes, all that feasting, and drinking would suit you perfectly. I can just see you as being Odin, the god of alcohol."

Piers shot her a sideways glance. "Has anyone ever told

you that you are an impertinent young lady, Miss Margaret Radley?"

She clapped her hands together and continued to laugh. "More people than I care to count. Perhaps even more than all the stars in the sky."

You really are a delight. I love being here with you.

I love you.

Those three words pulled Piers up sharp. It was clear that his heart had decided it would no longer remain silent. It demanded to have its voice heard.

These moments alone with Maggie were wonderful, when the silly banter between them made him forget all his worries. If only it could always be like this—sharing the simple, fun things in life. Being with this woman, was his heart's greatest desire.

She would be right at home here in Denford Park. With me.

But not while his future lay so uncertain.

"We should have brought food with us," said Maggie.

Now that was a problem he could solve. Piers quickly dug into the rucksack and produced a cloth bag. "Huzzah!" he cried, holding the bag aloft triumphantly.

This wasn't his first-time night-gazing. Being out in the cold made a man hungry. He had paid a visit to the Denford Park kitchens earlier in the evening and begged them to show him a little kindness. The friendly servants had, of course, made good.

"I think you will find what you are looking for in there," he said.

She took the bag, shaking her head in mock disapproval. "Of course, you brought food. What was I thinking? I also expect that there is a hipflask hidden somewhere in your coat." The tone of her last remark held a certain level of expectation mixed with a thinly veiled threat. He had better have a hipflask with him.

Piers patted the sides of his coat, relieved when his hands touched the solid shape of the hidden object. He reached into his pocket, and with a flourish, produced the flask. While Maggie rummaged inside the bag for food, Piers helped himself to a stiff dram of whisky.

She unwrapped a cloth and sniffed at its contents. "Bacon and fried egg sandwiches. Piers Denford, you are a genius; these are my favorite."

After removing her gloves, Maggie took a hold of one of the sandwiches and bit into it. She hummed her approval as she happily chewed away. When she had finished her first mouthful, she waved the sandwich at him. "It needs a touch of piccalilli to give it a little bite."

"Piccalilli? I should try that some time, though I must say, I particularly like chutney in my bacon and egg sandwiches. I just wasn't certain that you would, so I didn't ask our cook to put any in," he replied.

Piers removed his own gloves before gladly accepting the sandwich Maggie offered him. He handed her the flask in exchange.

The food kept them quietly chewing for the next short while. When Piers downed the last of his sandwich, he searched in the bag, and produced two napkins. While he waited for Maggie to finish, he wiped his hands and face.

Hot bacon and egg sandwiches. So delicious.

She stepped toward him and took the other clean cloth from out of his hand. When her fingers brushed against his, Piers sensed a shift in the mood. Maggie's gaze went to his chin.

"You missed a spot," she said.

His breath caught as Maggie proceeded to wipe his face with the napkin.

"You left a bit there too," she said. The cloth moved closer to his lips, and Piers's heart began to race. It had been some time since they had been this close. The moment was heavy with promise.

He leaned forward, their faces now barely an inch apart. "Anywhere else?" he asked.

She nodded and touched a fingertip to his lips. "There. Especially there."

His hands were in her hair in an instant, holding her to him as he claimed her mouth with a deep, passionate kiss. Temptation had left him hungry, yearning for her. For the taste of Maggie. Their tongues met in a fevered, needy tangle. There was nothing polite or graceful about this embrace; it was messy, desperate, and he wanted it to go on forever.

Maggie clung to Piers like a limpet. Her hands were tightly fisted as she gripped the lapels of his coat. Over and over, they worked their lips and mouths together in a glorious kiss that took his breath away.

When they finally did break apart, they were both sucking in air. One brief exchange of glances and they were back kissing one another again.

Piers couldn't care less about the stars or the glory of the heavens which shone above—he just wanted Maggie. Every inch of her.

The first drop of rain landed in the middle of Maggie's forehead. Lost in the toe-curling kiss, she ignored it. Then came the second, followed by the flash of lightning which lit up the sky. A low rumble in the distance heralded oncoming thunder. She and Piers broke apart just as the heavens opened.

"You get the blanket. I'll get the telescope," he cried.

Maggie scurried around, quickly snatching up the blanket and tossing it over her arm. While Piers collapsed the telescope and tripod, Maggie took a hold of the rucksack. She held it open, and he stuffed the precious instrument inside. She added the blanket to the pack and as he hoisted it on his back, she picked up the lantern.

The rain was now coming down in torrents. "We are going to be drenched if we try to make it back to the main house. We had better head to the barn," he said.

Maggie's romantic notions of getting caught in the rain evaporated as they sprinted through the wild tempest. By the time they reached the barn, they were both thoroughly drenched. Piers threw the bolt back and wrenched the door open. Maggie dashed through it with Piers following close behind.

"Oh, that's a relief," she sighed.

The door clattered closed, and Piers threw the interior bolt to hold it shut fast. He took one look at Maggie's wet and bedraggled state and winced. "My mother is going to kill me for letting you get a soaking."

Inside the barn was surprisingly warm. Maggie deftly worked the buttons of her coat free and shrugged out of it. She shook off the beads of water that sat on the surface. Piers did the same with his overcoat.

Standing around in wet clothes was never a good idea. The rain drumming loudly against the wooden shingles of the barn roof let her know that they wouldn't be going anywhere anytime soon.

Piers gently tugged the blanket free from the rucksack and handed it to her. "Here, put this around you. It will keep you from getting a chill. Your gown is wet." He nodded toward a pile of clean hay. "Let's go and sit over there while we wait for the storm to pass."

They found a cozy corner in which to shelter. Piers wrapped his arms around her, holding Maggie close. "Are you alright?" he asked.

She snuggled in. "Yes. Just a bit cold. I'll be warm soon. Just hold me."

Piers brushed a tendril of damp, wayward hair behind her ear. Maggie shivered. Whether from the cold or Piers's touch, she wasn't sure.

The candle inside the lantern was now burning low, and it gave a warning sputter. If it went out, they would be left totally in the dark.

Outside, the rain continued to thrash down at an unrelenting pace. She ought to be worried about getting a chill, but Maggie's mind was focused on that kiss.

They were stuck in the barn. Alone. Together. This was an opportunity she shouldn't waste. Gathering up her courage, she decided it was time to act.

Carpe diem, and all that.

Maggie pulled out of Piers's arms. She gently pushed his legs apart and knelt between them. The blanket fell from her shoulders. As their gazes met, she gave him a shy smile. This was a risk—one she felt compelled to take. Not just for herself, but for the both of them.

"I love you, Piers."

There—she had said it. For the second time in her life, Maggie had put her heart on the line. In making such a bold move, she could only pray that she hadn't read Piers wrong.

He slowly nodded. "I love you too, Maggie."

Relief washed over her. She wasn't alone in wanting them to be more than just friends. For them to claim a future together.

I want him to be mine forever.

His hands settled on her waist as she bent and placed a tender, tentative kiss on his lips. Maggie wanted nothing more than to deepen the kiss, to return them to the place where they had been before the rain, but she held back. This moment called for measured steps.

As they continued their easy, languid kiss, she reached and grabbed a hold of her skirt, tugging it up. Slowly, deliberately, she raised the hem. The gown bunched around her hips. Cool air kissed the skin of her thighs as the bottom of her dress rose higher.

And higher.

She shivered, a heady mix of being both chilled and aroused. Maggie broke the kiss.

Piers's Adam's apple bobbed up and down as he swallowed deep. "Maggie."

"Touch me."

His gaze dropped to her exposed flesh, to her sex, and he groaned.

She could sense his hesitancy in his every breath. Things between them teetered on the edge; this was a moment which could go either way. The only thing of which she was certain was that after tonight, their relationship would have changed. No matter the outcome, there would be no going back.

Piers's hands slid down her waist, then rested on her hips.

Please.

He lifted his head and offered her his mouth; Maggie greedily took it. Their tongues danced together in a heated exchange, but when she sought to deepen the kiss, Piers broke away.

"Slow down. There is no need to hurry," he said.

"What do you want me to do?" Maggie feared she was pushing too hard. That in her haste to confirm their love, she might force Piers into taking a step back.

"Just kiss me. Let me do the rest," he replied.

When their lips met once more, it was in a tender, unhurried kiss. But Maggie's heart was still beating fast in her chest. She was holding onto her self-control by the merest of threads.

Piers's hands slid slowly up Maggie's inner thighs; from her knees all the way to the dark curls of hair at the entrance to her sex. He paused for a moment, and whispered, "So beautiful."

"Please," she breathed, rising up on her knees and spreading her legs wider. Her hands rested on his shoulders.

Piers nodded. "For you? Always." He gently parted her soft folds, then slowly slid a finger deep into her slick, wet heat.

Maggie whimpered. "Oh, Piers."

As he stroked her, his thumb traced exquisite circles around her sensitive bud. Piers could read her body so well. Shifting his angle and depth of penetration, he drove Maggie's need for release to an ever more frantic pace. He slipped a second finger into her sex, and she clung to him. It was better than anything she could ever have imagined. Every caress had her panting for breath. Wanting more.

He thrust in deeper, faster, and she shattered on a sob, reaching her climax in a moment of unbridled ecstasy. "Piers."

He caressed her through the aftermath, slowly bringing her down. But when she reached for him, intending to open the placket of his trousers, he placed a firm hand on her wrist. "No."

"I am ready. Make me yours. Take freely what I want to give. Piers, I love you."

Her skirts were tugged back down, and he lifted her off his lap.

"Piers?" she pleaded, confused.

"Maggie. Don't ask it of me. I can't."

Can't or won't—it all meant the same. He didn't want her. Memories of that night with Robert flashed through her mind. The searing pain of rejection.

Another man whom she had lost her heart to; another

who didn't feel the same way that she did. Piers's declaration of love was empty of meaning. His words were hollow.

"I'm sorry. I thought we meant more to one another. It's clear that I was mistaken. Next time you offer up words of love to a woman, I would suggest perhaps you should hold your tongue." Maggie got to her feet; bitter tears of disappointment stung her eyes. Why she kept falling for men who were only content to toy with her, she couldn't fathom. Piers was yet another in a disappointing list of males who'd said that they cared for her, but in truth, didn't.

She hurriedly straightened her skirts, then reached for her coat. It was soaked through; putting it on would serve no purpose. But she wasn't concerned about the coat. All she wanted to do was flee. Her moment of ecstasy was gone, replaced with heartbreak and humiliation.

Piers came and stood behind her. Taking Maggie gently by the shoulders, he turned her to face him. He lay a large warm hand over hers. "Maggie, please don't take this the wrong way. I care deeply for you. It's just that my life is complicated. Ruining you would be the worst thing I could do. It's too much of a risk."

She shook her head. "I have never thought that love-making between two consenting adults was ruining anything. I'm sorry you view it that way. I just don't understand why you brought me all the way to Denford Park if you weren't serious about us. Or was this just another trifling encounter, which you males seem to excel at?"

She tugged the coat free of the hook and headed for the door.

"It's still raining. You will get drenched," he replied.

The bolt slid back with a clang. Maggie ignored the rain as she dashed out into the tempest. She just had to get away.

Chapter Forty-Two

T he knock came at her bedroom door just after first light. A half-asleep Maggie opened it to find Piers standing in the hallway. He looked like she felt. The bags and dark circles under his eyes were evidence of him also not having got much sleep.

"Get dressed. We need to talk," he said.

After leaving the barn last night, she had stumbled through the darkness and driving rain back to the main house. Piers had followed, but she had ignored his pleas for her to stop.

"I don't know if there is anything left to say after yesterday. I'm planning to speak to your mother this morning and ask for her to arrange a carriage to take me to my cousin David's estate at Sharnbrook. I shall make my own way back to London; you needn't bother with me after today."

His splayed hand slapped loudly on the door panel, stopping her from closing it. "Please, Maggie. Let's not do this. We have to talk. I owe you an explanation. It isn't fair for me to keep you in the dark any longer."

As much as she wanted to tell him to go to the devil, she

also knew there was no point in being stubborn and refusing his offer. He was offering to give her some answers. It was what she had wanted all along.

"Give me a minute to find some warm clothes," she said.

Piers let his hand drop, and he moved away from the door. "I shall wait here."

While he lingered outside in the hallway, Maggie quickly found her boots and her cloak.

A short time later, she opened the door. "Where are we going?" she asked, stepping out of her room.

Piers, who was leaning against the wall, pushed off and stood upright. "Back to the barn where we were last night. I want to have our conversation again, but this time, I am going to get it right."

A perplexed but resigned Maggie followed him downstairs, out the garden gate, and across the rain-soaked top field. The ground under her boots squelched with her every step and Maggie struggled to keep up with Piers's fast marching pace.

At the barn, he pulled the bolt back and opened the heavy door. As with the previous evening, Piers closed it again as soon as they were inside. He hadn't brought a lantern with him this time, and the pale morning light barely filtered through the slats in the walls. It left the barn in an eerie state of semi-darkness.

"Please have a seat," said Piers.

Maggie dropped onto the dry hay. She was doing her best to beat down her humiliation of the prior evening. It wasn't easy. Anger simmered in the back of her mind.

Piers, meanwhile, paced back and forth, his hands clasped behind his back. His shoulders were stiff, his spine, ramrod straight. While she sat and impatiently watched, he continued marching up and down.

Finally, an infuriated Maggie got to her feet and cried, "Piers. Stop!"

He came to an immediate halt. His shoulders slumped as he bent and rested his hands on his knees. Maggie made tentative steps toward him but halted before she got within reach. Piers was struggling—that much was obvious. It pained her to see him in such distress.

"Do you trust me?" she asked.

Standing this close to him, in the faint light she could make out the deep lines of worry on Piers's face. It made her anxious. She feared what might come next. What was so terrible that he had to take her all the way from the main house to the isolated barn just to tell her?

"Yes, Maggie, I do trust you. It's myself I am not sure of. I'm afraid of what will happen if you find me lacking."

She took another tentative step forward but stopped when Piers flinched. He raised himself to his full height and faced her. "Answer me this: what do you know of what happens between a man and a woman in the marital bed?"

What?

She was innocent of such things in the physical sense, but she had a pretty good idea what they involved. Of what went where. If she hadn't, she wouldn't have openly offered herself to him. This didn't make sense.

"Is that what you are worried about? That I am afraid of sex? I would have thought what happened here only a matter of hours ago should have shown you that I am not. And yes, I am aware of the marital act. My mother sat and gave me the talk when I first started my courses. I might not have actually ever done *it*, but I understand the physiology that it involves."

She had also been privy, on more than one occasion, to her male cousins walking naked out of the lake at the Key in Scotland. She had caught sight of their manly appendages swinging to-and-fro before they made a mad dash into the lodge to dress.

But something told her that Piers wasn't in the mood to hear another Radley family holiday story.

He raked his fingers through his hair, gripping tightly to the ends. Frustration oozed from him. "No. I," he huffed.

Maggie waited, suddenly sensing it was something far worse than her lack of sexual experience.

Finally, he drew in a deep breath, and let it slowly out. "You understand what is possible between a man and a woman. Well, there are things which can also happen between men."

Her brain took a minute to absorb that fact, to come up with an answer as to how that was possible. She hadn't ever considered that such a thing could occur.

"I see. I think," she said.

"It's actually a crime in this country, punishable by death. Which is why no man wishes to ever have his name mentioned whenever the subject is raised."

A horrible cold dread gripped her. Was this the real reason why the British Army was holding onto Piers? Had he done something illegal?

"I served under the Prince of Orange as an assistant aide-de-camp. What is not widely known in polite society is that the prince regularly conducts sexual liaisons with both male and female lovers. It was a closely guarded secret amongst those of us who served with him—that some of the prince's other aides-de-camp were what could only be described as special close friends."

Maggie felt close to tears. "And were you and he . . ." She couldn't finish the sentence. The thought that Piers would never be hers was heartbreaking. Not after all she had gone through with Robert.

Was that why he hadn't wanted to consummate their relationship? His love for her perhaps being different to how she felt for him?

Piers shook his head. "No. I was an aide-de-camp—nothing else. I was appointed to serve the prince in a military capacity; and in the few months that I was a part of his entourage, he never treated me as being anything other than a fellow officer."

He and the prince were not lovers. Then what is the problem?

It was only when Maggie sucked in a desperate lungful of air that she realized she had been holding her breath. "Go on."

Piers visibly relaxed, letting go of his hair. She could just imagine how fearful he must be. If he'd gotten this wrong, she may have never spoken to him again.

"The fact that there was nothing untoward with the relationship between me and the Prince of Orange hasn't, however, stopped some in the British Army from trying to make up rumors and circulate them. I have told you about Major Hall, under whose command I currently serve."

"Yes, the officious one."

"He had my name mentioned in dispatches from the battle of Waterloo as being incompetent, which in army terms means I am a coward. I was fighting alongside his men when the Prince of Orange suddenly decided he wanted to go off and engage the enemy elsewhere. I followed. Major Hall was furious. When the prince took a musket ball in the shoulder, I had to take him away to receive urgent medical attention. By the time I got back, the battle was all but over."

"And you had made an enemy."

"Yes. In Major Hall's opinion, the only reason why I would have gone after the prince was because he and I were involved with one another. The real reason, of course, was because it was my job to help the prince."

"Have you tried to speak to Major Hall?"

Piers sighed. "It's not that simple. There are deep prejudices within some men, and Major Hall seems to think that if the prince can't be punished for what the major considers to be an unnatural act, then he is going to make it his business to find someone who can be held to account. When I returned to England, I was shocked to discover I was placed under his command at the Horse Guards."

"And this Major Hall has taken it upon himself to make your life a misery ever since."

Piers's explanation went a long way to filling in the gaps which had sat in Maggie's mind.

"I take it that is one of the reasons why Lady Dinah kept up the pretense of the two of you still being betrothed?" she replied.

If Piers had a fiancée waiting in the wings, it would make it harder for any accusations of sexual impropriety against him to stick.

"Partly. Though she doesn't know about the prince's private relationships. Lady Dinah agreed to keep things quiet because we were both concerned how a failed engagement would reflect on the two of us. Major Hall's battle report has never been a secret; nor has the fact that I am still in the army. If Lady Dinah jilted me, then society would naturally think she believed me to be a coward. That the reports were true."

Now Maggie understood Piers's frightening dilemma. Her doubt over him, and why he hadn't dared to lay with her the previous night, was all too painfully clear. It wasn't a case of not wanting, but a case of not daring.

"And you think that because the army is still holding the threat of punishment over your head that you are not in a position to take on a wife. Is that it?" He was keeping her at arm's length because he was afraid of what the military might do to him.

"You deserve to have someone who is able to be your husband in every sense of the word. My current predicament precludes me from being that man. Maggie, if there was a way out of this mess, I would gladly take it. I've wasted two years of my life thinking I would get fair justice."

It was tempting to offer him her sympathy. But hugs and soft kisses wouldn't do anything to remedy the situation. This problem called for action. They had to come up with a plan.

He should have known by now that she was a woman always ready to help solve a problem. Maggie's mind moved at a fast clip, figuring out their next move. Of how the two of them could come up with a way to get Piers out of this mess.

Piers didn't deserve to be stuck in the army—left in limbo while powers unseen decided his fate. It was time to set her own needs and wishes to one side and think of what she could do to help him.

"Let us forget about last night. Everything that was said and done doesn't matter. All that is important is finding a way to stop the army from further punishing an innocent man," she said.

Piers grabbed a hold of Maggie and pulled her roughly into his arms. "I will never forget last night. Nor will I take back my declaration of love. You have no idea how hard it was for me not to make you mine. All I wanted was you. You were right there, all warm and willing. So damn lovely. It took every ounce of my strength not to give in and take you. The only thing that stopped me was the fear that in doing so, I was possibly going to ruin your life. If I face a court-martial and I am found guilty, I could be transported to the colonies —or even worse."

Maggie fisted her hands and lay them on his chest. "Jonathan was right; you are your own worst enemy. Piers, you need friends. Powerful people who are on your side."

Raising her head, she met his gaze fully. She had to make

him understand just how determined she was, how stubborn. "My uncle is the Duke of Strathmore. My father is the Bishop of London. You must appreciate the sort of clout my family is able to wield. Believe me, it's more than just getting me in the front door of the Horse Guards. And if that isn't enough, I have my Cousin Will who I can call upon to take up your cause."

"Will?"

"Yes Will, or Sir William Saunders, as he is shortly to be known."

"The spy?"

Maggie nodded. "Next week, the Prince Regent is coming out of official mourning for Princess Charlotte for one special public engagement. He is going to knight my cousin for services to king and country. If anyone can get you out of this pickle, it is Will."

Beyond her family, few people knew just how powerful Will Saunders really was. Even Maggie doubted she was privy to all but a slight and carefully constructed vision of the truth. Will not only knew powerful people, but he was also extremely adept at bending them to his command.

Piers slowly shook his head. What was there to say? Of course, she had a relative who was close to the future king. Why was he even surprised? Just when he thought he knew everything about Maggie, she threw some other precious gem of knowledge into the mix.

He knew who William Saunders was, having heard of the man who had been a spy for the British Crown, and who had operated undercover in France for a number of years prior to the fall of Napoleon. It was rumored he had fed vital information to the commander of the allied forces, the

Duke of Wellington, just prior to and during the battle of Waterloo.

Maggie's cousin was also more than likely the one responsible for the miraculous delivery of the messages the Prince of Orange had frantically sent from the battlefield at Quatre Bras to Wellington, who at the time was still in Brussels. Those coded dispatches had begged the British commander to urgently send more troops. Before the reinforcements had arrived to fight alongside his regiment, Piers had feared that they were about to be overrun by Napoleon's commander, Marshal Ney.

Will Saunders was the type of man who got the impossible done. If he could get Will to take up his case, Piers might actually stand a chance of getting a fair hearing. Of getting his life back.

But before then, there was another important matter which they needed to discuss.

"What do you mean, Jonathan said I was my own worst enemy?"

"I tell you about my cousin, who is more powerful than my uncle and father put together, and you focus on what your brother said? Heaven help us," she huffed.

Piers snorted. "Oh, Maggie. I think heaven has already heard and answered my pleas. Because surely only God could have sent you."

Chapter Forty-Three

I t was a pity that they had to leave Denford Park so soon after arriving, but Maggie and Piers agreed that it was vitally important that they return to London as soon as possible. If there was any chance that Will Saunders could help Piers, they shouldn't delay. Lord and Lady Denford were naturally disappointed but also in furious agreement.

"I am so glad he met you, my dear," said Lady Denford. She embraced Maggie, then whispered in her ear, "My son is a good man. He just needs to believe he deserves happiness. I think he may have found that in you."

Maggie glanced over to where Piers and his father were talking. "He is lovely. But I don't want to place him under any further pressure than he already is. There is more than enough at stake without Piers having to worry about me."

Lady Denford nodded, then smiled. "But he does worry about you. That's the nature of Piers—always thinking of others."

To the detriment of himself.

"Well, I promise you, he has friends who care what

happens to him. I am going to do everything in my power to make sure he is free of the army."

"And then he will be free to make other decisions. Like finally being able to offer marriage to the woman he loves, and hopefully, start a family. I want my son to be able to live his life again."

The light of hope shone in Piers's mother's eyes. Maggie hoped that Lady Denford would have her wishes come true. That her son would indeed be once more in command of his own life. Only then would he be truly free to choose love.

She would be waiting for him when he did.

A week or so away from town wasn't nearly enough. Piers liked London, but he loathed being back at the Horse Guards and being under the continual crushing boot of Major Hall.

"So, you didn't find a single thing about this missing captain? What a waste of army resources," huffed the major.

Piers took a slow, deep breath in, then let it out. "No, that is not what I put in my report, sir. I did find the baptism records for Robert Eustace Taylor, but I couldn't find anything further regarding his army career. I told Miss Radley that I believe her late fiancé may have not been fully honest with her."

On the journey back to London, he and Maggie had come to a decision. As far as the world was concerned, the Robert Taylor that Maggie had known had indeed died a tragic and heroic death at Waterloo. The Robert Taylor who still lived in Coventry with his wife and children was merely a man who shared the same name.

It was a lie, but one they were determined to maintain. Jonathan and Elizabeth could be trusted to keep their silence.

Lord and Lady Denford need never know the truth. When the time was right, Maggie would confide in her parents, but no one else.

As for the rest of the powerful Radley family, they would be happy that she was ready to move on with her life. While it wasn't fair that the guilty had gotten away scot-free, protecting the innocent was more important than revenge.

Not all of it sat well with Piers, but in the end, it was Maggie's choice. She was the one who would have to explain things to her family. It was the thought of what Maggie would endure if word ever got out that finally sealed it for him.

He loved her, and he wouldn't stand for the rumor mongers of the *haute ton* to inflict their pain on her. The daughter of the Bishop of London being taken for a fool by a married man who had not only faked his death, but who'd left her to grieve for more than two years was the sort of shocking scandal that some members of London society could only dream of getting their hands on.

Maggie had suffered enough.

Now, it was Piers who was enduring the fallout of their trip to Coventry. Major Hall made no effort to hide his delight in making Piers squirm.

"I don't recall Miss Radley undertaking the journey with you as being any part of the plan, Denford. This was army business," said the major.

Piers nodded. "You are correct sir, she wasn't. Miss Radley and I crossed paths after I had left London. As she was travelling unaccompanied, I felt obliged to offer her my protection."

"Well at least her virtue wouldn't have been at risk from you."

The ugly taunt went unanswered.

"You have been gone for two weeks; don't tell me it took

you all that time to figure out that Miss Radley had been duped. What the devil have you been doing?"

Piers hated hearing Major Hall utter Maggie's name. It made his skin crawl.

"Miss Radley took ill in Coventry. We had to stay until she was recovered. As she is the daughter of Lord Hugh Radley, I had to make certain she was well when I returned her safely to her family. His grace the Bishop of London was most grateful for my efforts," he replied.

I also have powerful friends.

"Just make sure the final report is on my desk by end of day," snapped the major. The door of Piers's office rattled in its frame after his commanding officer left.

"Self-righteous prig," he muttered.

He finished up the report, lies and all, then handed it to a private who delivered it to Major Hall.

By the time Piers left the Horse Guards, it was late in the afternoon. One day, back in London and he already missed Maggie something fierce.

When he had returned home to Denford House the previous night, it had been with a heavy heart and a deep yearning to hold her in his arms. The night when he had come so close to claiming Maggie still burned brightly in his mind.

He had taken himself in hand as soon as he retired to his bedroom. Laying on his bed, stroking himself while thinking of her, was the only way he was able to find a modicum of peace. It had taken the memory of watching her while he had brought her to completion in the barn for Piers to finally achieve his climax. Mercifully, sleep had soon followed.

I want her. I need her.

So much now hinged on him meeting with Will Saunders and them finding a successful way out of this situation. For the first time in a very long time, he was filled with resolve and purpose.

He was going to make Maggie his wife and hold her love forever, and no one, not even Major Hall, was going to stop him.

"Someone has to know something to prove my innocence."

Chapter Forty-Four

Newport Street, London, wasn't somewhere that Piers regularly frequented. It didn't have quite the same luster as the area around St. James's. But it wasn't too far from Denford House in Park Place—a mere fifteen-minute stroll.

Arriving home from his day at the Horse Guards, Piers shed his Grenadier Guards uniform and replaced it with his ordinary about-town clothes. It had been two days since he and Maggie had last seen one another, and it seemed an eternity. It wasn't the proper thing for an officer to be seen out and about in civilian dress, but he had reached a point of not giving a care about it.

They think they have enough on me already. They may as well throw a charge of being out of uniform in with the rest.

From Park Place, Piers took a short walk via Jermyn Street, past Leicester Square, and then turned right into Newport Street. From out of his coat pocket, he retrieved the note he had received from Will Saunders, and checked the address.

Number forty-three was close to the end. The house sat

behind a high brick wall. Piers pushed open the iron gate and made his way to the front door.

He checked his coat, brushing off a stray piece of lint from its left sleeve, then paused. His heart was pounding hard. This wasn't just a friendly chat with Maggie's cousin. Piers's whole future might well hinge on the outcome of this appointment.

"Come on, Denford. You can do this. Ask the man for help."

Taking a hold of the brass knocker, Piers rapped it hard. He took a polite step back and waited.

The sound of shuffling came from within, and then the glossy black door slowly opened. On the other side was an elderly butler, who peered at Piers over the rim of his spectacles. "Captain Denford?"

"Yes. I have an appointment with Mister William Saunders."

The butler ushered him in and upstairs to an elegant sitting room. As Piers entered the room, his gaze fell on two men who were standing warming themselves by the fireplace. One, a tall dark-haired man, stepped forward and immediately thrust out his hand.

"Will Saunders."

The second man in the room, who bore a striking resemblance to Will, gave a tip of the head. "Bartholomew Shale."

Piers finished shaking Will's hand, then bowed to the other man. "Lord Shale."

He had been expecting to meet with Will, but not Earl Shale. His memory dug into the past and reminded him that Earl Shale was yet another of Maggie's many cousins.

Will motioned toward a cluster of ornate antique chairs. "Please, have a seat."

While Piers and the earl settled into their seats, Will

headed to a nearby sideboard and poured three generous brandies.

Lord Shale leaned forward and offered Piers his hand. "It's nice to finally meet. Maggie told us all about you this afternoon. She seems quite taken with you, Captain Denford. Will we be hearing wedding bells shortly?"

Piers scowled. He had come here expecting to discuss his problems, not have the Radley family poke their noses into his and Maggie's private relationship.

But if these men can help me, they are likely going to be family very shortly.

"Lord Shale, Maggie and I have become friends of late. As for the rest, a gentleman never tells."

The earl grinned. "Excellent answer. And please, my friends call me Bat."

Will handed both men a drink, then sat. "Bat and I were both agents for the crown at one point. We lived undercover as clerks in Paris for a number of years."

That was a surprise. He had known about Will having been a spy but hadn't ever heard about the earl.

Bat chuckled knowingly. "My work in France was rather limited. I returned to England before Napoleon was overthrown for the first time as my father had died and the Shale bloodline wasn't yet secure. I had to leave behind the machinations of war and find myself a wife."

Will casually sipped at his brandy. "Took you long enough to convince Rosemary to marry you. Poor girl."

Piers caught the glare that Bat shot his cousin, followed by a mumbled, "Cheeky devil." Both men chuckled.

"But I am sure that Captain Denford isn't here to listen to us go over our war stories. It's his which are the issue at hand," said Will.

"Would you care for me to give you a summary of what happened that day at Waterloo?" asked Piers.

Will waved his offer away. "No need. I've read the dispatches that your Major Hall sent, along with those from various other high-ranking officers. Oddly, his is the only one which makes mention of you having done a poor job. The rest of the reports are either silent, or simply state the facts—those being that you aided the Prince of Orange after he had been felled by a musket ball."

Piers narrowed his eyes. "How did a civilian like you get a hold of the military records? They are meant to be secure."

"Will and I were not in the military, but we have our connections. The army might not recognize our work as spies, since it is considered less than honorable, but rest assured, it is valued. There are few doors which are closed to men like us," said Bat.

"And for those that remain shut fast, we have a set of skeleton keys," added Will.

Piers wasn't sure where this conversation was headed. He had been hoping that Will could provide him with a list of influential people who could be relied upon to come to his aid. At the moment, he didn't have anything.

Will set his glass of brandy on the floor. "Let us get down to the business of things—the first being that you have been waiting on letters from the Dutch royal family. Letters to support your case. If you have those, then they will go a long way to convincing the army that you were merely doing your job as an assistant aide-de-camp."

"Yes."

"And as far as you are aware, those letters never made it to England."

Piers's jaw tightened, his teeth grinding as a horrible sense of foreboding gripped him. What did 'as far as you are aware' mean? He met Will's gaze. "Go on."

"Maggie came to see me and explained the whole situation in great detail. I must say, some of what she told me, I would never have expected to hear from the lips of an unwed woman. But I accept the need for her to understand what is at stake. After she left, I went to see the Prince Regent."

"I meant to ask, how is Prinny?" said Bat.

"Not good. For all his faults, no man deserves what he is going through. I wouldn't have troubled him if I'd thought a few weeks' delay wouldn't change your circumstances, Denford. But my sources tell me that the army is finally going to press charges against you. You are going to face a court-martial for dereliction of duty. Don't be surprised if they add a few more charges to the sheet before you face a trial."

Piers gripped the sides of the chair, his knuckles turning white. A large hammer was about to come down on his life. His future would be shattered to pieces. He and Maggie wouldn't get their happily ever after.

My love, I am so sorry. Maggie, you deserve better than this.

Will leaned forward in his seat and pointed a finger at Piers. "And this is where things get interesting. I spoke to the prince, and he was adamant that letters had come from King Willem and the Prince of Orange earlier this year. In their correspondence, they both made mention of your efforts to save the heir to the Dutch throne. The Prince Regent's private secretary confirmed it. Unfortunately, the letters were forwarded onto your commanding officer, Major Hall."

It was as if someone had punched Piers hard in the gut. The air whooshed out of his lungs. For a moment, he feared he would be sick.

How could that be? The major never mentioned receiving—oh, no. He wouldn't dare, would he?

Bat placed a comforting hand on his shoulder. "You look as if you have had a bit of a shock, my friend. I take it this is the same Major Hall who slandered you in the dispatches and under who you are currently serving."

Piers nodded. "Yes. I can just imagine what he thought

when those letters arrived. If they contained words of support for me, then they would undermine his efforts. I hate to think what he has done with them."

Little wonder Piers hadn't ever heard about the letters, let alone seen them. They were probably kept hidden under lock and key in the major's office. Or worse, had already been destroyed.

"Well, then you need to rectify that situation, and quick smart," said Will.

Easier said than done. But what could he do? March up to a senior officer and openly accuse him of withholding information and lying to the army? Not likely. He would be clapped in irons and thrown into a prison cell within minutes.

Piers considered Will's words, and a small spark of hope lit in his heart. The expression on the face of the former spy was that of a man who had already come up with a solution.

"Just tell me what you want me to do," said Piers.

"Go home; try and get some rest. I know that won't be easy. I shall send word to Denford House later tonight and let you know of what is likely to happen tomorrow. There are some people I am still waiting to hear from, but I would strongly suggest that you should prepare yourself for an interesting morning," replied Will.

The three of them rose from their chairs. This whole disaster had hung over him for two years, but to know that it was now moving to a decisive point filled Piers with a degree of apprehension. He wasn't naive. Will Saunders may well have plans in hand, but it didn't mean that things couldn't still go awry.

"Thank you, gentlemen. I appreciate your assistance. It's a relief to know that someone is prepared to help."

Bat nodded. "Just be ready to deal with whatever comes tomorrow. If this Major Hall, has it in for you, he won't go quietly."

"No, he won't. He has done his best to make my life a misery. I've lost count of the times I've tried to talk to him, but his mind was made up that day on the battlefield. If he can destroy me, he will," replied Piers.

Piers left Will and Bat to finish their drinks. He resisted the temptation to ask Will who it was that he was waiting to hear from, deciding it was wiser to trust Maggie's cousin rather than to appear as if he were questioning his efforts. He had a powerful friend—one who had already gone out on a limb for him. When Will got in touch with him, Piers would do exactly, as he was instructed.

His whole future depended on the next twenty-four hours. He just wished Maggie was here, that he could tell her he loved her. And that he was going to fight for them.

Chapter Forty-Five

H *orse Guards*
London

Piers reached to adjust his cravat, then stopped himself. If he tightened the knot any further, it would strangle him. Though, from the furious way that adrenaline coursed through his veins, a quick and painful death might be the lesser of two evils.

Under his arm was the satchel of papers he intended to present to the Commander-in-Chief of the British Army, Prince Frederick, the Duke of York and Albany. Taking his cue from his meeting with Will Saunders and Earl Shale, Piers was making certain he was not going into battle unarmed.

Maggie, my love, I am going to fight for our future.

From out of the main office, the duke's private secretary appeared in the hallway. He gave Piers a small nod. "You can come in now, Captain Denford."

He had barely taken two steps toward the door when the heavy thud of military boots echoed off the walls in the narrow corridor. Piers turned. His gaze settled on the immaculately dressed Major Hall. The only thing he had under his arm was his swagger stick.

Piers saluted his commanding officer. "Sir."

The sly grin on the major's lips had a lump of dread settling in Piers's stomach. Why the devil was he here?

"You didn't think you would get to have a private audience with the head of the army, did you? Foolish boy," he sneered.

Piers did his best not to respond to the obvious taunt. If he were to let the major get the better of him now, he may as well give up, go home, and abandon all hope of ever getting out of the army or having a future with Maggie.

"I expected you would be here, sir. You did write the dispatch report, and that is the subject of today's hastily convened meeting."

Not that you have ever let me forget that it was you who put me in this situation.

Major Hall gave a derisive huff, and Piers quickly stepped to one side as his superior officer pushed past. He fell in behind the major.

Will's personal note informing him that a meeting with the Duke of York and Albany had been arranged for eight the next morning had arrived at Denford House just before the hour of midnight. At the Horse Guards, the official notice had only been handed to Piers at ten minutes to the hour of eight. It was clear that someone was determined to ambush him.

But today, he was going to have his voice heard. If the army was going to try and tear him down, Piers Denford was not going to go quietly.

Once inside the Duke of York's office, Piers was shown to a chair positioned in front of a large oak table. Major Hall made his way around to the other side. They both stood waiting for the head of the British Army.

The door at the far end of the office opened and the duke appeared. A civilian secretary trailed behind him. The Duke of York and Albany walked with the self-confidence and purpose of a man who had been born to the high rank of prince.

"Good morning, gentlemen," said the duke.

Piers and Major Hall both saluted, then stood stiffly to attention.

The duke stopped at the end of the table, took one look at Major Hall's chair, and frowned. He turned to his secretary. "This isn't right."

The secretary stepped forward, made a hurried apology, and picked up Major Hall's chair. He moved it to the side of the table where Piers stood. It might have been but a minor change in furniture arrangement, but it spoke volumes as to how his royal highness viewed his position. They may all be officers in the army, but only he was of royal blood.

"Gentlemen, take a seat," said the duke.

Major Hall cleared his throat. "Your Highness, I must protest. You cannot expect me to sit on the same side of the table as the accused."

The duke shot him a look of disinterest. "This is not a military court-martial, Major Hall. Captain Denford has not been charged with any offense. We are simply here today to get to the bottom of the matter. The only protest I wish to hear is my own, which is that you have let this matter drag on for as long as it has. It should have been dealt with at least a year ago." He motioned to the chairs.

Piers sat, placing his satchel on the floor beside him. He kept his eyes focused forward. At the same time, he sent a silent prayer to heaven, hoping that Will Saunders had come through for him.

"The business of the army doesn't stop just because the guns have fallen silent," grumbled Major Hall.

You might want to hold your tongue; I hear the duke has a decent temper.

It was obvious that the major had been rattled by the sudden early morning summons to meet with the duke because a calm and rational man wouldn't dare to talk back to the commander of the British Army in such a disrespectful manner.

The secretary stepped forward and placed a large, bulky folder of papers on the desk in front of the duke. The duke nodded, then waved the man away. "Have a seat out of the way, but make sure you take accurate minutes of the meeting."

"Yes, Your Highness."

Piers tore his gaze away from a spot on the wall and glanced at the voluminous amount of paperwork. Where had it all come from? He couldn't fathom how a minor misunderstanding on the battlefield could have turned into something so big.

"Major Hall, take a seat. I won't ask again," said the duke.

Major Hall wisely sat in his chair.

The duke banged his hand down on top of the enormous pile of papers. "I had plans to enjoy the evening with a lady of my acquaintance last night, but instead, I spent many hours going through these. And what I uncovered disturbed me greatly."

Major Hall shifted in his seat. "With respect, Your Highness . . ."

A raised hand from the duke silenced him. "I don't think you understand what the word respect means, Major Hall because the original papers which I finally received from you only last week didn't include all the relevant documents. A man who respects his superiors wouldn't have made that mistake."

You dirty swine. You waited until I was out of London to finally push for me to face charges and a court-martial.

The major's easy acceptance of Piers's request to accompany Maggie to Coventry now made sense. With Piers out of the way, the major could make his move.

But in the last day, things had changed. The worm was surely turning.

Hope flared in Piers's heart, but he resolutely pushed it down. Too many times he had thought that the end of the nightmare was in sight, only to have his expectations dashed.

The duke plucked the topmost piece of paper from the pile and brandished it at the major. "This document, Major Hall, was not among those in your submission."

He flicked through another good inch of the stack, before lifting it, and then dropping it with great vigor onto the table. The papers scattered in all directions.

"I can only assume that all this correspondence, including a number of first-hand accounts of the battle was missed being sent to my office, purely due to an oversight on your part. Because there is no other reason, aside from pure malice, that I can think of as to why they were not included in the first place. I am surprised that an officer of the British Army would behave in such a manner."

For a moment, Piers feared that his heart had stopped. He turned to the major, unable to hold his tongue any longer. "Do you hate me that much? That you would go to all that trouble just to ensure I faced a court-martial and imprisonment? What did I ever do to make you want to destroy me, or to deny me the justice to which I am entitled?"

"Justice? You don't deserve it." The major got to his feet and pointed at Piers. "You abandoned your responsibilities in the heat of battle and went running after that fancy man of a prince. The secretary is welcome to quote me in his notes. What you did, Captain Denford, was not only incompetent, but also the act of a coward. It's exactly what I wrote in the dispatch report. The Duke of York and Albany may have all the piles of papers in the world, but nothing changes what you did."

They had finally got to the heart of the matter. It had taken over two years and countless hours of bastardry, but the major had given voice to his hatred.

Piers quietly ran through his response in his head. He had waited a long time to be able to say his piece. He got to his feet, then bowed to the duke. "Your Highness, may I have the floor for a moment?"

"Yes, you may, Captain Denford." The duke shot Major Hall another dark look. "Major Hall, resume your seat or resign your commission. I am fast running out of patience."

Piers waited until the major had sat down, then cleared his throat. "The details of what happened that day on the battlefield at Waterloo are well known. We were in the heat of the conflict. Major Hall and his men were fighting close to where the Prince of Orange and his party were stationed. I was with the prince, acting as an extra aide-de-camp."

"Is that what you call it?" replied the major.

Piers ignored the remark. He wasn't going to give any ammunition to his foe. Up to the eve of the battle, there had been plenty of rumors about the prince and his sexual proclivities, but none of them had involved Piers.

"I was tasked with ensuring that the future King of the Netherlands survived. That was my sworn duty. And while I fought the skirmish alongside your troops, the moment the prince moved away and pressed into the thick of the battle, I was duty-bound to follow him," said Piers.

"Were you and the prince close?" asked the duke. It didn't need saying that the question had a double edge to it. Major Hall muttered a less than subtle, "Molly," under his breath.

"Just because a man does not frequent the whorehouses

does not mean he engages in acts of sodomy nor dresses as a woman. Some men are simply better at discretion," snapped the duke.

Piers caught the anger in the duke's voice. Major Hall was fast losing this battle.

Still, Piers paused for a moment, choosing his words carefully. The next few minutes could well determine the outcome of this hearing and his whole future.

"I was under the Prince of Orange's command. As were others. I respected him as a soldier. The prince is a fierce warrior. It took a French musket ball to bring him and his horse, Vexey, down, but even then, he didn't wish to retire from the battle. His Royal Highness had already lost a great deal of blood by the time I got to him. He was pale and unsteady on his feet, leaning against another officer's horse. I was about to offer him my own mount when he suddenly collapsed."

That moment was forever etched in his memory. The fear that the prince was about to die in his arms had given Piers many a nightmare over the past year or so.

"Then what happened?" asked the duke.

Piers shrugged. "Exactly what was written in the dispatches. We got the prince onto my horse, after which a number of his personal adjutants helped to lead him away to the nearby hamlet of Mont Saint Jean where a surgeon attended to his wounds."

It was the truth. Nothing embellished. Exactly how things had happened that day. How it had gone from him simply doing his job as an aide-de-camp to being written up in the dispatches as being incompetent Piers had never fully understood. But the more he listened to the conversation, to its dark undertones, the clearer the picture became.

I can't believe I was so naïve as to think they would judge a man on his contribution to the battle, to his bravery. Not his sexual appetites.

The Prince of Orange had been a solid commander, trusted and promoted by the British commander, the Duke of Wellington, but that wasn't enough for men like Major Hall. Piers worried it might also not be enough for the Commander-in-Chief of the British Army.

The major cleared his throat. "What happened to your fiancée, Denford? Why aren't you married?"

"I don't see the relevance of my betrothal to this meeting," replied Piers.

The duke glanced at his papers. "Answer the question."

They weren't even going to bother dancing around the subject any longer. If he didn't deal with it here and now, the next step would be outright accusation.

Piers wasn't going to take the bait; he was determined to keep his temper. If he didn't control the situation, he stood in grave peril of having to defend himself against charges of sodomy. He wouldn't put it past Major Hall not to have already thought of that option.

It was time to finally let the world know the truth of the women in his life.

Sorry, Dinah. I have to do this or else they will not stop until they see me hung.

"Lady Dinah Gibney and I decided that we didn't suit. And rather than marry and be miserable, we made the choice to remain friends. Why we haven't made this public is because it is no one else's business. And also, because there is another lady in my life. She is the woman I plan to make my wife."

The duke raised his head and met Piers's gaze. There was an unspoken threat in his eyes, one which silently cautioned Piers against being reckless enough to attempt to lie to him. "Who?"

"Miss Margaret Radley. Her father is Lord Hugh Radley, the Bishop of London. Her uncle—"

"Yes, I know the family," snapped the duke.

"Rather convenient," mumbled the major.

"But compelling. As is this . . ." The duke produced a letter from his pile of papers and held it up.

An odd mixture of fear and hope coursed through Piers's veins. Could this be his salvation?

"This letter was received by my brother, the Prince Regent's personal secretary, some ten months ago, along with two other subsequent missives. All of which I am led to believe were delivered to the Horse Guards. More specifically to you, Major Hall. Though why they were not forwarded onto me, I am yet to understand." The duke spread the letter and several others out across the top of the desk, then pointed to them one by one. "Letters from both the King of the Netherlands, and the Prince of Orange. This one from King Willem specifically mentions Captain Denford and offers his deep gratitude for his assistance in helping save the life of his son."

Piers swallowed deeply. Somehow, the letters had finally found their way to the Commander-in-Chief.

"How did you come by those?" asked Major Hall, his voice icy with anger.

The duke glared at him. "You mean these documents which were anonymously delivered to my home late last night? Who knows how they found their way from *your* locked desk drawer and into my hands? And to be blunt about it, I don't bloody well care. All that matters is that they have finally reached their destination. No, thanks to you, Major Hall."

Piers could only imagine what had transpired last night. While the major was at home, someone had broken into his office and taken the letters. That someone had then made a late-night visit to the Duke of York and Albany.

Tension simmered in the room, but he paid it little mind. The truth of his actions during the battle had finally seen the light of day. Pride and stubborn minds could do what they wished.

"Major Hall, I would suggest that we are doing Captain Denford a grave disservice by holding him in the army. By keeping him from both his potential bride and his future role as Viscount Denford. Wouldn't you agree?" said the duke.

The major closed his eyes and slowly shook his head. His shoulders slumped in defeat.

Not the outcome you had been hoping for, you dirty cad. Where is your honor now?

"I beg your pardon. I didn't quite catch that," the duke added.

"Yes, Your Highness. I think it best that Captain Denford be relieved of his duties."

Fearing his knees may buckle from under him, Piers dropped onto his chair.

"I have decided that the only way justice can be served to the captain is for him to be given an honorable discharge and also granted the letter of commendation which the King of the Netherlands personally requested," said the duke.

What?

"The Prince of Wales and I have concurred about the need for both the discharge and the commendation. My brother was most insistent about the matter when I spoke to him late last night. The subject of your dispatch note from the Battle of Waterloo was also discussed. I would strongly recommend that you, Major Hall, consider correcting your report, as I am sure that it was purely an oversight for you to write incompetent next to Captain Denford's name."

The duke reached into his jacket pocket and produced a

folded-up note, waving it at the major. "This should do. You just need to change a couple of words and initial the document. I expect to see the amended entry delivered to my secretary before the day is out."

I can't believe this is happening.

Piers waited patiently, praying that Major Hall wouldn't do or say anything foolish. To his relief, his nemesis simply rose from his chair and took the note. He examined it, huffed in obvious disgust, then nodded. "I understand, Your Highness. The amended note will be with your private secretary this afternoon."

Pity your resignation won't be with it.

The Commander-in-Chief hadn't requested the major give up his commission and Piers had his suspicions as to why. The British army needed hard men like Major Hall. What they didn't need was Piers Denford.

Thank God.

He had what he wanted. A way out of the army. Any thoughts of revenge or confronting the major were immediately swept aside. Like Maggie, he, too, had to put the past behind him and move on.

The Duke of York and Albany closed up the file and got to his feet. Piers quickly stood to attention.

"This meeting is at an end. But, Major Hall, I must mention one last thing before you go. In future, I expect to receive all relevant paperwork from you in a timelier fashion. You are dismissed. Captain Denford, a word, if you wouldn't mind."

Major Hall glared at Piers, then saluted the duke before heading for the door. The stony expression on his face said it all. His hopes for ruining Piers's life had been foiled.

The door was closed firmly. "Horrid man," muttered the duke. He nodded at his secretary. "That is the end of the meeting. Gather all these papers and then you may leave. I will sign the minutes later."

As soon as the secretary was gone, the duke beckoned Piers over. "Drink?"

"That would be most welcome, Your Highness," replied Piers.

The duke collected a brandy decanter from a nearby sideboard and poured them both a generous glass. He handed one to Piers, who gratefully accepted it. He was in desperate need of a stiff drink.

"To you, Denford. Before those letters were discovered last night, I was worried that you might have to ask for a royal pardon. This has been a rather ugly business. And while I don't agree with the way the Prince of Orange conducts his private affairs, I have even less regard for those who lie. Major Hall had no right to withhold such important correspondence."

Piers sipped his drink, the alcohol burning his throat as it went down. "I won't ask how the letters came into your possession," said Piers.

"No. I wouldn't. All I can say is that you are a fortunate man. Few would be able to achieve what your friend did and manage to get away with it. I doubt anyone has even noticed that Major Hall's office was broken into last night. The major certainly hadn't."

Piers coughed, the brandy going down the wrong way. Will Saunders had somehow stolen into an office at the Horse Guards, one of the most heavily protected places in all of London. He had then broken into a desk, stolen papers, and made his getaway without anyone being the wiser.

How the devil did he manage that?

It really did pay to have friends in both high and low places.

"Now you can understand why my brother is giving your friend a knighthood."

"What will happen to the major? I mean once he has amended the dispatch note, and after I have gone."

The duke downed the rest of his drink in one smooth gulp, then set the glass onto the sideboard. He shook his head. "Nothing. The major will go back to sorting the records, overseeing letters to widows and families. Waiting for the next war to begin. He might not be the sort of man who thinks twice about smearing someone's reputation, but he is exactly the kind of man the British Army needs when it comes to leading troops. Major Hall gets the job done. And that is what wins wars."

While he didn't exactly like what he had just heard, Piers wasn't the least bit surprised. There would be little point in the army making an example of a decorated war hero. He didn't want revenge; he just wanted his freedom.

"Will you allow me to vacate my office today, Your Highness? If it's all the same to you, I would rather not spend another minute at the Horse Guards while I wait for the army to grant me a discharge. If those letters from the King of the Netherlands and the Prince of Orange had been handled correctly in the first place, I should have been released from service many months ago." It was a request, but it held the weight of a demand.

"I think you will find that the official paperwork will be processed promptly by my office. But since I am the Commander-in-Chief, I can't see anyone stopping you from clearing out your desk today."

A sigh of relief escaped Piers's lips. "Thank you. I shall do just that. If our business here is at an end, I should like very much to depart the Horse Guards within the hour. This past year or so has been difficult—my future constantly uncertain.

Now I just want to leave, and then go and find the woman I love and ask her to marry me."

The duke nodded. "Good luck, Denford, I am pleased that this is over. But I think you know the gentleman whom you should be giving the most thanks to, and it's not me."

After one final salute, Piers wasted no time in leaving the Commander-in-Chief's office. Seconds later, he was out the door and racing down the hallway as fast as his legs could carry him. Reaching his office, he threw off his jacket and tossed it onto the desk. His pistol and decorative gorget followed. If he didn't know that it would surely cause a huge scandal, he would have stripped off every piece of his uniform and walked home naked. He even abandoned his greatcoat.

When they did eventually arrive, he would accept the letters of commendation and army service release graciously, after which they would be stuffed in a drawer never to see the light of day again. He wanted no reminders of his military career, nor of the miserable years he had wasted serving under the command of a tyrant.

Not an hour later, his farewells spoken, the honorable Piers Denford marched out the front door of the Horse Guards for the last time, no longer a captain, but a civilian.

It was bitterly cold without his jacket and coat, but he didn't care. Hastening his steps, he marched home to Park Place to change.

His next stop? Fulham Palace and an audience with the Bishop of London. Then he would finally be able to ask for Maggie's hand in marriage.

Piers couldn't wait to start his life with her.

Chapter Forty-Six

It was late afternoon by the time Piers managed to track down Hugh Radley. His impulsive journey out to Fulham Palace had been in vain. None of the Radley family were at home. But he didn't mind. There was no pressing need for him to race back to town; the army no longer held sway over where he went and at what time. His life was finally and completely his own once again.

He was in such a happy mood, he verily skipped up the steps of St. Paul's Cathedral and into the five o'clock evensong service, ignoring the odd looks his light dance garnered from other worshipers as he went.

Once inside the cathedral, Piers scanned the crowd for Maggie. According to the head butler at the Radley family home, she would be in attendance along with her mother and sister. Rising up on his toes, he peered over the heads of the multitude gathered inside the front door. *Where are you?*

For the first time in a long time, he was filled with excitement, giddy with a thousand plans for the future. He just had to find the woman he intended to share them with—the woman he loved.

He finally caught a glimpse of Maggie as she headed toward the front of the nave. She was joined by two other dark-haired women who suddenly appeared from out of the crowd. The site of his future wife and her female relatives had him grinning from ear to ear.

Maggie. He couldn't ever imagine not having his heart skip a beat at the sight of her. She was his everything. He made as hasty a dash as was permissible in a church and hurried to join the parishioners at the front.

"Excuse me. Excuse me. Pardon."

He scuttled around a couple who were deciding where to sit before dropping into a seat just as the opening strains of a hymn filled the domed great space. Hugh Radley appeared from out of the choir and climbed the steps of the pulpit. As he did, Piers leaned back in his seat and tried to catch Maggie's attention. She, however, was being a dutiful daughter, and her gaze was fixed firmly to the front.

It was another forty agonizing minutes before Piers was finally able to seek her out. He made his away over to where Maggie and the other members of her family were gathered at the end of one of the pews.

"Hello. I wasn't expecting you here tonight." Her eyes narrowed, but a smile danced on her lips. She could read him only too well; she could tell that something good had happened.

"I have news. Wonderful news," he said.

Her eyes grew wide. "Piers! You are out of uniform. Please tell me that means what I think it does."

He grinned. "It does. An honorable discharge. I am a free man as of this afternoon." He gave a nod in the direction of Lord Hugh Radley. "Though hopefully not for very long. I was planning of speaking to your father this evening."

Maggie stepped back as Mary Radley appeared at her side. Piers dipped into a respectful bow. "Lady Hugh."

"Captain Denford, what a pleasure to see you in church. And please, call me Mary, I rarely use my formal title with friends and family," she replied.

Slipping her arm into his, Maggie grinned. "Piers is Captain Denford no longer. He is simply Piers."

"Piers, is it? Not Lord Woodford?"

He caught the hint of a teasing chortle in Mary's words. No doubt Maggie had already spoken privately to her mother and informed her of their plans for the future.

Piers hadn't used the title of Lord Woodford since joining the army. But now that he was on the cusp of getting married, it made sense to revert back to being referred to as Baron Woodford, one of his father's lesser titles.

"I was hoping to speak to his grace this evening, but he looks a busy man. Should I request a private meeting for tomorrow morning?" Piers asked. Disappointment was in his tone, but he could understand that Hugh had many parishioners to serve. Evensong at St. Paul's was busy, and hundreds of people were gathered under the dome.

"My husband will be in his private office shortly. I shall speak to one of the deacons and arrange for you to meet him there," replied Mary.

"And in the meantime, you and I need to talk," said Maggie. She took a hold of Piers's hand and began to lead him away. "I shall bring him back presently," she called back over her shoulder to her mother.

Piers didn't protest as she towed him toward a side door. Clearly Maggie knew her way around the cathedral and all its secret entrances and exits.

They stepped out of the main nave and into a darkened lane way. A high wall separated it from the main street. The fresh night air chilled his cheeks, but Piers shrugged it off. He was with Maggie, and that was all that mattered.

He barely had time to register what was happening before

Maggie pulled him into a secluded doorway and threw her arms around his neck. Their lips met in a heated, desperate embrace. She was hungry for him, her need feeding his own.

They were kissing in the courtyard of London's foremost public cathedral, one where her father had just given a short sermon about social rules and how they helped bind people together. What he and Maggie were doing was surely breaking at least a half dozen of those.

This is wonderful. I have missed you.

He wrapped her up in his embrace, not caring if they were caught. After all they had both been through, they deserved happiness, and today, he was going to seize the moment and make it their own.

The temptation to deepen the kiss and then offer to find a place where they could repeat the heady experience of the stables was strong. The loud toll of the cathedral bells, however, tore his lusty thoughts away. Hugh Radley would soon be finished with the final parishioners at the service and Piers was keen to speak to him.

Maggie drew back. "We should go. The steeple master will soon be down from the tower. He comes this way after the quarter hour chiming of the bells post evensong."

"And I need to go and speak with your father," he replied.

"Aren't you forgetting something?"

In the dim light Piers couldn't make out the expression on Maggie's face, but her words were filled with joy—just like his heart.

"I think you have already said yes to whatever I might wish to ask. The moment you let me touch you in the barn that night, you agreed to a future with me. To becoming Lady Woodford," he replied.

She mewed with feigned disappointment.

Piers pulled her hard against him. "Be mine forever, Maggie. My lover. My life. My wedded wife."

Maggie fell silent for a moment. To Piers's utter relief, so did the cathedral bells. He waited with bated breath for her answer.

Then, from out of the still darkness, came the word he had longed to hear her say.

"*Yes.*"

Piers bent his head and kissed his fiancée one more time. "Come. Let's go and find your father. I want to be able to announce our engagement tonight."

He also had in mind to set the wedding date. The sooner, the better.

"If we can arrange one, how do you feel about an early December wedding? It could be just after your birthday. I know it will have to be quickly organized and a common license secured, but I want you to be Lady Woodford as soon as possible."

Maggie sighed happily. "Yes, let's not wait. And if you speak nicely to my father, he may even agree to waive the bond for a license."

Piers softly laughed and took hold of her hand. "I think my own pockets are deep enough to pay for one, if need be, but since I am going to ask his grace to marry us, we should be fine."

The sooner he and Maggie were able to begin a new life together, the better. As they walked arm in arm back into the cathedral, there was a lightness in his heart. The warmth of hope and the promise of happiness pushed his dark days firmly into the past.

Maggie glanced up at him and smiled. "Don't forget you promised me a birthday cake. I shall hold you to that, Piers Denford. I mean Lord Woodford."

"I expect you shall. Future Lady Woodford."

~

"It's beautiful. And I am so happy for the both of you. I still can't believe that you are getting married," said Claire.

Maggie continued to stare at the ruby which sat on her finger. After Piers had spoken to her father and received his blessing for their future marriage, her new fiancé had suddenly produced a stunning ring from the depths of his coat pocket and placed it on her finger.

Piers was a man full of wonderful surprises. Even now, every time she glanced over at him, tears threatened. Seeing him dressed in a dark gray jacket with light beige trousers instead of his usual officer's uniform was an odd sight. It would take some getting used to, but she approved of his new look. She'd had her fill of army uniforms—enough to last a lifetime.

The most significant change of all in Piers was the constant smile on his face.

"Papa says he can fit us into the wedding schedule next week. My fiancé is keen for us to be wed as soon as possible," Maggie said.

Her sister took her by the hand. "I am so glad that you met Piers. After all you have been through, you deserved to find happiness again."

A little while earlier, Maggie had shared the truth of Robert with Claire. It was a secret too big to keep from her best friend. And while Claire had been all for heading straight to Coventry and giving the lying cad a piece of her mind, she had also agreed that it was something that should never be mentioned again.

"Now we just need to find you a suitable husband," Maggie said.

Claire shook her head. "All the so-called suitable bache-lors are boring. They haven't done anything in their lives. I am going to wait to find a gentleman with something inter-esting to say." She leaned in close. "I'm seriously considering stowing away onboard the ship that our cousin Gideon is taking after Christmas when he is due to sail to Italy."

"Don't you dare. He is going after his mother and sister to bring them back to England. He wouldn't appreciate you suddenly popping up in his luggage."

Maggie would be having a quiet word with her uncle, the Duke of Mowbray, and warning him against inviting Claire to his home anytime soon. Her sister had a way of talking people into things that were not always in her or their best interests.

"It was just a thought. A fanciful notion—nothing more," replied Claire.

Thank heavens. This family has had enough drama of late. Anymore and we shall have to take up the stage.

Maggie turned, smiling when she caught a glimpse of her father leading Piers into his study and closing the door behind him. A private chat. She hoped there would be many more moments that the two most important men in her life would be able to share.

"I am getting married. And this time, it's for real. And forever."

Chapter Forty-Seven

Lord Hugh Radley mouthed *'thank you'* to Maggie as she turned away from him and went to walk back down the long aisle of St. Paul's Cathedral. Her father didn't need to explain his words of appreciation. She had married Piers in a traditional Church of England ceremony in the right church, at the right time of day, and in front of many of London's elite —all without a hint of scandal.

With luck, it would put many of the rumors about the Bishop of London's children quietly to bed. Not wishing their own scandal to overshadow Maggie and Piers's big day, James and Leah Radley had made the wise decision not to come up to town for the service. A beautifully wrapped gift, one of James's stunning landscapes, had arrived earlier in the week. Maggie couldn't wait to hang the painting in the downstairs foyer of Denford House.

Piers glanced at her and grinned. "Happy, Lady Woodford?"

Maggie swallowed a lump of emotion and whispered, "Deliriously so, Lord Woodford. I can't believe that this day has come, and we are man and wife."

Upon his marriage, Piers had officially taken back one of his father's courtesy titles and was once again known as Baron Woodford. But as far as Maggie was concerned, he would always be just Piers. Her Piers.

And while she would have been quite content with a small wedding, her family had convinced her otherwise. A grand *ton* nuptial service was as much about making a statement of both Piers's innocence and her reentry into society as it was about them celebrating their marriage.

The only concession to her desire for a simple celebration was the wedding breakfast. It was being held at Denford House rather than in one of the grand ballrooms of Strathmore House. Her parents would have to pin their hopes on Claire and the notion she would marry someone who was happy to endure a ball for a thousand people.

Just as long as she doesn't go sailing off into the sunset.

As Maggie and Piers made their way toward the sweeping stairs of the cathedral's west front, Maggie searched the gathering. Her eyes sought out one person in particular.

Tradition dictated that Sir William Saunders sit with the family of the bride toward the front of the cathedral, but Maggie had long ago accepted that for her cousin, the rules did not apply.

At the end of the aisle, just before the doors, she caught sight of him. Will was standing alongside his wife, Hattie. She was yet another member of the Radley clan who was heavy with child. Hattie grinned at her husband, then gave him a gentle shove. He stepped out in front of the bride and groom. "My wife suggested that I come and offer my congratulations. I don't think we will make the wedding breakfast. Hattie needs her rest."

Piers slipped his fingers from Maggie's and shook his hand. "Sir William, how can we ever repay you? So much of today is as a result of your efforts."

"As long as you are both happy, that is all the payment I shall ever need. Justice has been served. And my lovely cousin is finally happily married to the man of her dreams. Well, something like that."

An emotional Maggie mouthed her own '*thank you*' as Piers took her hand once more. They continued on their way out into the chilly London morning as the bells of the cathedral chimed.

Chapter Forty-Eight

Toasts and speeches took up the better part of the wedding breakfast. First up was Lord Denford, who welcomed Maggie into the family. She cried all the way through the speech. Then came her father, regaling everyone with tales of his daughter's childhood, including all the things she thought she had gotten away with long ago. A highly amused Piers was wiping tears from his eyes by the end of it.

By the time the groom rose to make his speech, Maggie was hoping her new husband would make it a short one. Piers cleared his throat and the gathering fell silent.

"Friends, family, and new family, Maggie and I would like to thank you for joining us on this most joyous of days. When she stormed into my office barely a month ago—my apologies. When she walked with purpose into my office . . ."

The ripple of chuckles eventually died down and he continued.

"Who would have thought but a short time later she would be my wife. But in all seriousness, Maggie and I have been blessed. Without every one of you, we wouldn't be here today." Piers raised his glass in salute. "To you all." He turned and faced a now blubbering Maggie. "And especially to my darling wife. I love you."

~

It was another hour before they finally managed to steal away from their guests. Maggie had assumed they were headed upstairs, but as Piers led her from the ballroom, they went straight out the front door and into a waiting carriage.

"Where are we going?" she asked.

"It's a surprise. A special place that I think you will love."

They curled up together in the carriage under the same warm blanket Piers had wrapped Maggie in after their trip to Kenilworth Castle. It was also the same one they had used in the barn. He was more than likely just being practical, but to her, it was supremely romantic.

"Do you remember when you looked after me when I had that anxiety attack on the way back from Kenilworth to Coventry? You were so attentive. I wasn't sure if my light-headedness was because I was over-tired or because I realized that you had come to mean more to me than just a friend. That you genuinely cared," she said.

Piers dropped a kiss on the top of her hair. "I was worried, but I knew you were strong. All you needed was someone to believe in you. To listen."

Maggie lay her head against his chest and closed her eyes. Without the many buttons of his military waistcoat and the heavy work on the front of his dress coat, cuddling with Piers was a more comfortable prospect these days. If she never saw him in uniform ever again, she would be happy.

The streets of central London slowly disappeared as the carriage continued on its way. They passed by Fulham Palace, her old family home, and she leaned forward in the seat. Last night had been the final time she had slept under her father's roof.

She was a married woman. Lady Woodford. Piers believed in her. His love and strength were all she would ever need.

"Where exactly are we going?" she asked, sitting back, and snuggling in once more.

"Richmond. We have a small manor house there. It's a modest country retreat. My parents are not ones for town and all the crowds. It's where they usually stay, but for the next few days it is completely ours."

Now Maggie understood why her luggage had not been sent to Denford House. Piers had arranged for it to go to their secret honeymoon home.

The carriage turned left off the main road which led to the village of Richmond. Maggie knew her way around this part of outer London, but she couldn't recall having ever been down this road. They passed by what was clearly a gatehouse, but it was of such a grand stature it could easily be a manor house.

I can't wait to see inside.

Maggie pulled out of Piers's embrace, expecting the carriage to stop. But it continued on. Piers gently laughed. "The head butler and chatelaine live there. Keep watching the road ahead, my love."

She did as he instructed. Her mouth dropped open at the sight which loomed up in front of them as they crested a small rise. It was an enormous red-brick, Jacobean manor house. Maggie pressed her face to the glass. As the carriage swept up the drive which ran across the front of the house, she quickly counted the windows. Nine, plus two three-windowed bays. The house rose over four floors.

"Now I understand why you were not daunted by the size of Kenilworth Castle. It's a small palace," she said.

"Not quite. And before you ask, no, I have no idea how

many rooms there are under the main roof. All the Denford children tried counting them one year, but we kept losing the tally. There are more bedrooms than we could ever need, even if we are as blessed as the King and Queen when it comes to children," said Piers.

Maggie shot him a glare. "Don't you dare get me with fifteen children. I shall have the door of my bedroom nailed shut if the count goes past eight."

He pulled her back into his arms, placing a tender, inviting kiss on her lips. "I make no promises, apart from one —you and I shall never have separate bedrooms. Where I sleep, so do you."

What a wonderful idea. She couldn't wait to spend the rest of her life sharing her nights with this man, ending each day tucked up in bed with Piers and forever knowing that he was hers.

She was still considering the daunting prospect of a large brood of children when the coach finally came to a stop out the front of the grand manor house. The small army of servants who were gathered around the steps, promptly stood to attention.

Modest country retreat, my foot.

"I assumed that when I saw Denford House, you were a family used to understated elegance. Now, I realize it's all a myth. You let people in town think that you are poor country mice when you have this splendor right on the outskirts of London."

"The Grange came to our family, your family, as part of my mother's marriage settlements. It now belongs to me, but I have always shared it with anyone who wishes to stay. It's where we can have the best of both worlds—a beautiful garden for our children to play in, while we are still close to town."

"And it's near to my parents. Fulham Palace is only a short distance from here. Oh, Piers, this place is perfect."

Piers pulled the blanket away. The moment the footman opened the door, Piers climbed out. Maggie followed, grinning as her husband spread his arms wide and lifted her down. She was still smiling as he carried her up the steps, through the front door, and across the threshold. The servants followed at a respectable distance.

It was wonderful that Piers was determined to observe all the wedding traditions for the bride's arrival at her new home.

He thinks of everything.

"Now you are officially Lady Woodford of the Grange," he announced, setting Maggie on her feet.

Her wedding slippers touched the hard, marble flooring, and she glanced down. Elegant lines of gold and amber stretched across the foyer. The walls that they eventually touched were painted a rich burgundy.

Maggie lifted her gaze up past the giant tapestry of a hunting scene all the way to the ornately decorated ceiling. Now she understood why Piers hadn't been overwhelmed at the sight of the grand ballroom at Strathmore House when she had first shown it to him. While not as stunning, the Grange could certainly hold its own.

"It's wonderful," gushed Maggie. She stepped away and, lifting her skirts, gave an impromptu twirl. Happiness made her light of foot and eager to dance.

It's been forever since I felt this happy.

"Come, let me show you the rest of the house," said Piers.

Maggie slowly shook her head. "Not now. Later, perhaps." She pointed to the white marble staircase which led up to the next floor. Moving in close so only he could hear, she whispered, "The only place I am keen to see is our bedroom. I want us to be alone. You still haven't claimed what I was willing to give you that night in the barn."

A blushing Piers cleared his throat. "Right. The guided tour can wait. You, clearly, cannot."

He scooped her up in his arms and headed for the stairs.

Chapter Forty-Nine

O nce upstairs, he carried her along a long hallway that was also decorated with various paintings and tapestries. Maggie didn't bother to look too closely at any of them. Instead, her focus was solely on trying to keep her nerves from getting the better of her.

Halfway along the hall, Piers stopped and set Maggie on her feet in front of a plain brown door. He fished in his pocket and produced a key. After slipping it into the lock, he opened the door and pulled Maggie inside.

She was met with the sight of a simple unadorned bedroom. A large bed with a blue-and-white-checked coverlet sat in the middle, but there was not a single painting or hanging on the wall.

He caught her questioning gaze. "I don't spend a lot of time here, so decorating my private apartment hasn't ever been a priority. Now that you are the lady of the Grange, I am trusting you will remedy whatever you feel is lacking in both our room and the rest of the house."

"To be honest, I haven't taken much of anything in since we arrived," she replied.

The expression of concern on his face was more than just endearing—it was beautiful. Knowing that the man who was now her husband understood her so well had Maggie blinking back a tear.

Piers drew her into his arms, placing a tender kiss on her lips. She shivered as his kiss drifted from her lips, across her cheek, and to her ear.

"Just like I said that night, we will take things slowly," he whispered.

"I don't mean to be a timid bride; it's just that I've heard all manner of first-time stories. But I am sure once we have been together, things will be fine," she said.

Piers drew back. "I have a confession to make. I'm also nervous." He licked his lips and softly chuckled. "It's my first time, too."

You could have knocked Maggie over with a feather. The thought that Piers, tall, dark, and commanding, could possibly still be a virgin hadn't ever crossed her mind. She had naturally assumed that he would be like so many other men of London society—experienced in the bedroom.

But she wasn't disappointed to discover that she would be his first. It was exciting to know that no other woman would know Piers. That for all time, he would be just hers.

You are mine. And none other shall have you.

"Well then. I guess, we are going to take things slowly," she replied.

They held one another for a short while, simply hugging, offering reassurance. Hundreds of other couples faced this same situation every day. There was no reason why they couldn't successfully navigate their way through things.

In time, they would learn the secrets of one another's bodies, discover pleasure together. That thought was enough to have Maggie relaxing into Piers's embrace. She loved that he had been saving himself for marriage. It was touching. Respectful.

"May I unlace your gown?" he asked.

"Yes."

He turned her in his arms and set to work on the ties at the back of her dress. Maggie slipped her arms out of the sleeves and the dress dropped, pooling at her feet. She stepped over the fabric and toed the gown aside. All that remained were her stays and petticoat. Piers rid himself of his jacket, and waistcoat.

When he reached for his cravat, Maggie lay her hand over his. "I want to do that. I've always itched to slip the knots of a man's necktie open."

She might have been an innocent, but she understood temptation. And lust.

His hands fell to his sides as Maggie loosened the knot. She hummed softly, drawing the cravat from around his neck, then dropped it to the floor where it joined the rest of their discarded garments.

Piers sank to his knees before her. His hands rested on either side of her hips, drawing her to him. For a man with no experience of sex, he made surprisingly short work of her undergarments. He glanced up at her. "There are some book-shops in London which sell what they politely describe as titillation tomes. Very thorough with their descriptions, while others have quite detailed drawings."

Maggie gasped. She could just picture Piers reading and absorbing every word and illustration. Reclined on his bed, book in one hand and . . .

She bent and tapped her finger gently on his nose. "Tell me, Lord Woodford, with these books—did you pleasure yourself while you read them?"

The last of her clothes disappeared from her body, leaving Maggie naked. It came as somewhat of a surprise. She had been so caught up with imagining Piers and his naughty books, she had forgotten her husband was slowly stripping her clothes away.

"I did. And that night after we returned to the house from stargazing, when I almost broke and made you mine, I knew you were angry with me, and I couldn't sleep. So, I read a whole chapter of one book and touched myself while I thought of you."

A whoosh escaped her lips. He had been thinking of her. As his gaze drifted appreciatively over her body, Piers drew in a deep breath and whispered, "Beautiful. I am so fortunate, happy beyond words to know that you are mine. I love you, Maggie."

She blinked back a tear. "I love you, Piers. Being your wife is a dream come true."

He cupped his hands over Maggie's buttocks, pulling her hips forward. "Rest your hands on my shoulders. I am going to show you exactly what was in the book I read that night."

She did as he asked, biting down on her lip as his knee pushed her legs apart. The instant his tongue touched the tip of her sex, she closed her eyes.

Sweet heavens. He might not have done this before, but he certainly took good notes.

His tongue delved deep into her heated core. Maggie cried out as Piers dragged his lips up her length and then sucked hard on her bud of pleasure. Her moans and sobs urged him on. Her grip on his shoulders tightened with every lash of ecstasy that he gifted to her. By the time he finally withdrew his mouth and tongue and sat back on his haunches, she was a quivering, needy mess.

"Oh, that was incredible," she gushed.

"I am not done with you yet."

Piers got to his feet, stopping partway to lift Maggie up

and toss her over his shoulder. He carried her over to the bed and set her down.

She lay in a heated, lust-filled haze while Piers rid himself of his shoes and then set to work on the buttons of his trousers. When he released the second clasp on the folds, his hardened cock sprang free.

Open mouthed, Maggie stared in wonder. She hadn't ever seen an erection before. It was big. And there was a lot of it.

"Please tell me the book explained how that is supposed to fit in me?" she asked.

Piers climbed back onto the bed and sat between her spread thighs. "Believe me, I heard enough about this part while I was at school. I also know that women are supposed to enjoy a man with a certain amount of girth."

His thumb rubbed over her bud, back and forth. Then he slipped a finger inside her heat and began to stroke. "You are so wet, Maggie. Do you like me touching you this way?"

"Yes. It feels good."

"Good. I want you to enjoy pleasure between us. To be hungry for my touch." He withdrew his fingers, then positioned the broad head of his erection at her entrance. Slowly he pushed in.

Maggie braced herself. There was a slight sting, and some pressure. She flinched and Piers immediately withdrew.

"Are you alright?"

"Yes. Try again."

When he entered her a second time, there was still a little pressure, but no pain. Piers captured Maggie's lips with a deep, loving kiss. She gave herself up to him as he rolled his hips, thrusting in and out. The length of his hard cock dragged over her most sensitive of places and she groaned into his mouth. "Oh Piers, it's so good."

The aching need, the bone-deep desire for release built with his every stroke. She knew enough about her own body to sense where this was leading. And from the deep moans of her husband, it was clear Piers was also enjoying the experience.

"Harder, deeper, please," she begged, urging him on.

"I don't want to hurt you."

"You're not. It's wonderful. But I need you to go faster." Maggie closed her eyes, concentrating on the pleasure as it coursed through her body. Piers increased the pace of their coupling, his strokes becoming frantic. He hit her pleasure bud at exactly the right time, and she screamed. "Piers!"

The orgasm hit, wave after wave crashing over her. She was certain she could see stars. Maggie was still riding the crest of her own climax when Piers suddenly stilled and swore.

She opened her eyes. Piers, head hung low, was sucking in breaths like he had just run a hundred-yard dash. Beads of sweat glittered on his brow.

He raised his head and their eyes met. A deep, rumbling laugh rose from within his heaving chest. "I think we more than just got through that, if the volume at which you cried my name is any indication."

"Says the man who swore as he reached his crisis."

Piers rolled off her, landing on the bed in a heap. "Come here, wife," he commanded.

Maggie turned over onto her side and snuggled up against him. Piers wrapped his arm around her. Her fingers came to rest on the dark hairs of his chest. It was still rising and falling as he slowly caught his breath.

"That was superb, husband. I'm up for doing that again before the day is over."

They shared a tender kiss, after which they lay on the bed simply grinning at one another for the longest of times. Fingers touched and roamed. Explored.

This was what Maggie had always dreamed her wedding

day would be like—a public declaration of their union followed by loving moments of privacy.

"I am so glad we are here. That you and I made it," she said.

"Just think, if I had refused to see you that day at the Horse Guards, none of this would have happened. You wouldn't be mine from this day forward." He slid his hand under her waist, dragging Maggie up and over him. As she settled her legs over his, she bent and kissed him once more.

She tapped her finger lightly on Piers's chest. "That will teach you for sending me a terse letter. You now have a lifetime in which to regret it."

He pulled the coverlet over them and as Maggie nestled against him, Piers whispered. "I will never regret anything with you."

Chapter Fifty

❦

T he official letter from the head of the British Army arrived at the Grange a week later. Piers's gaze was still on the letter's wax seal as he strode into the breakfast room.

"I received a letter," he announced.

Maggie gave a mere *hmm* to his words.

"This morning's newspaper has a report from a special correspondent in Amsterdam. Rumor has it that the King of the Netherlands is going to commission a great statue and monument on the site where the Prince of Orange was injured. They say King Willem plans to spare no expense," she said.

Piers looked up. His wife's nose was firmly in the daily newspaper. Had she even heard him? She most certainly hadn't noticed the letter.

"I can't imagine how much that is going to cost," she continued.

Clearly not listening.

He tried again. "I received a letter from the British Army this morning."

She lifted her head from the paper, took one look at the letter, and sighed.

"Why didn't you say so? We have been expecting that."

Piers lifted an eyebrow. In the week since their wedding, he had already learned a great deal about his bride—one of which was her habit of scanning the morning's newspaper each day, cover to cover, looking for interesting pieces of news.

From his jacket pocket, he produced a second letter. This one had been marked as having been sent from Europe by the Thurn-und-Taxis postal service.

"There is another letter. This one, interestingly enough, appears to have come from Brussels."

Maggie scrunched the paper closed and tossing it onto the table, quickly rose. She was at Piers's side in an instant.

How wonderful it was to have such an enthusiastic woman in his life. From the bedroom to the breakfast table, Maggie was full of vigor. Especially in the bedroom.

A hand slipped under his arm and snatched the second letter away. She waved it in the air. "First, the letter from the army."

Piers wasn't about to argue. He was as keen as Maggie to read the contents of the letter from the Commander-in-Chief.

The wax seal gave a loud, satisfying crack as he broke it open. The single page opened to reveal a scant few lines.

HRH The Duke of York and Albany
Commander-in-Chief
His Majesty's British Army
Horse Guards, London

To Captain Piers Denford,

I wish to thank you for your service and sacrifice as a member of the British Army's Grenadier Guards. Your request to resign your commission has been accepted and you are hereby granted an honorable discharge. A separate letter of commendation will come from His Royal Highness, the Prince Regent, in due course.

His Royal Highness, the Duke of York and Albany
Commander-in-Chief

Piers stared at the letter. After all he had been through, it was finally over.

A gentle hand on his arm stirred him from his musings. He met the sapphire-blue eyes of his wife. All thoughts of the army and how badly they had treated him melted away at the sight of Maggie.

"It's over. They have granted me an honorable discharge," he said, his voice lacking emotion.

"That's what you wanted. Congratulations, my love. You are officially a free man."

Piers gazed at the letter once more. Maggie was right; this was what he had wanted. What he had feared he may never receive. He was no longer an officer; he was just Piers Denford.

"I'm finding it a little difficult to believe. In truth, my army career ended the day I walked out of the Horse Guards, but actually seeing my notice of discharge, holding it in my hand, makes it now real."

Maggie rose up on her toes and gave Piers a kiss on the cheek. He turned and stole one from her lips. Kissing his wife was fast becoming one of his favorite hobbies.

"Now, open the other letter and let's see what the news is from Brussels. By the way, who is in Brussels?" Maggie asked.

Piers dropped the letter from the Duke of York onto the table. Later, he would find a safe place for it.

Maggie tried to snap the seal of the second letter in the same way as Piers had done the first, but she only succeeded in ripping the page. With a huff of disgust, she handed it to him. "They must have put a special seal on it to make sure it survived the long journey."

The seal broke cleanly for Piers, and he let out a gleeful, "Huzzah!" Even Maggie's playful batting of his arm couldn't quell his mirth.

Every moment with this woman is a delight.

He scanned the second letter, taking in the salient points. "It's from the Prince of Orange. He says he and his good lady wife have been busy with continuing the remodeling and decorating of Soestdijk Palace. I expect that will have cost his father some serious blunt."

And now, King Willem was going to keep spending money on what Piers suspected would surely be a magnificent monument to his son. Something impressive that would forever mark his place on the battlefield at Waterloo.

He wasn't entirely certain how he felt about that. Thousands had died on that rain- soaked battle ground, but only the prince was going to get a public shrine to his heroics.

"The Prince of Orange also mentions how well his son is doing, and that he and the princess are hoping for another child in the new year."

Rumors of the prince conducting yet another extra-marital affair with a gentleman had reached Piers, but he wasn't going to make mention of it. Nothing was going to dampen his day. Nor the spark of happiness which shone in Maggie's eyes.

You are so beautiful. I am truly blessed.

"Oh, and they are staying in Brussels. Apparently, the princess prefers it to Amsterdam. It's more like her home in Russia."

That explained the postmark of Brussels on the front of the letter. Piers quickly ran his eye over the rest of the missive, not caring to take much of it in.

The second letter joined the first on the breakfast table. He might read the rest of it someday. Perhaps not.

"Are you done with breakfast, my petal?" he asked.

Maggie snorted. "My petal. Are you serious?"

In the week since they had been married, Piers had been trying various terms of endearment for his wife. Petal was his latest offering.

"Well, you are a precious flower. I thought it rather sweet," he replied.

She drew close, her hand settling on the top of his trousers. "You don't like sweet. Well, that is what I'm sure you said in the early hours of this morning," she purred.

He kept his gaze on her. "Please tell me there are no footmen in here."

She slowly shook her head, and his relief was palpable. "I sent them away while you were fetching the mail. Thought we could do with some privacy. If you get my meaning." She batted her long black eyelashes at him and offered up a knowing grin. His wife was incorrigible.

Piers was sorely tempted. But he had paperwork to do this morning. *Later.* He promised himself.

"Alright, petal goes on the discard pile. We are going to have to come up with something. I can't just call you Maggie whenever I look into your eyes."

"Why?"

He brushed his hand over the top of her glorious raven mane. Because Maggie was more than just her name. This woman had stormed into his life in a fury, swiftly laying claim to his heart. He had been hers from the very first day. And it meant she would always be more.

"I don't know how to put it into words—perhaps that's why it might take me some time to come up with a suitable term. All I know is that you have changed my life. Given it back to me."

Maggie's smile grew tremulous. Tears shone in her sapphire eyes. "You can't possibly imagine for one minute that it hasn't been the same for me. I was lost before you. My heart had shattered into a thousand pieces. But you put it all back together. Made me whole again."

"I think I have the right words now. Nothing clever—just pure, honest emotion. From my heart. Maggie Denford, you are my love. *My love.* Will that do?"

Piers slipped an arm around his wife's waist and drew her close. Maggie met his gaze and gently nodded.

"Always."

Epilogue

❦

The wedding was lovely, and he wished Maggie and Piers all the happiness in the world, but Francis Saunders was in a foul mood by the time he left the wedding. A sensible, sober man would have gone straight home; however whisky and his bruised pride spoke louder.

If only my life wasn't a constant battle with idiots and bloody stubborn neighbors.

It was bad enough having to deal with ships which arrived late at port and clueless captains, but now he had a new and worrying problem on his hands. Someone had taken over the lease of the warehouse next door to Saunders Shipping at London Docks.

The very warehouse he had intended to use when he won the lucrative spice contract, which was shortly to be announced. He had coveted the warehouse for over a year. Done everything to secure the lease. And now someone else had captured his prize.

He hailed a hack and headed east toward the London Docks; causing mischief was at the forefront of his whisky addled mind.

I will show this interloper who is the master of the North Quay.

As soon as he alighted from the hack out the front of Saunders Shipping, warehouse number twelve, Francis saw red. Tossing a coin up to the driver, he slammed the carriage door hard. "I am going to commit bloody murder."

He continued to curse and utter foul threats as he angrily marched across to the pile of flotsam and jetsam which had been dumped right in front of the door of his warehouse. Barrels and ropes blocked his access to the building.

A note, nailed to the nearest of the barrels, caught his attention. He swiped at it, tearing it away. Holding the letter up close to his face, Francis strained to read it in the dim light.

With paper tightly held in his fist, he marched back toward the entrance of the docks and the gas lights which blazed outside the superintendent's office. As he drew close, he slowed his steps. There were a few people about the place, the docks were never empty.

Whatever the contents of the note, he didn't need other people to bear witness to his anger. Trying to calm the rage which boiled within, Francis took a deep breath, then held the letter up to the light.

Saunders,

I have reached the end of my tether. The end of my patience. The end of being polite.

Keep your cursed barrels from out the front of my warehouse. Take your confounded ropes. If your bloody barrels cross the line between our buildings one more time, I will throw them off the dock and into the water.

I have moved your rubbish twice now. Trust me, the third time will not be the charm.

Yours, fed-up to the back teeth.

P. Basden
Basden Shipping Line.

It was fortunate that Francis was a healthy young man as the contents of the note sent his blood pressure rocketing to a dangerous level. For a moment, he swayed on his feet, utterly gob smacked that someone would think they could do this to him.

Who the devil does P. Basden think he is?

Francis screwed the paper up into a ball and stuffed it into his coat pocket. He wasn't about to throw it away, no, he was going to shove it down his neighbor's throat.

"I'll show him what a man at the end of his tether looks like."

He returned to the front of his warehouse, picked up an empty tea chest, then carried it over to the edge of the wharf and threw it into the water. Sanity threw up its hands at that point.

"See, I can throw my own rubbish into the dock."

The tea chest landed with a splash. But being empty it didn't sink. Instead, it gently bobbed up and down on the waves, taunting him.

"That's it. I am going to have it out with this blackguard, and right now."

Francis stopped outside warehouse number fourteen and glanced up. The top floors were all in darkness, but there was a faint light shining through one of the ground floor windows. Someone was in the building.

Hand fisted, he pounded on the door.

"Open up Basden!" he bellowed.

When he didn't get an immediate response, he attacked the door once more.

Bang. Bang. Bang. It hurt his hand, but in his drunken rage Francis was beyond sensible thought.

"Open up, you foul dog!"

The clang of a bolt being drawn back had him making ready to rush into the warehouse and confront his nemesis.

The door opened barely a crack. Light shone through the gap, but he couldn't make out who stood on the other side.

"You might think you can send me threatening notes, but I am Francis Saunders, and you clearly have no idea of the sort of power I can wield," he said.

The door opened a little more and Francis moved forward. The sight of a pistol had him skidding to an abrupt halt. It was pointed directly at him.

He might be drunk, but Francis wasn't stupid.

To his surprise, a young woman stepped out of the warehouse. A woman with long, fair hair which tumbled down to kiss the top of her naked shoulders. *Her naked shoulders.*

As his gaze settled on her pale, cream flesh all thoughts of violence fled his mind. She held him spellbound. Even the fear of the pistol couldn't stop Francis from sneaking a peek at the swell of her bust. It was generous, buxom. Perfect.

It was only when his brain finally registered the click of the gun being cocked that Francis finally tore his gaze from ogling the woman and back to the weapon.

"You have until the count of three to move away before I put a bullet in your head," she announced in an eerily calm voice.

"I..."

"One."

"I need to talk to P Basden," he replied

"Two."

A now frantic Francis rummaged in his coat pocket, hurriedly searching for the note. He held the screwed-up paper in his trembling hand. "I have a letter. This is London. You can't just go shooting people," he stammered.

"Three."

The loud echo of gunfire rang in his ears, and he dropped like a stone.

All is Fair in Love coming May 2022.
Mixing Business with Pleasure.

***

Join my VIP readers and receive your FREE copy of A Wild English Rose.

Click here for your Free Book

Love Audio Books ?

audiobooks

Click HERE to listen to the first chapter of all audio books
by Sasha Cottman

Audio titles are available at all major retailers and lending
libraries.

Author's Notes

The Lion's Mound (*Butte du Lion*) is a man-made hill which stands at 43 meters in height and is situated on the site of the Battle of Waterloo. It commemorates the location on the battlefield where a musket ball hit the shoulder of William II of the Netherlands (the Prince of Orange) and knocked him from his horse during the battle. It is also a memorial for the Battle of Quatre Bras, which was fought two days prior to Waterloo, on 16 June 1815.

King Willem I of the Netherlands ordered its construction in 1820 and it was completed in 1826. If you pay a small fee, you are allowed to climb the 226 steps to the top where a statue of a lion overlooks the battlefield.

Kenilworth Castle holds a particular place in my heart. My late aunt and uncle lived close to the castle grounds and often took an evening stroll among the ruins.

A few years ago, the Elizabethan gardens were restored by English Heritage, and you can visit them.

The Two Virgins tavern is now called the Virgins and Castle and does a hearty Sunday roast.

St. Michael's Cathedral, along with large parts of the city center of Coventry was destroyed during the Coventry Blitz in November 1940. The ruins still remain as a memorial garden, and a new cathedral was built next door.

Also by Sasha Cottman

SERIES

The Duke of Strathmore

The Noble Lords

Rogues of the Road

London Lords

For other releases and international editions please visit

www.sashacottman.com

The Duke of Strathmore

Letter from a Rake – eBook, Audio, Print

An Unsuitable Match – eBook, Audio, Print

The Duke's Daughter – eBook, Audio, Print

A Scottish Duke for Christmas – eBook, Print

My Gentleman Spy – eBook, Audio, Print

Lord of Mischief – eBook, Audio, Print

The Ice Queen – eBook, Audio, Print

Two of a Kind – eBook, Audio, Print

A Lady's Heart Deceived - eBook, Print

All is Fair in Love - eBook, Print

Mistletoe and Kisses (novella) – eBook, Print

A Wild English Rose – exclusive eBook, Print

The Noble Lords

Love Lessons for the Viscount – eBook, Print

A Lord with Wicked Intentions – eBook, Print

A Scandalous Rogue for Lady Eliza – eBook, Print

Unexpected Duke– eBook, Print

The Noble Lords Boxed Set

Rogues of the Road

Rogue for Hire – eBook, Print

Stolen by the Rogue – eBook, Print

When a Rogue Falls – eBook, Print

The Rogue and the Jewel – eBook, Print

King of Rogues – eBook, Print

London Lords

Devoted to the Spanish Duke – eBook, Print

Promised to the Swedish Prince – eBook, Print

An Italian Count for Christmas – eBook, Print

Wedded to the Welsh Baron – eBook, Print

Bound to the Belgian Count – eBook, Print

About the Author

USA Today bestselling author Sasha Cottman was born in England, but raised in Australia. Having her heart in two places has created a love for travel, which at last count was to over 55 countries. A travel guide is always on her pile of new books to read.

Sasha's novels are set around the Regency period in England, Scotland, and Europe. Her books are centred on the themes of love, honour, and family. Visit her website at www.sashacottman.com

For international editions of novels, please visit www.sashacottman.com